THE CUBAN PROSPECT

THE CUBAN PROSPECT

A NOVEL

BRIAN SHAWVER

THE OVERLOOK PRESS
Woodstock & New York

First published in the United States in 2003 by
The Overlook Press, Peter Mayer Publishers, Inc.
Woodstock & New York

WOODSTOCK:
One Overlook Drive
Woodstock, NY 12498
www.overlookpress.com
[for individual orders, bulk and special sales, contact our Woodstock office]

NEW YORK:
141 Wooster Street
New York, NY 10012

∞ The paper used in this book meets the requirements for paper
permanence as described in the ANSI Z39.48-1992 standard.

Library of Congress Cataloging-in-Publication Data

Shawver, Brian.
The Cuban prospect : a novel / Brian Shawver
p. cm.

1. Baseball scouts—Fiction. 2. Baseball players—Fiction.
3. Illegal aliens—Fiction. 4. Cuba—Fiction. I. Title
PS3619.H3575C8 2003   813'.6—dc21   2002193107

Book design and type formatting by Bernard Schleifer
Printed in the United States of America
ISBN 1-58567-344-7
FIRST EDITION
1 3 5 7 9 8 6 4 2

To Mom, Dad, and Erin

CHAPTER ONE

THE DEFECTION BEGAN, APPROPRIATELY ENOUGH, WITH ME crouching at the cusp of a dirty field, waiting. There was nothing unusual in this; almost half the days of my adult life, until my retirement less than one year ago, have at some point found me squashed into that position, waiting for something—for a ball to be thrown at me, for a batter to swing before me, for an umpire to bark a call into my ear. Most of the time I did not even know what I expected to happen next, or what I would do when it came. I just knew that my job was to wait.

This is not to say that crouching in this field at the outskirts of Rios, Cuba, two months ago bore any real resemblance to the way I had crouched and waited on the countless baseball fields upon which my career had passed. I just mean that, at that moment, I felt the old comfort of squatting in the night air, bouncing occasionally with the toes and quadriceps to keep the muscles awake. I felt my haunches pestered by the familiar ache, and these sensations and the hot breeze reminded my body of what had once been an inevitable part of my days. I spit out the side of my mouth with the dexterity only baseball players have

7

(it's a strangely difficult skill to master) and I punched my open left hand the way I used to punch my mitt.

In the old comfort of this position I was reminded that this simulation, the resumption of this stance, would be the only physical reminder of baseball in the journey I was about to begin, a journey that was completely about and because of baseball. In the course of a year I had been removed several degrees from the actual playing of the game, and now my role was so ancillary to it as to be almost bizarre. What I mean is this: if my impending journey—from Rios, Cuba, to a spot off the Florida Keys at latitude 24°4'/longitude 81°1'—were to be recorded on film without sound, the viewer of the tape would have no reason to suspect that my role in life had anything to do with the sport of baseball. At the time I found this to be more terrifying than ironic, since I had never shown competence in any aspect of life except for baseball (had, in fact, rarely been asked to participate in much else), and even in baseball the word "competence" never completely applied to me.

In any case, this is what occurred to me at the time, and it was enough to make me flush a bit and shiver with a mild embarrassment, and to stand and lean up against the fat trunk of a cedar tree with one hand in my pocket as if I was waiting for a bus.

In fact, I was waiting on a pitcher, just as in the old days. This time I was not waiting for him to throw to me, but to meet me at the edge of the meadow that separated Rios from the trees, as had been arranged by a man named Charlie Dance. The pitcher was named Ramon Diego Sagasta, and he played for the Matanzas Toronados. We were to escape together. He was left-handed, threw a fastball in the high nineties, but had three other pitches that he used almost 60 percent of the time. He was six foot two, two hundred five pounds, unmarried, reportedly twenty-six years old. He had tried to defect before, while touring with the national team in Bulgaria, but had somehow botched it and hadn't even gotten close to the Italian border. I had never seen Ramon before, but I had pretty well memorized the statistics that were available to me, and so I knew Ramon Sagasta in the theoretical way that scouts believe they can come to know prospects through statistics. We tend to have more faith in numbers than in anything else, including our own perceptions.

When I removed myself from the catcher's crouch it was a little past midnight, meaning that Ramon was over an hour late. From my post I could see him in profile clearly—I had binoculars, and used them once or twice to scan a piece of shoreline about a mile to the south, but I didn't need them. The squat, square Sagasta family home sat about 10 yards from the lip of the forest, across the dirty field, at the beginning of an open cluster of houses that were similar not so much in color and shape, but in their common dilapidation and smallness. The village of Rios was the size of the average major league ball field, and it did not conform to any kind of grid; the houses were haphazardly situated and close together. It was perfectly suited for communism, since there could be no secrets here—there could not even be the desire for secrets here, it seemed to me, because someone from Rios must never in his or her life have truly known what it was like to be alone. These were daunting thoughts, since Ramon's defection absolutely had to be the securest of secrets, for my neck's sake at least.

Each house had a yard, but most were overgrown with sustenance gardens and weeds, and so they only looked like shorter, enfenced versions of the forest. None of the yards were large enough for children to play proper games on; the dirty meadow that separated me from the houses wasn't marked off in any way, and only with great imagination could it be reckoned a diamond, but I felt certain this was where Ramon had learned and practiced his precious skills.

The edge of the forest bordered the community like a coastline, and I had taken cover at this margin, at the confluence of jungle and village plain. When I arrived, I had easily spotted the rose-colored siding and strangely tilted cedar tree that I had been told would mark the backyard of the Sagasta house. For two hours I had watched the family through its branch tips and listened through the open window.

I could see the lean figure of Ramon—or who I felt certain must be Ramon—at the head of the table; and what looked to be Ramon's mother close beside him; and even closer beside him, to his right, what must have been his girlfriend, who sat with exaggeratedly straight posture. Her black hair was pulled back so tight that the candlelight reflected against it and at times she stroked his hair. An adolescent in a tank top—a cousin or a brother—showed his back to me, and occasionally the hand of another family member would come into view to grab something from a serving plate. For two hours, I had watched as they feasted and toasted Ramon's farewell. The noise of the family's chatter—giddy, high-pitched, with voices overlapping voices and rising to be heard—came to me clearly, bouncing off the fully bloomed foliage of the jungle.

Occasionally Ramon would become somber and gesture for quiet. He would stand, speak, and lean across the table to hug someone for long seconds. At one point, the teenager to his left teased him for his sentimentality, and Ramon returned the teasing with an exaggerated hug and kisses to the boy's head—one of those gestures between brothers that is so pure with affection that it is embarrassing to watch.

I paid special attention at these moments, trying to listen

to Ramon's speeches, but he mumbled and lisped in a funny way, and the wind rustled the leaves above my head, and I could make out very little of what he said. I heard "Estados Unidos" and *"beisbol"* and "mama" and "Rosa," but I didn't catch any complete sentences, although I was fluent enough. The rest of the table clapped at these speeches, but Ramon's mother and girlfriend watched stoically, lips stretched in gracious, depleted smiles, the kind of smiles women give to men who wrongly believe they are doing them a favor.

Ramon's girlfriend, thin and much younger than him, did not speak, though she sometimes reminded herself to smile along with the jokes and the chatter. Her back never touched the back of her chair; when she relaxed her posture at all it was to lean towards him. She held her left hand lightly between his shoulder blades throughout the meal, and whenever he paused in eating she reached out with her other hand to take his. A gorgeous girl, probably not yet out of her teens. She wore a yellow dress and cast her eyes downward. In the candlelight the tan skin of her arms and face looked flawless, like a baby's. In the tumult of the dinner, I believe I was the only one who noticed that she didn't eat a thing.

Frequently, all activity stopped at the quiet and absolute insistence of the mother, and the diners would bow their heads. The mother kissed beads in her hands as she prayed, and she ran through the prayers in Spanish so automatic and rapid that I doubted even the people at the table followed her words. I assumed they practiced Catholicism, or whatever Santeria-flavored strand of it might have developed here, and she seemed to be invoking all the saints and blessings her religion had to offer—she interrupted the meal to pray more than Ramon did to gush; it was no surprise that things were running late.

I could guess a few of the saints she may have been

pestering, having spent plenty of time in the Latin American winter leagues. Saint Christopher, certainly, for safe travel, and Sebastian, who watches over athletes. Saint George, perhaps, for physical strength. Possibly a direct communiqué to the Virgin herself, a prayer for Ramon's soul in advance should things go badly. Ramon and his brother kept their heads bowed, but I could see them poke at each other below the table.

When the mother began what I reckoned to be her eighth mid-meal prayer, I found myself muttering, in Spanish, that the only saint she should bother contacting at the moment was the one in charge of cloud activity and tidal flow, and perhaps whichever one could get Ramon off his ass and out into the forest—the saint of getting the lead out, as it were. I'm sure the Catholics have one. The dinner had gone on too long, and a wave of panic swept upon me like a predatory bird.

If I could see him now, I would say only this: *Ramon Sagasta, why did you keep me waiting that night?* It's a useless question, since it's doubtful things would have changed if he'd met me on time, and since he wouldn't understand how to respond. But I am curious. How is it that he did not feel that fire at his back? How could he have sat there with them, babbling and feasting? If I had been him, I would have kissed them off in the morning and slept by the forest to wait for the man who would smuggle me out of Cuba. But he felt it reasonable to sit and wait. I have come to see it as a glorious quality of his, this blindness, perhaps just another manifestation of his greatness.

At first it had been easy to indulge their farewell. I had just come six miles through the jungle—all I wanted was a patch of soft ground to plant myself upon as I waited for my sweat to dry. I found this spot, up against the cedar tree, and I was treated to the vision of their family. It had been a welcoming sight, a sign that things were right and regular. I had taken it as an assurance that nothing had gone awry, that nothing I'd said or done during my five days in Cuba had tipped off the National Revolutionary Police about the defection. The sight of their mundane gathering calmed me, slowed my breath, swelled my empathy. I bobbed my head and pursed my lips when they hugged each other. It was a dreadful thing Ramon was going to do, I realized this.

But now, after these hours, my sweat had dried, my rear end ached (thus the crouch), and I felt the presence of a host of dangers that I had simply never considered before. For example, it suddenly occurred to me that the moon was nearly full that night, and along with this came the similarly spectacular realization that I had not considered checking on this beforehand (nor, even more disturbingly, had any of our sponsors). It had been a simple, obvious thing to check off the binoculars, the Swiss Army knife, the contour maps that I couldn't even read— but I hadn't once thought of the moon. For the first few hours after dusk, it had been obscured by thick Gulf clouds, but in the past half hour it had abruptly rid itself of cover, and the landscape had become noticeably brighter, as if someone was turning up a dimmer switch on the world. I could identify the color of almost every house in Rios, now that I had my night vision and the clouds had shifted. It barely mattered that it was well past midnight; it seemed to me that we might as well have been trying to flee at noon.

And so I dwelt among the many discomforts: a cold sweatiness, a gnawing impatience, and the understanding that my incompetence had already begun to reveal itself, in concert with the moon. This last was a familiar discomfort. I am one of those men on whom many things are lost, and to whom many concepts cannot be explained firmly enough to take root. It made perfect sense, in retrospect, that an American who had traveled surreptitiously to Cuba and was in the process of smuggling out an electrifying pitching talent might want to check to see what the moon might be doing on the evening of said escape. And yet I was not at all surprised that I had not done this; in fact, it would have surprised and pleased me greatly if I had.

This is by way of saying that I accepted the existence of a thousand other dangers that I simply hadn't anticipated, and wouldn't even know about until Ramon and I tripped over them. Perhaps they would not be so substantial as to end things for us, but this was hardly something I could assume.

I cursed him. "Fuck you, Ramon," I said, and even though I was alone and frightened there was gentleness in my voice, a kind of deference.

It wouldn't have been out of the question to walk up to the door of the house and get him. In spite of the disrupting mirth of the Sagasta home, no one in the village seemed to be awake. At one point I actually took six sharp strides across the field, having been frightened giddy by some kind of jungle rodent that scampered over my foot. But in the end, I realized that I could never do this. I had my orders, and they were almost all I had; I could not abuse them. I was to remain anonymous during this ordeal, not just during the escape but also in the aftermath. I was to speak to no one about this, I was to be remembered by none of the participants. My supervisors' belief that I could easily be nondescript seemed to be the strongest faith they had in me, and it was matched only by their absolute confidence that, whatever happened between us or to us, Ramon would not remember me a week after our acquaintance ended. My supervisors know baseball players very well.

The family knew I existed, they knew I lurked in the trees like the rodents and the crickets, that I had come because it was in my power to take Ramon away from them, whoever I was. While they didn't seem at all affected by this knowledge, I relished my role as this mysterious presence. I wondered what they thought about me, how they envisioned me, whether they were now talking about me at the table. I had wondered this twenty-two hours earlier, as I stood and inspected myself in the leased room on Santa Teresita Street in Matanzas. I've always been somewhat slight—my first minor league scouting report called me "pretty wiry for a catcher"—but I had cut a dashing figure in that hotel room. The thin black turtleneck, loose gray Army surplus pants tucked into tall hiking boots, a rakish tint of beard stubble—Ramon could have asked for no better cocksure American guide. I wondered if his family was expecting a figure like this to come and take away their boy, I wondered if I was what they hoped for. At various moments in the forest I had remembered that image from the mirror, and I had been pleased—it is maddening to remember my idiocy—that I simply looked prepared, and dangerous.

Dangerous, I turned out to be. Prepared, as I've already established, was another matter, and as the moon rose—passing through another stripe of clouds at 1:15 exactly—my apprehension had become so profound that nothing could have comforted me, and certainly not the façade of my appearance; I might as well have been wearing bunny slippers. In frightened boredom I opened the duffel bag, which was marked in stenciled letters with Charlie Dance's name, although the idea that Dance had ever served in the military still mystified me. I pulled out the contents to rearrange them more efficiently; they had shifted during the hike.

The maps: one for the Florida Keys, one for northern Cuba, one for the specific six miles between myself and the launch beach, one for the hilly country to the west, which, if we were to need it, would mean that we were woefully lost. The maps were marked with contour lines, a concept that I had always been able to grasp in the abstract but which I had never been able to use in any practical way. Charlie Dance had been overly pleased with himself for procuring them, as if we wouldn't stand a chance if we didn't know the contours. It didn't seem at all important to me, or even desirable, to know the heights and depths we faced, in both a literal and figurative sense. The maps were rolled up and stored in a lightweight metal tube that was like a short fly rod container.

There was a pair of hiking boots, size thirteen American, in case Ramon didn't own good shoes, and a pair of sweatpants should he be wearing shorts. There was the Swiss Army knife, which I found deep in the bag's recesses and then put in my pocket. Its weight gave me a mild sense of confidence, the gentle heft of a useful tool, although as with the maps I couldn't foresee any immediate need for it. It might serve to help us with engine trouble somehow, or even to cut kindling if we became stranded, but I didn't know a thing about fixing an engine or starting a fire. I had begun to view the contents with the perspective of a castaway, seeing only instruments of final recourse. The binoculars would let us know, minutes before the steel shaft of Kalishnikov rifles were pressed to our temples, that the police had found us. The sheathed Buck knife might allow us to dispatch some local beachcomber who would snitch on us, if Ramon had the nerve for that sort of thing (I certainly didn't). The blocks of cheese, encased in Tupperware, might be used to lure seagulls close enough to our stranded boat to whack them with oars. Unable to see in them any purposes but these, I squinted and scowled at the scattered contents of the duffel bag, as if accusing them of betrayal.

An uproar from the Sagasta house drew my attention away from this. The sharp noise of sudden laughter made me crouch again at the base of the tree. I shivered and, though I realized immediately the noise was benign, I couldn't stop. Through the empty limbs of the cedar tree, I saw Ramon slap the table with the flats of his hands, red-faced and breathless, and to his left his brother did the same. Even his mother seemed amused, and no longer stared alternately at her rosary beads and Ramon, but looked to the other end of the table with wide-eyed interest at whoever had caused this merriment. I decided it was a crazy uncle showing off a magic trick or contorting his face (I had encountered my share of this race of crazy uncles in Latin America, when I would court local girls in the winter leagues)— perhaps he was drunk enough now to fart or to share a dirty joke in the presence of the women. Only the girlfriend remained humorless, looking now not so much at Ramon as past him, at me, towards or through the fingers of the tree that tapped the glass. With the window's reflection and the shadows of the forest she could not have seen me, and yet I was stared down in an instant. I looked back at her through the binoculars, protected by them, and she kept her eyes locked on mine. I pretended to believe that she looked at me because I was the only one not laughing, I was the only one equally aghast that Ramon found in this moment an opportunity for merriment. It was true, as I recognized in an instant, that she and I wore the exact same expressions. This was an expression that said one thing: I am not ready for this. She was not ready to let him go, I was not ready to take him away. Ramon kissed her on the cheek. She blushed, and resumed her melancholy. She was a gorgeous girl.

I put the gear back in the duffel bag, leaving out one of the three plastic gallon jugs of water. Though I wasn't really thirsty, I drank until I was breathless, because I had remembered the weight of the things on the hike, and that I had planned to get rid of as much as possible, or else make Ramon carry them. The water jugs were the heaviest things I had to carry. And the heaviness, I was surprised to learn, had been the greatest problem.

On the maps this forest was labeled as *Selvaroto,* and it was cluttered with so many contour lines and circles it looked like someone had been doodling on it. All the lines, of course, meant that there were many dips and heights, and I could acknowledge this as truth based on my trek through it, and the presence of the contour lines and circles had done nothing to ease my legs. The knowledge that my trip would be bumpy, in fact, took root in no part of me except in an irrelevant part of my brain, the same part that kept Ramon's statistics even though I had never seen him throw a pitch.

The map told me that I had hiked, trudged, jogged, staggered, and limped for six and a half miles. This had taken me a little under four hours, though I had budgeted for five. The greatest surprise was that the weight and awkwardness of the duffel bag had offered much more resistance on the journey than had the flora, temperature, and fauna of Selvaroto. Selvaroto, in fact, wasn't occupied enough for me even to think of it as a jungle, although I suppose technically it was. The trees and leafy bushes were expansive and strange, but never so dense that I couldn't squeeze through—circumventing was not an option. I had to follow the straggling stream (which was labeled on the maps simply as *Agua*) or I would be lost. There had been no murderous snakes or insects, so far as I could tell, no chattering monkeys or fantastic amphibians. The shimmering eyes of starved predators never peeked through the long-fingered leaves, the way they had in my worst fantasies of what Cuba held for me. Through most of the journey I had stood upright, sometimes whistling, careful to watch where my feet stepped, but in general ambling along as if I'd been hiking the Appalachian Trail.

It had been humid, of course, but this did not bother me as much as Charlie Dance had insisted it would. I had spent almost a week in Cuba now, and was generally unimpressed by its weather—everything else about the place was much more oppressive than the heat. I have played baseball in Mexico and Venezuela, Alabama and Central Florida, and a dozen other places that seemed to consider themselves the sister cities of Hell (and many of those seasons were spent during the dreaded scratch-polyester uniform phase of the 1980s), and none of them had impressed me much. The torture of climate is often overstated. My nomadic life has taught me that people value the suffering that weather offers, they value the chance to lay themselves on the altar of climate, because people believe that suffering confers a kind of greatness. This is absurd, since greatness is rare, and suffering is common. But I digress.

At once the chatter in the Sagasta house ceased, and the silence was as sudden and conspicuous as a cannon blast— the immediate lack of noise actually made my body jerk. The Sagastas were all standing, the girlfriend still with her hand on Ramon's back, but she stood stiffly with her shoulders hunched a bit, and she gazed at the floor, holding herself in a deferential stance, like a geisha. I didn't want to watch them say their goodbyes—I was fatigued from their tenderness, which seemed gaudy and showy, even though I was their only audience. I did not want to see the girlfriend collapse with the mother into a weeping ball of women, as I felt certain they must do. I looked back down to the duffel bag, packed in the contents a little tighter and closed it up. I would be ready when Ramon came. I would toss him the bag and bounce out of my crouch without introduction, and lead him briskly towards the stream with a coarse "follow me," to let him know how I fumed at his tardiness.

I looked up again, expecting to see him still clutching to his mother or brother or lover, but I only saw the rest of the Sagastas, again seated at the table. Each of them stared in silence, fiddling with their silverware, except for the pretty young girl, who covered her hands with her face as her shoulders heaved. The boy laid a hand on her back, trying in his gawky way to be a man, now that Ramon was gone.

Ramon walked towards me. He strolled, in fact, glancing up at the moon-conquered sky, veering in his path as if he had been drinking, but I could tell that he hadn't been, that he was simply wistful. I was told this by the casual placement of his long hands behind his head, by the way his languid steps kicked at swatches of grass. Although it was only a moment away, I could not imagine our encounter. I could think of him only in terms of Charlie Dance's exaggerations, the organization's calculated ambitions. I could imagine Ramon Sagasta only in terms of a blood-red jersey with his name blocked across the back, in terms of my possible salvation or destruction—Ramon had been theoretical for so long, a dream tied to the controlling dream of my life, that it seemed ludicrous for us to actually meet and interact. Instead of anticipating the impossible moment that was about to pass, I could think only of Charlie Dance.

CHAPTER TWO

WHEN THE ORGANIZATION INFORMED ME, BY WAY OF A TERSE phone call from the chief scouting director, that I was to smuggle a left-handed pitching prospect out of Cuba, I was halfway through my first year as a scout, ten months removed from a career as a minor-league catcher. I was spending that year in Mexico, based in Tampico, and this may or may not have been the main reason they chose me for the mission; getting to Cuba is much easier for an American if you've been living abroad to begin with. In any case, I didn't have much trouble buying the plane ticket from Mexico City to Havana, and shortly before I left I received a delivery of two thousand dollars and a letter from the organization. The postscript in the letter instructed me to burn it as soon as I'd memorized the key points, a thrilling little addendum if ever I'd heard one.

The letter offered the specifics about our rendezvous with the charter fishing boat in the Florida Keys, which would be manned by people from the organization who were versed in the intricacies of defection. Apparently, if we touched down in the wrong spot, or in the wrong way, or at the wrong time, the Coast Guard could turn us away, or—even worse—we could lose the rights of our prospect to free agency. The letter advised me in stern verbiage that I would be expected to honor a life-long silence about my adventure. It told me how to get to Matanzas from Havana. It told me how to avoid the police, what to say to them if they stopped me. I say "it" because the letter, written on unmarked typing paper, was unsigned, for the sake of plausible deniability should I screw things up. The letter concluded with the following: *Your contact in Matanzas is a scout of long standing with the organization, named Charles R. Dance, or "Charlie." You will find him at El Refugio, a restaurant at the corner of Salamanca and Santa Isabel Street, not later than 9:00 P.M. June 10. He is American and very large. He's quite hard to miss, and he will be waiting for you. Do as he says.*

I had imagined that these kinds of meetings took place in dark alleys or seedy bars, and so the idea that Charlie Dance and I would discuss things over dinner sounded unexpectedly civilized. When I got to El Refugio, however, exactly one week after receiving the letter, I found Charlie Dance already well into a plate of fried bananas, a collection of beer bottles posted on his table like a centerpiece arrangement. When he saw me, he shook his hand in the air and motioned for me to sit, although there was no other chair. He resumed eating.

I don't think it's necessary for me to describe the ruthless way that some dark emotions can descend, drop upon you in an instant pang, and completely usurp whatever had been deluding your thoughts up until then. We've all had these moments, and the only thing surprising about them is how fast they come, how stealthily they swoop. I had entered El Refugio with a confidence that had showed itself so clearly in my aspect and swagger that in Havana people had stared at me on the street. They must have thought I was a spy, or a European mercenary advisor to Castro, or an American congressman. There was no position more glamorous than mine. I was spy, jock, playboy, soldier. I was nearing greatness as I envisioned it, snuggling up to the part of my life that might provide me with a legacy. I could fight any man in Havana, I could seduce any woman, I could smuggle any pitcher with a solid fastball to Miami, right under the nose of the Revolutionary Navy. With this swagger and smirk I entered El Refugio.

In the five heartbeats that passed from my entrance to the first vision of Charlie Dance, the swagger and smirk were punctured; I could almost hear the hiss of air as they collapsed into a broken posture, a forehead wrinkled in anxiety. I had been a mercenary, and now this blob of a man, without a word, had me roaming the restaurant in search of a chair, like a batboy sent out to shag flies. What is more, I could not find one, or was suddenly too meek to ask the other diners if I could borrow an empty one, and so I took a stool from the bar and sat at the end of Dance's table, perching above him like a parrot as he ignored me to finish his food.

El Refugio was a *paladeres*, one of the restaurants that had been illegal mom-and-pop type of places before the government starting demanding half their earnings. Now most of them were official and regulated, and something like the Cuban version of chain restaurants. Even so, the place was tiny, not all that much bigger than my leased room, and it had no windows. Naked high-watt bulbs lit the place with the kind of intense whiteness you get in dentists' offices, but I'm certain it never once occurred to anyone there to complain about it; it probably was a bit of a miracle that they had been rationed light bulbs at all, or that the electricity worked.

It was late, and most of the dozen or so people in the restaurant were done eating, but no one left the entire time I was there. Empty plates and glasses remained on every table, and I noticed that this must have been a pretty good *paladeres*, since some of the table scraps were different from others—I hadn't yet been in a restaurant in Cuba without being told that I had my choice of only two menu items, and the second option was usually sold out. The men and women were all pressed and combed and dolled up for their night on the town, surely the only one they'd get for a while, and they brushed away fruit flies as they leaned forward to speak without being heard by the others. This, like in Ramon's village, was unavoidable. Charlie Dance remained absorbed in his meal—the pile of fried bananas shrunk in front of me. I decided that he had never been here before, that the restaurant had been chosen arbitrarily, no thought given to privacy—perhaps it was not possible to find privacy in this nation, and so he just selected the *paladeres* that he knew would have a bit of a selection. Or perhaps he had not chosen it at all—it was suddenly obvious to me that it had been chosen by the sponsors back home, who had never been to Cuba but who liked to micro-manage, who held their meetings in an air-conditioned board room the size of an infield. Perhaps they had leafed through a guide book and chosen this place because of its name.

For all my previous confidence, I had been desperate to assume the competence of Charlie Dance—somewhere in myself I had admitted that everything depended on him, and on what he would tell me in this restaurant. No doubt few men could have lived up to the expectations I had placed on this name. Yet the actual Charlie Dance, the one guzzling beer and fried bananas and tapping the fat fingers of his left hand on the table to the rhythm of his gullet noises—he astounded me, he changed my perspective to such a degree that from that moment on all of Cuba would seem to conspire against me.

It was not necessarily that he was obese; lots of people in

baseball are, even some of the players. In fact, often the best scouts are very fat men—their fatness speaks to endless hours perched on bleachers, gazing motionless at the game, guiding countless hot dogs into their maws. But Charlie's fatness seemed especially vile. I guess I've seen fatter men in my life, but none who wore their heft with such contempt. The way he maneuvered his arms around his girth, the way he contorted his face and groaned when he had to move—he was clearly angry at his body for being the way it was, and he managed to make you feel that his obesity was somehow your fault. I'm getting ahead of myself—much of this I figured out later.

Charlie Dance had thick, dark gray hair that he didn't seem to have ever tended to, and despite his girth, his face was narrow, almost skinny. His shoulders were also narrow, covered in a faded polo shirt that flared out dramatically as it dropped towards his waist. Given my elevated seat, I could see the great expanse of his middle, which hid every bit of the chair from sight. The middle of his body could not have been circumscribed by a hula hoop. Sadly, I began to imagine the body beneath the clothes. I had a certain familiarity with this body type because I'd been in locker rooms with coaches who had enthusiastically let their bodies go to seed. I knew that Dance's thighs, massive and dimpled, would work in concert with the rampaging fat of his belly and sides to almost completely swallow up his genitals; his penis would look like it was sinking in quicksand. I could not get rid of this heinous image, and I know that it was simply a way I had of making an obscene situation as obscene as it could get, so that there would be no more surprises. I could have no worse a savior than the hideous, naked Charlie Dance, and so that is how I pictured him. I wondered what, in Ramon's mind, was the worse-case scenario for the man who came to rescue him?

I stared at him without compunction; I assumed that he

was the kind of man who had absolutely no pride in his appearance, that there was nothing you could say about the way he looked that would truly injure him. I had come to learn that scouts like Dance—that is, top-level scouts in third world nations—had no pride in anything, not even in their remarkable understanding of the game of baseball. I had known a few in Venezuela and Mexico (it had, in fact, been my role over the past winter season to serve them and learn from them). They enjoyed their checks from the home organization, were pleased with the Latin American cost of living, the weather, the easily purchased women, the food. Not all of them were fat, certainly not as fat as Dance in any case, but all of them seemed to be the kind of men who could wake up to discover that they had gained eighty pounds overnight, and not be concerned by this in the least. It had not occurred to me that Charlie Dance would be one of these men, but in fact he was the prototype for this kind of man.

This was how he began our relationship: "I don't know shit about you, I'm sorry to say."

He had a flat, unaccented American voice, although I would later learn that he had not been out of Latin America in nine years. I thought he might be from the Midwest, or else, like me, he might be from everywhere.

"It must be difficult for you to communicate with the organization out here," I said.

"I communicate with them plenty. Plenty." Charlie Dance wiped his face, picked his back teeth with his tongue. He had a very small mouth, and his lips were chapped. "About important stuff, though, just the important details. They told me they got a way to get the kid out, and that's all I wanted to know. They told me they're sending some old player, some low scout, and I say 'That's fine, just tell me where to go.'

They told me I got to rig you up, well okay, I guess I'll do that then, won't I?"

"Rig me up? You need to tell me everything. I don't know shit. They just told me to find you, that's all I know. They said you'd be here and you'd take care of everything." They hadn't really told me this, but they had put me in a position to assume it. It was equally likely that they hadn't told Charlie Dance much of anything either. For a moment I wondered if the organization had simply decided to get rid of me, and this was their way of making me quit, but I realized this was self-flattery. I had no contract—if they wanted me gone, it would not require elaborate measures.

No one seemed to work at the restaurant. The plates remained on the tables, the flies swarmed. The men and women chatted, continued to squint against the insidious glow of the light bulbs, continued to wave at the fruit flies. I began to notice that they glanced at us often, probably just because we were American and because Charlie was so fat, but it was difficult not to be made paranoid by them. I had heard somewhere that one in twenty Cubans is an informer.

It began to seem odd how abandoned the restaurant appeared, as if the owners were too tired to deal with customers and had just trusted the last one out to lock the door. Even the cash register, an old model that might have been stolen from an American diner or museum, was unattended, in a far corner close to the door. It came to me that I could easily rob the place. I can't imagine that anyone would have acted if I suddenly sprang up and stole the money, and I could have been out the door before Dance pried his fat body off the seat. It seemed a completely benign notion, no risk involved, at least compared to my present situation. Robbing the restaurant, bursting off to begin a fugitive life in the Cuban night with a few thousand pesos, along with the emergency dollars in my money belt, seemed infinitely preferable to remaining at the table with Charlie Dance, and working out my dangerous fate with this man.

"Yeah, well it's all arranged I guess," he said, as if to comfort me. "You know about the boat? Not the charter boat, I mean the one you're taking."

"I don't know shit! I don't know shit!" My protestation caught the attention of some of the diners, and a waiter peered out from the kitchen. I held one of the empty bottles up to him and pointed to my mouth.

"Well, there's a boat," he said. "Not much, a kind of skiff. Better than the rafts they usually escape on. Yours has an outboard motor. Fifteen horses."

I could only reckon the strength of this machine by imagining a line of fifteen horses towing a boat through the water, and in my imaginings the horses did not move very quickly. "Is that a lot? I mean, it's the ocean."

"Most of the poor bastards make it to the Keys on swimming pool toys. Go to Miami, ask around," he said, then leaned back and took a sip of beer, as if to indicate that he'd wait while I skipped over to Miami for a few minutes to confirm this. "A thousand or so make the trip every year, and compared with what they leave on, a motorboat's like the *Queen Mary*."

"I looked at a map. It's an awful long way."

The waiter brought two beers. Dance explained more to me about the boat, how to start the engine and prime the gas. He drew a diagram on a napkin, which I put in my pocket. In a moment of absurd hope, it occurred to me that this was the kind of artifact that could someday be in the Hall of Fame. There were a lot of contingencies, to be sure, but in the grimy paper of the napkin, and in the firm lines of Dance's outline, I sensed a piece of something ordinary that could be made exquisite. It simply looked like the kind of thing that they keep behind the glass at Cooperstown, and I realized that, of all the things I have touched in my life, only this had the chance to actually make it there, if what they had told me about Ramon Diego Sagasta was true. This possibility was small when weighed against my fear, but it was suddenly a presence in my mind, where before there had been just trepidation. It was strange to be comforted by this, by a smeared napkin, but it was something—I had somehow become closer to Ramon by imagining the glorious fate he could give to this object, and I had distracted myself from the moment's menace. I would become very good at this during my time in Cuba.

The motorboat would be hidden, Dance explained, on a thin beach, at the lip of the forest below a cover of frond leaves. It had been stashed by some Cubans he knew. On one of the contour maps, Dance had drawn the pathway from the boat (it would serve as my starting point—I could take a cab to a pier and hike two miles up the beach to it) through Selvarota to the Sagasta house. He described the house and the forest and the village of Rios. "It's a shit-bag little village," he said, "it makes me itch just to think of the place."

The waiter brought another plate out to Dance, although I hadn't noticed him order anything. His dessert was a lumpy mass of *natilla*, a kind of off-white pudding that tastes like overcooked vegetables but which is certainly made from an eclectic mix of animal parts. Some fruit flies swooped in to taste it and got stuck in the syrupy coating, but Charlie didn't notice.

"It's got a compass attached to the gas tank. You don't even know how hard it was to get one of those here. A good compass, and a boat and gas tank in Cuba—it's like trying to get a whore in the Vacitan."

"Vatican," I said, and he nodded.

"It's like getting a whore in the Vatican."

I knew how to read a compass, but I wasn't sure how this would help me get to the Florida Keys. I tried to imply this without sounding foolish.

Charlie Dance said "Ramon will know." I couldn't tell if he was making this up, but it was a comfort to me to let the matter drop.

I was thus briefed in a haphazard way—it became clear that Dance had no prepared list of things which I should know; he simply began thinking of things and he told me. He told me what to do if we were caught (don't mention the organization, and claim to be Canadian), how much water I would need in the jungle, how to deal with rough waves (approach at an angle—he did not say which angle), how many times he'd done this sort of thing before (too many to count, which turned out to be exactly the opposite of the truth), what to do if we got lost (don't ever call the organization from a pay phone). He told me the container of contour maps was under the table, that I should at some point before I left the restaurant slide it into my pants leg. His pauses became more frequent, as he tried to think of more nuggets of wisdom. It seemed obvious to both of us that there should have been more, that there must be things he was forgetting to tell me, things I was forgetting to ask. Or else it became obvious that anyone embarking of this kind of action should not need to be briefed on such matters at all, at least not by someone as ridiculous as Charlie Dance.

It occurred to me that he had not really given me anything other than the diagram and a roll of maps—he had not, in any sense, rigged me up. "What kind of equipment and provisions will be in the boat?" I said.

He took the last bite of his desert, probably to give

himself time to think—he held up one finger as a gesture that he would speak momentarily, as if his sense of decorum would not allow him to talk with his mouth full. After swallowing, he spoke emphatically. He had decided the exact lie to tell. "Jugs of water. Flares, just in case. Cheese and salami. Cigarettes. Ramon loves cigarettes. Lots of other stuff."

"Blankets?"

"Oh yeah, of course there are those. Of course. Trust me, it's all there."

"Matches, extra clothes?"

"You bet."

In general, I have a poor nose for deception. I virtually never know when someone is lying to me. When I discover that someone has been untruthful, I am immeasurably surprised, though I often realize I shouldn't have been (I will not go into detail about my two broken engagements.) At this moment, however, I was certain that Charlie Dance was lying about having stocked the boat, and that when I found it, it would contain nothing but an oar or two and a tank of gas.

"Charlie, you need to tell me the truth. Do I have everything I need? Will I be able to do this?"

"You better do this kid. You had better do this."

Charlie Dance reached into a kind of backpack at his feet and flopped a stack of papers onto the table in front of me. I recognized it as a scouting report. It was typewritten, not word-processed, and spotted here and there with gray stains and marginal notes. The sentences were skewed a bit, slightly diagonal to the paper. It looked anachronistic, again like something you might see behind glass at Cooperstown, and again I accepted this as a distant possibility, but it no longer felt so much like hope.

I read the cover page out loud:

SCOUTING REPORT ON RAMON DIEGO SAGASTA, LHP
FOUND AND RECOMMENDED BY CHARLES RAYMONT DANCE
MATANZAS, CUBA, 1996

In general, scouting reports are desperately boring and poorly written. I have always taken care with the ones I write, and I get the sense that they go unread by everyone but the players themselves. The prose in Dance's report was straightforward and emphatic, peppered with misspellings. I skimmed through the first paragraphs, where Dance had recorded his long history of proven acumen and loyalty. I learned there that he'd spent only two months in the major leagues, as an infielder with the Cardinals, and that he'd been a Latin America scout for over fifteen years, but only in Cuba for the last year or so. The report began discussing Ramon on the second page, under the heading "Overall Technique":

> He hangs his arm low on delivery. One time I saw his knuckles touch the ground when he reared back. His arm goes kind of like a windmill, if you know what I mean. Its almost strait up and down. I can't rember any pitcher I ever saw do that. But it works for him, even on breaking stuff. As you'll see in the charts, he has great breaking stuff, even though he pitches strait up and down. And of course his fastball. I don't even want to talk about his fastball, because it makes me sad that I didn't find him sooner, before he was 26, which now is how old he is. In his village they line up coconuts on fenceposts and he throws at them and breaks them open.

"He's pretty good then?" I said, to show that I was reading it.

Dance nodded. "Yeah. We're always saying that, you know. The chief scout in Santo Domingo last year said he'd found the next Roger Clemens, and now the kid's stuck in Oxnard. We're always saying stuff like that, always exaggerating. Sometimes they make it to the States, and sometimes they work out, but they're never really the next Clemens. But I'm serious this time."

I didn't say anything.

"I don't care if you believe me."

"No, it's not that, I believe you. It's hard up there, though. I know that from experience, it's just too hard sometimes."

If Dance had been more agile, he probably would have stood up—his face clenched into a weird, feral grimace, and it seemed to call for some accompanying gesture of the body. Instead of rising he leaned forward, which forced a gurgling, involuntary burp out of him, and he stared hard at me. "I fucking know that. I know it's hard. You think I was born in Cuba? You think I think the rest of the world is like this? I know this is a fucking—" he waved his arms around the restaurant "—whatever it is. Cuba. I'm serious this time. This kid is real."

I tried to appease him with an earnest expression and a quickly nodding head, although I don't know why—there was nothing remotely intimidating about the man, even in his mild rage. He wiped his face with a cloth napkin and leaned back. The chair squealed. I looked back at the scouting report. "Ramon Diego Sagasta. If they don't believe you, what am I doing here?"

"What, it's some big risk? Who are you?"

I had no answer. I might have even lowered my head and eyes, like a scolded child, and this encouraged him to continue. He was amused, but not smiling. "Like they've sent down their top guy? Like they read my report and said 'Send our best man down there, pronto'?" He was smiling now. "I don't know shit about you, but if you're the one they sent, I'm gonna go ahead and assume two things." He held up two fingers. "One, you speak Spanish, probably from playing on shit winter league teams in Puerto Rico. Two, you don't know how to coach, and they don't need no more scouts, so they got nothing else to do with you. They care about me just enough to send some guy down—you know, to humor me, and maybe on the off chance that I'm partly right. But they sure as fuck aren't going to send me any guy they need, or any guy they care about." He laughed, a sinister thing.

The cash register remained unguarded, beckoning. I had seventeen hundred dollars in my money belt already—I couldn't know how much was in the till, but all of this would surely be enough to get to the Bahamas. I wore good traveling clothes, good boots. I immediately and desperately wanted out, not just because of what Dance had said, but because everything about my present situation encouraged flight. I couldn't take it on faith that Ramon Sagasta was a great pitcher. I couldn't assume that helping him defect would somehow confer greatness on me. I could no longer assume some great destiny awaited me in baseball.

That is not entirely true. It is not true at all. I wanted out simply and exactly because of what Dance had said.

Up to that point I had not given much thought to the organization's reasoning in selecting me for the job, though I was vaguely aware my Mexican residency and language skills had much to do with it. This hadn't bothered me, though. Whatever their reasons, I would get a chance to prove myself, and this had seemed to be the main thing. They would let me show them what I could do. Having disappointed the organization more than once as a baseball player, to me this had seemed terrifically generous of them. After listening to Dance, it came to me with a dreadful weight that perhaps the last thing I wanted, the one thing I should have avoided at any length, was a chance to prove myself. It was not as if I had some latent talent as a smuggler of communist athletes that only I knew about—what did I think I could show them?

He beckoned our waiter. "That'll change, though."

I was clearly supposed to ask what he meant, but I would not. I didn't want to talk to him anymore. I itched for a silence long enough to end our conversation. I felt like I was interviewing for a job I didn't want.

"It's gonna change for you. For you, not me. You should probably be grateful, though I don't expect you will."

"It's not that I can't coach. They never gave me the chance. I think I can coach. And I am a scout. I watch the Mexican Pacific League in the winter." I knew how pathetic I sounded, even before Dance assumed a comical expression of mock interest and compassion. He made his eyes round, tilted his head, and touched his finger to his chin. I wanted to jam his head onto the table and suffocate him with his own food, but there wasn't enough left on his plate

I insisted on exposing this information. I was a scout—a low level scout it is true, but I was only thirty-four years old. They had never let me coach, they did not know if I had aptitude or not. These two facts were desperately important to me. I did not care how Dance reacted, so long as he knew.

"And who the fuck are you? Two months with St. Louis?" I said. "A Cuba scout, who the organization doesn't trust? At least I remember what a glove feels like."

"Would you shut up, you mope. You pissy bastard. Self-pity, that's something I can't fucking stand. That's you all over. And a shitty player, I bet. I bet you wouldn't even make my books. Here's a scouting report for you." Wheezing, he searched his coat pockets and eventually pulled out a pen and a small notebook. He scribbled, ripped out a page and slammed it on the table in front of me:

SCOUTING REPORT FOR THIS FUCKING MOPE: SHITTY, SHITTY, SHITTY. THE ONLY THING WORSE THAN HIS SWING IS HIS FUCKING SELF-PITY. PISSY WHINY MOPE. RECOMMENDATION: FLUSH HIM LIKE THE SHIT HE IS.

There was something so overwhelmingly offensive about every aspect of Dance—his oozing body, his filthy mouth, the way he belched and picked crust from his eyes, the way he used the end of his fork to root around in his ear—that made me immune from the offense he offered. It seemed to me that he tried so blatantly to be repulsive that there was no room for intent; he was so focused on playing this role that he could not have contained any free will or desire. He was what he had become, he had become what he long ago realized he should become, if this was indeed the life he would stick with.

We sat in silence, with some awkwardness—I, having read my scouting report, did not know whether to look up and acknowledge it, or instead to pretend that I was just a very slow reader until some diversion came up. The waiter, acting on an order I had forgotten about, suddenly placed two new beers on our table.

"This is Polar," Dance said. "It's the only thing I drink here, because it's made on the south shore. All the other breweries got workers that piss in the brew, cause the bosses don't give them pisser breaks. I know this, I really do. I got connections with all the vendors here, and that's what they say. At the Polar factory, the workers are allowed to go to the can every once it a while. What do you think?"

"It tastes okay. It's a little salty."

"Hmm." Dance drank a swallow from his bottle, and for some idiot reason I was thankful for this, for the fact that he trusted my opinion enough to taste the beer again. "Maybe they *have* started pissing in the brew then." He began to laugh. "Cuban piss is salty, you know—it's because of all the *jamonada*." He laughed some more. His laughter did not depend on anyone but himself. He didn't check to see if I was laughing along, or even smiling. I wasn't, and he didn't notice, and he wouldn't have cared anyway.

He treated his joke and subsequent amusement as a kind of breaking of the tension between us, as if he had apologized. "So, it's like I was saying, maybe you should be grateful to me, cause I might make your career, and I'm getting nothing out of it."

"How is that?"

Dance became earnest. He blinked his eyes tight and lowered his shoulders, as if he were about to jump at me. "I wasn't kidding before. He's the real thing. I've played and coached and scouted in nine different countries. I recommended Brent Borrester, way way back, when I first started to scout. Found him in Saginaw, where he wasn't hitting at all. But he had that beautiful swing, the one he's always had. And major league bat speed, and he could run a little, and so I sent him on, and I haven't heard a word about Brent Borrester from the organization since." I remembered that Borrester had retired only three years ago, so the "way way back" that Dance referred to was not so distant; I myself would have been in high school at the time he was called up. In spite of Dance's general repulsiveness, I guessed that he wasn't much older than fifty-five, but he seemed to want to give the impression that he was a very old man. Being an old scout could lend one an air of authority, after all, and Dance lacked any sense of vanity.

He continued. "So what I'm saying is, I've been around, and I know my baseball, especially pitchers. It's pitchers you focus on down here, cause there are too many wild cards with the other positions. Some kids down here hit a ton, but it's only cause they use those fat metal bats on some of the teams. But the pitching's pure. The pitching don't change from one place to the other."

I knew this, everyone knew this. My job, in fact, depended on what Dance was talking about. My previous role in the organization, in the Mexican Pacific League, had been as a condition scout. If the organization heard of a player with remarkable statistics—a .500 hitter or a 2-steal-a-game runner, for instance—I would be dispatched to the home park to check the truth of the reports. There was never any truth to the reports. Or, more to the point, the reports were always accurate, but the numbers had always been exaggerated by the conditions. Most of the time I would report to the organization that the numbers had been "conditionally inflated"—there was actually a Conditional Inflation form, with boxes to check for players whose home fields had short fences, whose opposition consisted of barely pubescent pitchers, whose games were played on gravel or unmown grass.

"I know," I said, for some reason feeling antagonistic. "I know about conditional inflation. But pitching can change too, sometimes. The cold especially can change things for pitchers. I bet your guy's never seen it below sixty degrees."

"That don't mean shit. He's not gonna be where you were, Slugger. He's not gonna be in Class A for ten years, having to help replace the spark plugs on the bus. Sleeping on the benches in rest stops. I bet you never even saw a major league clubhouse. Those clubhouses could be in Greenland and you wouldn't know it. The dugouts got heat blowing down. And the trainers know how to wrap you up tight and warm. I don't think the cold's gonna be a problem for Ramon. It might have been an issue for you, spending your career with the Toadsuck Butt-nuggets, or wherever you played, but it ain't gonna factor into Ramon's experience."

"What the hell is this, Charlie?" I called him Charlie because, for some reason, it seemed like the cruelest thing I could do to him. "I don't understand why you're assuming all this crap about me, and I don't understand why it has anything to do with anything."

"Are you gonna get this kid out of here? Are you? 'Cause I don't have the confidence in you I want. I want to feel like you're gonna do it, no matter what, and I just don't feel that. I don't feel that you're a winner. I feel that you're the kind of guy who'll let this all go to crap and then blame it on somebody else." He stuck out his lip and, I suppose, did an impression of me. "'Oh, we don't have enough food, oh, the boat's not stocked enough. Oh, no one's told me anything' And then you'll lose Ramon and it won't be your fault, right? Just like it wasn't your fault that you played with the Buttnuggets your whole life, that no one gave you a chance. Let me tell you this, smart guy," again he leaned forward. "You got your chance. You got more than one, more than ten. They don't leave guys where they left you if there's a Chinaman's chance they can play. Stop telling yourself you didn't get your shot. Wherever it was you were, you belonged there." He leaned back and resumed his previous volume. "Hope you invested your eighteen-twenty-five wisely."

A minor league player with more than five years experience in Double A ball makes $1,825 a month. Dance was guessing— I could have been in Class A or Triple A for all he knew—but he was right. For the last four years of my career, I made $1,825 a month.

Unbelievably, he was not finished. He said, "I just don't get the sense that you know how important this is."

"I understand that they'll shoot me if I get caught. Isn't that enough to make you confident?"

Dance wiped his tongue on a napkin. "They're not going to shoot you, you mope. Christ, you don't know a thing."

"How do you know they won't shoot me?"

"Fuck it all, I don't know that, that's my point! No one knows what the hell they're going to do. I guess they could shoot you, but then again they might throw you a damn parade and buy you a Cadillac. I don't know. That's not the point at all. Shit, just trying to save your own useless skin. How about thinking about something bigger than yourself for a change? Christ, that can't be hard. And don't give me your self pity."

Very abruptly, Dance became tranquil. He gripped the scouting report with both hands, a stripe of sweat slithered down his forehead. "He's not going to do anything for me. They'll forget about me. That's what I was trying to say before. He's going to be huge. I'm not trying to make you believe me really, I'm just trying to get you to accept it. Ten months from now, he will be in the starting rotation. They will be grateful. They will remember that your pretty fucking face delivered him. If they don't, *Sports Illustrated* will. I don't want you to be grateful just yet, there will be time for that. I just want you to know how big a deal this can be for you. Maybe that'll keep you from fucking up, maybe you'll put your heart in it if you think it'll land you a scouting job in Triple A. 'Cause it will."

Throughout his speech he stared at his bottle of Polar, and his voice stayed low, huskier and quieter than normal. "I've sent them twelve different reports, beginning last May, when I first saw him. They figured out I won't shut up about him, so they gave me you. You are a mope, by the way, but you're the luckiest fucking mope there is. I found him, but you can have him if you can carry him out. The organization will think he came from out of your ass."

I didn't feel sorry for him in the least, though I understood that I was supposed to, and though I understood that Charlie's position was perhaps unworthy of his skills and knowledge. Very little was asked of him down here. Recently some of the wealthier organizations had begun placing older scouts in Cuba, and dealing with the accompanying red tape and bribery, in order to set up a scouting infrastructure. The feeling was that the embargo would end soon, and when trade opened up baseball players would be the first thing on the market after cigars. Charlie Dance's job, basically, was to make contacts with managers and coaches, avoid getting arrested, write reports on the various field conditions and styles of play in the different regions, and wait for Fidel Castro to die. While doing this, he had stumbled upon Ramon, and no one believed him.

I shook my head at the waiter, who was coming towards the table with more beer. I stood. "You're full of shit about the provisions, and I don't care if you think I'm whining. We're going back to wherever you live, and you're going to get me the stuff I need, and I'm going to put it in the fucking boat myself. If I am going to do this, I am going to be prepared."

Dance smiled. "James fucking Bond of the Toadsuck Buttnuggets. Good God. What'd you think it'd be like down here?"

"I assumed there would be a contact who knew what he was doing. You're it. How about that?"

Charlie Dance acquiesced easily, and this didn't surprise me. He seemed worn out by our long discussion (is that the word for what we'd had?), and besides, he was going home anyway. He paid for his meal, but told the waiter to bring a separate check for my beers.

As we walked out of the restaurant, I laid my hand on the cold metal of the cash register. It was solid and cool—everything else in my world was hot, sticky, tacky. The button to open the cash tray was clearly marked, and I fingered it. I looked around the restaurant with an exaggerated expression of guilt; two or three of the diners looked at me with bold curiosity, not looking away when our glances connected. My heartbeat became audible as my adrenaline seeped, but suddenly Charlie Dance barked something at me, I shivered, took my hand off the register, and accepted that there was only one way out of Cuba. Some of my dreams are easily abandoned.

CHAPTER THREE

DANCE LIVED ABOUT A HALF MILE FROM THE RESTAURANT, IN THE top floor of an old motel. He was so thoroughly winded by the walk he could only gesture to the entrance of his building once we arrived, but he had, in the beginning, walked the streets with great confidence and purpose. He had actually pointed out a few spots of interest along the way, and he commented on nearly every *jinetera* we passed—there were at least ten on Salamanca Street alone—letting me know which ones might be bargains and which ones would clearly be nothing but trouble, the kind that think you're supposed to take them out to dinner or buy them some blue jeans before you do your business. The *jineteras* made me outrageously nervous, and Charlie was much amused as they all sensed this, and tried to outdo each other in making me blush. "Two things the *jineteras* know how to smell—money and fear, and you got both," he said.

The stairway to his apartment was cramped, and Dance had to twist his wide torso diagonally as he climbed. His door was unlocked, and he crashed himself against it and then lumbered in a beeline towards a reclining chair in the middle of the main room.

It looked like a large dorm suite at a college that was shutting down. One square central room, twice the size of the Sagasta house, served as the hub for the kitchen and a couple other rooms that Dance never bothered to show me. The interior had been repaneled with drywall and sheetrock, and on nearly every wall crumbled patches exposed the studs and wires, and in the kitchen the jerry-rigged pipes sprouted from underneath the sink like roots. There was a refrigerator, pale green and at least three decades old, standing alone in the middle of the kitchen. The main room was cluttered with several disparate couches and easy chairs—one plaid wool, one black Naugahyde. Beer cans on the coffee table left wet rings on a scattering of baseball magazines—not the *Sporting News* or anything like that, but the specialist magazines, the trade reports for scouts and general managers. The magazines were hard to find even in America, and of course strictly contraband in Cuba, and they were fairly recent. It said something about Charlie's contacts within the organization, I told myself, that he got someone to smuggle these to him.

On the back wall of his living room, Dance had taped up some of those old posters of major league players you used to be able to order from the back of sports magazines, the kind that still hang on the walls of my old room, in my father's house in Wichita. He might have done this for the benefit of players he cultivated there, people like Ramon who might have been captivated by them. They were the players of baseball's age of exuberance, players from the seventies and early eighties. In these posters, they wore gaudy uniforms (especially the San Diego Padres), and tucked frightful haircuts under their hats, and filled their cheeks to bursting with tobacco. On Charlie Dance's wall, Gaylord Perry heaved a slobbery screwball. George Brett smirked at the trajectory of a homer. Rollie Fingers twirled his bizarre mustache. I studied each one with grave surprise and something like delight. I could take delight in those players no matter where I was, no matter who I was with. And yet it suddenly occurred to me that if things were to go badly on this trip, if I were to be imprisoned or killed, my father would eventually have to take down these very same posters in my room. These happy, powerful men will confront him rudely in his grief, I thought. Mike Schmidt, Jim Rice, Catfish Hunter. They will mock my father, remind him of the disappointment that was the controlling fact of me. He will think of how, when my dream faded, I continued to worship these men and their greatness, how I worshipped them at thirty-four no less than I did at eleven.

I sat on the black couch as these thoughts worked on me, and Charlie Dance scuffled around the apartment shoving supplies into a duffel bag. He then sat on the couch and chest-passed the bag to me.

"What do you think? Look inside."

I made a big show of judging each item in the bag. Twice Dance interrupted to remind me that he didn't like doing business at his place. I had no way of knowing whether the bag was sufficient or not—I realized that clouding my judgment was the fact that I was very sleepy.

"Boots?" I said, holding them up.

"Ramon ain't gonna have his own. I bet he shows up in Bermuda shorts and bare feet, even though I told him to dress right. He don't listen all the time."

I held out the Swiss Army knife. "Is there anything else? For defense? Maybe even a gun?"

He gulped in breath. "If I had a gun, you fucking mopey puke, you'd be bleeding out in my bathtub right now! Nobody wastes my time like this! You're in my house, taking my food, and all you can fucking do is whine!" He wiped the sweat off his forehead, and with this gesture he seemed to clear himself of his rage.

He said: "Also, you need to remember that Ramon can't swim for shit. Just don't stand up or anything. Stay away from big waves. If anything goes wrong, if you don't meet up with the charter boat, remember that he just needs to touch dry land in Florida and he'll get asylum. And you got to be with him, you got to make sure to funnel him to our people, so that he don't become a free agent. If they get him in the water, he comes back. So if it comes to that, remember about the swimming thing—just try to drag him onto the beach."

The possibility of this happening—not the shit going wrong part, but the idea that I, in such a moment, would have the presence of mind, the desire, or the ability to drag the sodden, helpless Ramon Diego Sagasta onto the beach—this was so preposterous that I didn't even register it completely. I nodded with intensity, as if I relished the thought of saving Ramon in order to strike a blow against free agency.

We didn't speak for a while; both of us listened to Charlie Dance wheeze. His heavy breath made me feel bad for him, the only moment of pity he would ever earn from me. I felt the sudden need to speak to him without posturing. "Charlie, what is going on here? I mean, look at us—what kind of professional organization has its head this far up its ass to think you and I are just the men to plan and act out a defection from Cuba?"

If Dance had been a friend, or even someone I had developed any kind of rapport with, we might have started laughing at ourselves the way desperate, frightened men do—when our situation was put into plain words, it began to seem increasingly bizarre. Instead of laughing, Dance allowed for another long silence, during which we hung our heads, mirroring each other. He eventually took a beer from the coffee table—an open one that had been there when we arrived—and sipped ponderously.

"Well, it's like I said—I don't think they really believe me.

That he's that good. I'm as serious as I've even been. I'm serious as a heart attack. This kid will make it in the bigs. He's just fucking incredible. He's a phenomenon. But they just got my word to go by, really. Scouts from the other organizations don't even send reports home anymore—it's not worth the trouble. And this close to Havana, the Americans figure they'll hear about any kid worth taking a chance on. But the government hasn't let him play on the national team in three years, and apparently he's had some troubles in Matanzas. Getting hassled by the cops, harangued by his pitching coaches to change his delivery, and so forth. Whatever the reasons, I don't care—I seen him pitch, don't fucking tell me what his numbers are. That's all I know—I seen him pitch."

"So if they don't believe you, why do they even bother sending me down? There could be trouble, right, trouble for them, if I get caught? They'll figure out who I am, who I work for. Am I supposed to withstand torture or something, for the good of the organization—could they really expect that?"

Dance shook his head, and again let a long silence go by. "Not really. I mean the organization won't get in trouble, even if you rat them out. They'll say you misunderstood your mission or something. Besides, I don't even think the Cubans would ask, they'd just deal with you themselves." Dance had released a silent fart, which was coming to me like a mushroom cloud. "Alls they're risking is a motorboat and a crap-ass scout. They keep guys like you around for this kind of thing. Well, not this kind of thing exactly—frankly, they haven't gotten anyone out of here yet. But they got all sorts of guys, all sorts of risky little projects that are only risky for guys like you, and that can pay off big for them. Some poor schmo had to go into central Paraguay last year to look at a prospect, and he got some weird voodoo style malaria that made his fingernails fall out. But it's like I said, if this works out, you get him up there and he works out the way I know he will, they'll be grateful as hell. You won't be a crap-ass scout anymore." He finished his beer, shook more of the open cans on the table until he found another that wasn't empty. "But that's it, I guess. They think there may be a chance I'm partly right. That Ramon may wind up pitching middle relief. I also think it's got something to do with his name."

"What about it?"

"Ramon Diego Sagasta. It's a hell of a name. They'd love to put that on a jersey. Too many Martinezes and Gonzalezes and Rodriguezes in the league these days. Fans can't keep them all straight—some of the managers even have a hard time with it. That's the way these people think, that's the way they decide things."

He was completely deluded, of course. If the organizations had their way, they would identify their players by serial numbers. Yet Dance believed what he'd told me, and probably gave this pet theory of his more credence than he indicated. He had needed to find a reason why the organization had actually believed him, and he settled on the bizarre notion that they did not in fact believe him, not entirely, but that they liked the fact that the lies he told them were about a kid named Ramon Diego Sagasta, a name they wanted to see across a blood-red jersey in the concession stand.

When it came to that, I wondered for the first time if I myself entirely trusted his opinion of Ramon. I suspected his intentions in large part because of the magazines he kept on the table. They were study guides, reference materials—not light reading. There weren't any pictures or features; the rough pages just offered column after column of statistics and codes regarding North American prospects. He wouldn't have needed them, shouldn't have had them. Charlie was just there to do legwork, to get down the names of the managers, the styles of the clubs, the conditions of the ballparks. He would have known that this was his job, this is what his career had come to, but the magazines indicated that he still considered himself relevant to the game, that he thought he needed to keep himself current on the prospects in the U.S. Maybe accepting his fate as a Cuba scout was too much for him, maybe he had to talk himself—and everyone else—into thinking that he had finally, improbably, found something extraordinary.

I must have looked doubtful. He said, "They'll be laughing about this in two years—the idea that Ramon Diego Sagasta should pitch middle relief!" He settled down, slightly winded. "Trust me on this. They like the way his name sounds. It sounds crazy, but that's the way they make their decisions."

I agreed with him on that point, the caprice with which the organization seemed to decide the fates of those who depended on them. I thought of El Refugio, and why it had been chosen for us.

I looked past Dance, and became distracted by one of the posters on the wall. It was Don Sutton, the great Yankee, and the poster showed him from a distant side angle; it was the view the third baseman might have had of him. He was frozen in his reared-back position, the weight of his body entirely balanced on a geometrical point slightly behind the pitching rubber. In the far right of the picture, on the stretch of green infield over which the ball was about to travel, you could see the blended shadow of the catcher and the batter who were awaiting this pitch. I could not remember who caught for the Yankees back then, I doubt anyone does. This is all that is left of that catcher: his shadow waits for the revered Sutton to throw the ball in his direction. It seemed to me, at that moment, a very reasonable and valuable fate. To be the man who served the man who

49

triumphed over this moment. There are thousands of them out there. Vic Wertz, who hit the ball that Willie Mays caught and is remembered for. Dale Mitchell, who gave himself as the final out when Don Larsen threw the perfect World Series game. These names are trivia questions now, but it seemed to me that to be the answer to a trivia question could imply playing a great role in this game, to have given oneself to a great cause. For all my concern, a great hope still surged in me: to be the man who smuggled the man out of Cuba.

Dance smiled and leaned back on the couch, resting the beer can on his gut. "It's a crazy business. Back when some of the Latinos started coming up and performing, especially Clemente, a few of the managers were worried. There was the black problem, for one thing, but this was worse—they wanted their go-to players to be American at least, so that they could at least talk to them. Back then you got no points for finding a good spick, no matter what he hit like. All the really great players were still white back then, but it was like we were looking for the great white hope, like we were boxing scouts or something. Now they'll just settle for a spick with a great name." He sipped and sighed. "Roberto Clemente, there's a great fucking name."

I felt the dangerous and familiar presence of a tipsy old man who wanted to reminisce about his early days in baseball—hanging around with older scouts, most of whom could get me fired if they wanted to, had landed me in this position several dozen times. I dreaded hearing these stories, because of their inanity and casual racism and the fact that I was obliged to listen and look fascinated. It is as boring as listening to someone tell you about a dream they've just had. What is worse, they are told with easy cynicism—Charlie Dance had already been able to mitigate the greatness of Roberto Clemente by equating him with a collection of pretty syllables—the kind of cynicism that implies that greatness is a fabrication, that belief is always a delusion.

I stood up. "What about drinking water—I should have that. And you said Ramon likes cigarettes."

Dance stood up as well, perhaps embarrassed by his momentary nostalgia, even if it was cynically rendered. "Don't have smokes, but yes, Ramon will want them. Don't have water either. What you can do is just go to that bodega we passed. It's not three blocks down, you can buy all that stuff there. Pay in dollars," he said, but didn't offer me any.

"All right. I'll get it on the way back to my place." I shouldered the duffel bag, concerned now about whether I should shake hands with him.

"You're still a fucking puke!" He shouted suddenly, and moved towards me. "You're gonna fuck it up, I can just feel it. You got the bag now, and smokes and water, you think that's what'll get you home? You puke, you're gonna lose Ramon, I know it! You'll get busted, because you think that goddamn bag and that goddamn motorboat is what's getting him out. It's you, don't you fucking get it?! *You're* what needs to get him out, not all this crap, all this garbage that you won't even use anyway!"

"All right Charlie," I said, and took big strides to the door. "Hey, it was great meeting you."

"Wait, no wait, hold up. I get excited sometimes." He shuffled over to me. "What I mean is, you need something else, something for confidence."

"What, like drugs?"

"No. Like that, I guess, but no drugs. I wouldn't want to be a bad influence." He smiled, and he looked like someone who had just been ordered to smile at gunpoint. "Just say no, heh-heh." The smile left, the moment of good cheer had been completely unsustainable for Charlie. "No, I know what you need, and if you did it, it would really make me feel better. Because I'm being honest with you now. I've been honest all along. Except for the boat thing, I wasn't honest with that. But anyway, I'm giving you this kid, who's like a baby to me, it's like I'm his father, you know, and no one knows about his talent but me and a bunch of Cubans who don't mean anything. So it's like this huge gift, this huge responsibility I'm giving to you, and I've got to feel like you're not going to fuck it up. And frankly, I don't get that feeling right now. I don't feel like you're just gonna rush out there, grab Ramon, take him to safety, balls-to-the-wall, you know. I want to see Steve McQueen leaving right now, some guy who'll get the job done. Telly Savalas. And I just don't get that from you right now."

My smile was as impossible to resist as Dance's had been to sustain. "Telly Savalas?"

"Listen to me, goddammit!" He literally bared his teeth. "No, sorry, you've just got to listen, though. You need a shot of confidence, as I said, and in my experience, in all my years in the game and so forth, there's only one thing that can provide that confidence."

"What the fuck are you talking about?"

Dance spoke quietly. "Go out and get us two hookers."

"What? Are you shitting me?"

"I am not shitting you at all, and you need to hear me out. Hookers, sex, there's nothing like it for building confidence. Am I right? I don't need to tell you. You know it from the game. If you got problems with a pitcher, you get him laid, right, and then he goes out and he throws thunder. 'Cause he's got confidence. I don't need to give you all the examples, but just believe me on this. It's better than any drug you can take." He put a sweaty wad of dollars in my hand. "Just go out and get us two *jinateras*. They're easy to find, you know, you saw them.

Nothing too dirty—two good ones, use your judgment. Light-skinned for me. We need to restore your confidence levels. Fill those confidence tanks."

I took the money without speaking. I looked at him for several moments, up and down at least twice, then walked out the door, taking the bag and the money, leaving the sweaty fat man unsure as to whether sex would soon be brought to his door.

CHAPTER FOUR

As Ramon approached, I found comfort in objects. The simple bulk and weight of the duffel bag spoke of purpose and competence. I remembered that the boat had in fact been well hidden under a swatch of fronds and branches. The beach was narrow, so Ramon and I would have to drag it only a few dozen feet to the still, thigh-deep water of the shoal. The outboard motor had looked substantial, and gleamed in the sunlight—a sleek, sparkled gray, brand-new it seemed, or at least rarely used. The boat itself suffered in comparison, being well-used and scarred with rust, but it had no visible holes and it was long and wide, with high gunwales to block the spray.

Ramon paused, standing upright ten yards ahead of me. He rested his hands on his hips and looked puzzled.

"I'm right here, you dumb son of a whore," I whispered this in English, because Ramon was large and young, and I had learned that, no matter how justified, you should never insult someone's mother in Latin America. Ramon jerked his head spastically and then smiled in my direction.

"Where? Where are you?" he called out in a rich speaking voice. He made no effort to whisper, and he maintained his upright posture and easy gait as he approached the forest.

"*Callate! Shhhhh!*" I said, and stepped out of my cover. I maintained a low crouch, shouldered the duffel bag, and waved Ramon to come into the cover of the trees. He saw me, smiled, and approached with his hand outstretched.

"Ah, there you are. Dennis. Hello. I'm Ramon Sagasta."

I found it impossible not to shake the hand he offered, and in doing so I found it impossible not to stand up, like him, although unlike him I continued to whisper. We simply stood in front of the lip of the forest, shaking hands and making introductions—one of us in a loud, conversational tone of voice; it was as if we were meeting at an orthodontists' convention.

"You're not as tall as I thought you would be. Charlie said you would be a scout, someone who used to play ball in America. Is that right?" He asked this with a tone that said he would not entirely believe me if I told him it was true.

I nodded, and then said "We've got to go." Ramon was still looking me over, obviously judging me—he made no attempt to hide an expression that was made mostly of a smirk. I turned and heard him follow me into the forest.

For five long minutes, we plowed together through the leafy brush—we were off the path of the stream, since it ran south of Rios. It was clearly jungle here—the branches were wet and swatted us from all angles, painting us with berry juice, spider webs, and the carcasses of insects. Soon we reached the stream, at the point where it descended into a gully that ran above the cliffs of the shoreline. Here we halted, and I unlatched the duffel bag.

I pulled out a pair of socks and the boots for Ramon; he was wearing long pants, tied at the top with twine and cut off high above the ankle, but besides this he wore only sandals and a Matanzas Toronados T-shirt. Ramon took the footwear, sat on a rock and began putting on the socks. He did all this in a hasty, almost panicked motion, as if for the first time he realized we were in a hurry. He smiled when the boots slid on. "Charlie Dance remembered my shoe size."

"You should be very flattered. He's a noble man."

Ramon smelled bad. Even with the organic stench of the forest, and the saline air blowing from the south, I had noticed this immediately. I couldn't place the odor—it was as ambiguous as it was insistent. He smelled perhaps like a certain kind of cooking oil, or like bad oatmeal. In the moonlight by the stream, I could see that his skin tone was very dark, he was a *moreno*. His eyes were a kind of yellow-brown, the iris color you see on cats.

"I told Charlie I had shoes but he didn't believe me, and he was right. But I kept lying to him because I knew he didn't believe me, and that he would get me some shoes, so I didn't have to tell him the truth. That's the way it is with us—Charlie knows what I need, and gets it for me even if I don't ask." He said this with a broad, proud smile. His teeth were brown and crooked, the kind of teeth you would expect of a chain-smoker from the third world.

There was also something freakish about Ramon's ears— they jutted out from his face at a radical angle, almost perpendicular to the sides of his head. They were the ears of a little boy, which were coupled with the bad close-cropped haircut of a little boy, that only served to accent the abnormality of the ears. In spite of all this, I considered Ramon to be very nearly handsome. The childish face, the easy wide grin, the long lean body, the muscled arms of a pitcher—these factors mitigated the smell and the teeth and the ears. He would be popular in America, I thought, not just with the clubhouse groupies but with the media as well, and of course this mattered a great deal.

"Charlie is a great provider," I said, not knowing how to respond to his last comment. I then decided to drop the delicacy —the bastard had kept me waiting for two hours. "He gets you anything you need, huh? Like hookers?"

Ramon turned to me. His eyebrows stretched high, and the smile disappeared for a moment. "Hookers? Hah!" He leaned back on his rock and opened his mouth towards the sky—exaggerated mirth. "He did that for you? It makes sense. Charlie likes the hookers. But he always treats, right? Didn't he treat you?"

"Yeah, I guess he did." This reminded me that I still had the two hundred dollars in my pocket. I had forgotten about them. While Ramon stepped away to pee, I stashed them in the money belt.

He called over his shoulder. "Who did you have? Lucita? No? Lucita's very beautiful, although she has a scar on her shoulder that is kind of disgusting."

"Ramon, for the love of God, finish your pee already. I've been waiting for two fucking hours. If we don't hurry we won't make it before light. I'm serious. Fucking hurry."

When he came back, Ramon knelt to double-knot his laces. Very quietly he said, "Charlie likes any hooker, so long as she's not too dark." He stood and slung his bag over his shoulder. "Okay then, let's go."

The moon was overhead now, casting short shadows. I picked up the duffel bag and led him along the stream, deeper into the forest, and it quickly became dark. "It's tricky here, kind of muddy and steep," I said. "But when it levels off we're going to have to jog."

"I don't know about that," Ramon said. "Did you bring my cigarettes? I love cigarettes, but they make me not run so good."

"The organization will be very happy to hear that."

He giggled behind me. "What do you mean? I pitch, who needs to run?"

The terrain seemed familiar, although I had only crossed it once. I found myself remembering stumps hidden by leaves, thick patches of mud that I pointed out for Ramon to jump over, avenues through the trees where I knew there weren't any stickerbushes. I was suddenly frustrated that I hadn't been able to tear into Ramon for making me wait so long, and that I hadn't made him carry the duffel bag, and I didn't understand why I hadn't. It was not simply that it was difficult to speak harshly to his open, little-boy face (although it was); I found it awkward to speak to him in general. During our one brief conversation, it had seemed that I hadn't participated at all, that Ramon was simply listening to and responding to voices within himself, as he paid little attention to my words, and took no register of my tone. During most of our time together, Ramon and I were as isolated as we could be, and yet there were moments when I nearly looked around to see if he was talking to someone else.

I darted through the forest eagerly. Here it was too thick to jog, but in my haste I hoped to imply what I hadn't been able to say: that Ramon's farewell dinner had actually put us in serious jeopardy.

We were cutting it very close. If Ramon had lingered another half hour, the escape would have to be called off entirely; we wouldn't have made international waters by daybreak. As it was—1:25 A.M., six miles to the boat, another two miles to the international zone in the Caribbean Sea, sunrise around 6:00 (I guessed)—it would be a close thing. I could very well imagine us bobbing on the dark ocean as the sky illuminated itself above us, revealing us to any Navy cutter or fisherman who cared to look. It would be much the same kind of exposure as the moon had given back in Rios. The turning up of the world's dimmer switch to reveal Ramon and me caught in the act, sheepish and guilty, like delinquent schoolboys.

No one, of course, would be stupid enough to boat out of Cuba during the daylight hours, and so perhaps that in itself would provide a kind of cover—the fisherman and the cutter might simply refuse to believe the possibility of such idiocy, and continue to go about their business. I have learned, however, that just because no one is stupid enough to do something does not mean that you will get away with doing it; it simply means that you are more stupid than anyone else, and the authorities are always ready for that.

An example, a memory: One afternoon eight years earlier, catching a close game in Grand Rapids, I had inexplicably found that I could not remember the pitching signals, other than the call for a fastball. A jumble of signs came to me from other cities and other teams—at that point in my career, there had been at least a dozen—but they didn't help there in Grand Rapids. I might as well have been pulled straight from the bleachers and asked to catch the game, so total was my inability to call the pitches the situation demanded. Despairing, I called for fastball after fastball and, if the pitcher shook me off, I insisted or just shrugged. After two doubles and a home run, the manager came out.

Skipper, it's a strategy. It bombed, I'm sorry, but I didn't think they'd look for that many straight heaters.

No Birch, it wasn't no strategy. You're just lost. Go to the showers.

A bad memory, but a lesson learned: ignorance is almost always recognized as ignorance.

A bad memory. When they came, I simply had to remind myself that there were good memories as well, quite a few of them, moments of near greatness in fact, although just then I didn't have the leisure to savor them.

We jogged through the forest, the clump of Ramon's boots resonant behind me. He made it clear, through his gait and whining, that the boots were stiff, but he never fell more than a few yards behind, and probably could have passed me if the path had been wider. Because of the slopes and rises, the darkness that we still hadn't adjusted to, the jutting of the stream, the new boots, and the groping fronds of arching trees, we never moved at more than half speed. I felt healthy and strong—my steady breath a testament to the years of conditioning exercises, which are supposedly a little more severe in the minor leagues. The sweat of my body was encompassing and thick, layered on my skin instead of simply running off it. I felt like a baby newly arrived, sheathed in slimy liquid.

After two hours, we stopped. We perched on large, slanted shards of rock by the stream. The shore teemed with insects that stuck to our sweat and drowned in it. Together we drank an entire gallon jug of water, and I gave Ramon his cigarettes on the condition that he carry the other water jug in his bag, which he cheerfully agreed to do.

We rested in identical positions—arms flung over knees, heads hanging low—and we panted together until Ramon said, very softly, "You never told me what happened. Charlie made you get the hookers, right?"

"You're still talking about Charlie Dance's hookers? Good God, Ramon, this hooker fascination could be a problem. If you get to the big leagues and start to order hookers up to your hotel room, in about five minutes you'll be on the front page."

He shook his head with grave emphasis. "No, I'm not talking about the hookers. I'm talking about Charlie. He's my friend, I'm allowed to talk about him. You know why he made you get the hookers?"

"I have no clue, Ramon."

"Because they won't come if he goes to them himself."
Ramon's face was touched with a kind of awestruck intensity.
There was no humor in him anymore, but also no disgust, no
judgment at all in fact—he was simply fascinated with what he
was now telling me about Charlie Dance. He seemed to have
forgotten his cigarette.

"What?"

"Charlie is so disgusting, the hookers won't go with him,
even though he's rich. I guess there are always those he can get,
like the runaways and the homeless ones. But the regular
jineteras, the clean and pretty ones like Lucita, they won't sleep
with Charlie, even for all his money."

"You have a pretty high opinion of Cuban whores, Ramon.
It's been my experience that hookers will sleep with your grand-
mother if you pay them enough."

"Oh, I know, I know!" He flapped his hands before him, like
he was trying to cool himself off. "That's the point! Hookers will
do anything. Especially in Matanzas. But Charlie's too disgusting even for them. The ones that have done it with him, they cry
for hours and hours. They go back to the street and for a long
time they cannot even speak, and when they do they just tell
everyone to never, ever do what they've done. They say they are
polluted forever."

I took a cigarette from Ramon and lit it. With the exercise,
the urgency and anxiety of escape had left me. I'm not a smoker,
but we both had our breath back and I wanted to hear the rest of
what Ramon had to say, if only because he seemed so delighted
to get it out. I needed an excuse to linger. "What—just 'cause
he's a big fat guy? It's not like he's deformed or anything."

He gulped with solemnity. "He is like a whale, the hookers
say. It is like being with a whale. He won't let them be on top,
and so he crawls on top of them and they can't get out from

underneath him. Like a bug under the feet of a cruel boy. He gets tired so quickly that after a few seconds of plunging—" Ramon illustrated this with his hips "—he has to rest, and so he lays there, still on top of them, crushing them into the mattress."

Ramon had his face in his hands now, his lips moving between his fingers. He seemed bored and tired, or perhaps morose. For a while I had imagined this to be an anecdote—how could any story about a hooker and Charlie Dance not be?—but there was now a mood of profound sadness about us, as if we had been sharing stories of dead loved ones.

"And then she feels him come inside her and it's like she's being poisoned down there as well. And then when he's done it's impossible to get him to move. He's already snoring away—snoring and drooling and farting in his sleep. If she is strong, maybe she squeezes herself from under him during the night. But she probably will have to give in, she'll pass out from disgust. She will have to wait until he wakes up and rolls off her to go take a piss."

Sweat dried on my clothes and the insects had begun to bother me. I sat still, amazed by what Ramon had told me. I felt vaguely contaminated for having this information, for having this image entered into my brain. He had caught me off guard. I could not understand why he had needed to tell me this, and I would not find out for a long time.

He took his hands away from his face and looked at me. "Lucita told me this. You should have seen her bawling. Just from remembering it, months later, she bawled like she was on fire."

"How do the hookers know what it's like if none of them will do it?"

He shrugged. "Most of them have done it once. They didn't

know—they didn't believe the stories. He was just another fat American with money. So in the beginning, when he first came to Matanzas, he did most of them. When a girl finished, she told the others never to go up there, never ever, but no one listened, and only once they'd been, did they understand. Now he only gets them if they are tricked into it." Ramon paused and pointed an accusing finger at me. "You didn't have hookers with Charlie. I can tell. He wanted you to get him a girl, but you refused. Do you think it's immoral?"

"I'm not sure I need to explain myself to you Ramon."

"I don't think it's moral either. I feel sorry for Charlie, though, and plus he helps me with baseball, and so I get him the hookers."

"You don't sleep with them yourself?"

"Of course I do. I have to."

"And why is that?"

He leaned back on the rock and lit another cigarette. He had cheered up; he now seemed eager to speak, while before it had been like listening to a confession. "They won't come up if I don't. That's how Charlie gets laid, now that all the hookers know who he is. I go and find two girls on the Paseo, right? They know what's going on, because if they don't know I tell them right away where we're going. They won't do it with Charlie, they say, they can't—they say this every time. Then I say 'well come up anyway, and we'll see who does what with who,' meaning that one will sleep with me and the other with Charlie. I make sure to give each girl a wink at some point, so that she'll think I've chosen her.

"So we get to the apartment, and Charlie makes us drinks, and then, after we've had our small talk, and Charlie is getting sweaty, then I turn and kiss one of them and say 'Come with me, my angel,' and we go into the next room."

"And Charlie plows into the poor hooker who's left. That's quite a system, Ramon."

He smiled widely; his mouth seemed to be made of elastic. His empathy had vanished.

"Why do they have to fuck him, though?" I asked. "Why can't they just leave after you pick the other one?"

He shrugged. "They're whores. I think it doesn't occur to them that they could be in a man's apartment without fucking someone." He took a long drag and blew the smoke out his nose. "In a way it's like us," Ramon continued. "Baseball players. What else are we going to do? In school, if there was a soccer game going on, I'd pick up the soccer ball and try to throw a curve with it—a hard thing to do, but I've got big hands. What use did I have for soccer? That's what I mean—what use does a hooker have for sitting in a man's apartment without fucking for money? I've played here almost all my life, except when I was traveling with the nationals. What do you think that's like, playing here when I should be in Yankee Stadium? I tell you, Dennis, isn't it worse for me than for the whores? Playing for the Toronados is the same for me as fucking Charlie Dance is for the hookers. But what do you do? Do you quit? No. If you're a hooker, you fuck, even if it's Charlie, because that's what you do. If you're me, you play for Matanzas because you play baseball. I know you understand me, Dennis."

In fact, I did not understand him at all. That is, I was aware of the analogy he was making, aware of what it said about his feel for the game and his understanding of his situation—even if I was a bit surprised to hear him say it—but in no way did I understand him, or this feeling. He imagined I did because I was a minor leaguer—I had played for organizations similar to the Matanzas Toronados, in Venezuela, in Mexico, in Puerto Rico, in the United States Class A system. This much was true, but he assumed too much about my reasoning. I hadn't stayed with it because I was a baseball player, because of a devotion to my nature and to my game—I had stayed with it because I was terrified that I wasn't actually a baseball player at all. I had played in those places with gratitude, and with the suspicion that those places and players were perhaps too good for me; there was no resignation on my part, no grudging acceptance. In any case, I nodded as if I knew exactly what he meant—I was used to doing this.

"I'm glad I don't see their faces," Ramon said. "Once I decide who I want, I'm playing kissy-face, and I carry the girl into the room, so I don't get to see the look on the other's face, and I'm glad for that."

"Naturally," I said. I stood up and brushed my backside. "Well I'm glad I was spared the experience."

"Oh, it wouldn't have been like that for you. You might not have even gotten any hookers to go with you."

"What do you mean? You don't think I can get a hooker?"

"It's not that. By yourself you could, but I don't think the promise of a night with you would make a girl risk a night with Charlie."

I pondered this. Insulting and arrogant as his statement was, he had spoken it with such guilelessness, and his face kept such an earnest expression, I thought perhaps I had misheard him, or was letting frustration color my interpretation. "What are you saying, Ramon?"

"Forgive me, Dennis. I'm sure you're a virile man. But I am Ramon Diego Sagasta. To sleep with me is something the girls talk about for a long time afterwards. Of course, making love to Charlie stays with them as well, but as I've already said, they always think I will choose them. They've all seen me play, and their fathers and brothers talk about me. Some of them may

imagine that I will fall in love with them, if they please me
enough, and that I will send for them when I am a big player in
the United States. Hookers have dreams like that, I think."

I picked up a stick and doodled on the muddy ground.
"First of all, Ramon, getting a woman to fuck Charlie Dance is
not something to brag about. It basically means you would
make a very good pimp. And second, you're probably not going
to be a big player in the United States, since your goddamn
farewell party, and your goddamn stories and your goddamn
lollygagging have cost us about two hours, and we'll be hitting
a wall of the Cuban coast guard right about the time the sun
comes up. You and I will be the best players on the Cuban
National Prison non-traveling squad, but that's probably as far
as we'll make it."

He looked at me with a vacant expression. The smile was
gone, but he did not seem to be affected by what he'd heard. He
reached out suddenly and groped my calves, then my biceps.
"What were you, Dennis? Shortstop? Second base? You weren't
a pitcher, I can tell. And when was this, when did you play? I
want to know about this."

I felt an instinctive need not to answer, but I could not
withstand the silence for more than a few seconds. "I was a
catcher, mostly. Some outfield, towards the end. I finished more
than a year ago. This is all beside the point."

"Hmm. You were not a very good catcher, perhaps. You
didn't play in the big leagues?"

"Why would you say that? How the fuck could you know
that?"

"Your face tells me I'm right."

"You dumb bastard! Did you hear what I said? I lied, in
fact—I'll be the one who goes to prison, and you'll probably be
shot. So much for baseball then."

"Charlie has confidence in you, he told me. I think you'll get us safely there."

"Charlie hadn't met me the last time he talked to you."

"Nevertheless. I have confidence, I have faith. I am destined to become a great major league baseball player, and that's all there is to that."

"Yes, Ramon, it's that easy, isn't it? You have a great destiny, so you don't have to worry about it. You just traipse through the woods with me, and the next thing you know you'll be on *Baseball Tonight*." He didn't know what *Baseball Tonight* was, so I awkwardly had to explain ESPN to him—it put a small hitch in the momentum of what was becoming an argument between us, but I carried on with it. Yes, I was disturbed about what he'd said regarding my assumedly mediocre pimping and baseball-playing skills, but it wasn't just that, I'm not that quickly provoked. It was many things. The cigarettes and the two-hour wait. The foolish ears and strange odor, the easiness of his step. The fact that the hookers probably *had* slept with Charlie Dance just to be near Ramon. A fastball in the high nineties, and three other pitches. The greatness in him.

He looked at me with a quizzical face, searching for the source of my sudden bitterness.

"Do you ever think about anyone else, Ramon?" I said. By anyone else, of course, I meant me and players like me, but he took it in another sense.

He paused and nodded, closed his eyes against the gravity of his sudden sadness. "Yes, I think about them," he said. "I will miss them more than you can know."

I paused, having to readjust my attack, now that I realized he meant his family. "I never did understand defectors, Ramon. How is it that you can just up and leave everything so easily? Just because you want to play a game."

"Because I want to play a game," he repeated. "It's not what I *want*, it's what I *need*!" He screamed this, not in anger, but in absolute pain. Tears appeared on his cheeks almost immediately, as if they had seeped out of his skin. "They wouldn't let me play anymore! When the Nationals went to Atlanta last year— they wouldn't even consider me, because of what happened in Bulgaria. What am I supposed to do when I can't play? It's all I can do—there's nothing for me without that! There's nothing for my family without that! My family, my Rosa, I love them," He was bawling now, bent over, about to fall to his knees, "but I must pitch!" He sniffled noisily. "I know you understand me, Dennis."

This last remark ruined it for me. As before, I didn't understand him, and I now lost patience entirely. The tearful appeal to my sympathies as a fellow baseball player was ridiculous and insulting—Ramon would spend about two days in the United States before signing a contract welcoming him into a baseball fraternity that had consistently rejected me since I was twenty.

I walked away from Ramon, knelt at the stream bed and began tracing patterns in the water. "I don't know that I do understand. You're leaving everything. Your home, family, girlfriend. The streets you grew up on, fields you played on. You'll never see them again. I'm not sure I understand what would make someone do that. I love baseball in my way—but if you told me I couldn't see my parents again just so I could keep playing . . . there's no way." This was partly true. I wouldn't ditch my father just so I could play more baseball. If, however, I could trade in the right to see my father in exchange for skills that would take me to an everyday role in the major leagues, I would not think very long before accepting the offer. A lot of what I said to Ramon seemed to be half true.

Ramon had stopped crying. He watched the surface of the

stream. "You just don't know, so it's not your fault. Living as I lived here, you don't know. Yes, it's a hard thing, to leave them all." He whispered now.

The whispering affected me more than the tears had, and so I tried to sound jolly. "Well, you'll make a new life, and a very good one. You won't find another family, but there will be a different Rosa every night, trust me."

His eyes suddenly focused, and he aimed them at me. "There isn't another Rosa, Dennis. Do you understand me? When I make it to the States, I will get her out of here. I have it planned already. I'll get her out before I get out my brother and my mother. I will spend all the money the organization gives me—people can be bribed. I will send down others to get her if necessary. Someone better than you. What are you costing, anyway? Are you a fifty-dollar smuggler? I will pay millions, I will hire soldiers, I will buy a submarine to take her to me."

I shook my head firmly. What I said next was partly for his benefit—it was all true—but also because I needed to find out what would hurt Ramon, and I felt like I was getting close. I wanted to take away this dream of reunion in America. "Impossible, I'm afraid. They'll be watching her pretty closely once you're gone. Your family, too. They might even send them away somewhere. I've played with Cubans before, ones that made it out on their own. They say Castro pretty much makes sure they don't let a whole family slip away—what good Cuban wants to see you reuniting with your family on SportsCenter? It would be very embarrassing." He remained still. "Besides, what about the hookers? You're in love with Rosa, but you sleep with that garbage? I figured Rosa was just another whore." I was feeling playful, I had no sense for what would be going too far. "She must be a fantastic lay."

These words affected Ramon in a way that seemed almost

deliberate, dramatic, as if he were a bad actor in a pantomime who had heard his cue. He took a few staggering paces backwards, then raised a shaky hand to point at me. I knew in a few seconds, however, that there was nothing staged about his reaction.

"A whore?" He swiped at the extended branch of a birch tree and knocked off some small leaves. He stuttered over the next few words. "Did you just say that? Yes, I think you did. Rosa is a whore? A whore!"

The word in Spanish is *puta*, as everyone knows, and I could see the spittle of rage career towards me as he pronounced the hard consonant.

The statement had felt wrong, severely wrong, coming from my mouth. I had not thought I would say anything like it, and could not even guess what I could do to soothe him. I could almost see the wrath escaping his body, like steam. Yes, it had been a large mistake, but it seemed that all I could do was wonder how large.

"Ramon, I am sorry. Really, really, really. My mistake. I didn't mean to call her that." And I hadn't meant to, of course, but I knew he wouldn't buy this. It's why apologizing is generally such a useless thing—there's no way to express your sincerity except by repeatedly expressing it, and that's just not convincing.

His rage would just have to exhaust itself of its own accord, I could see that clearly enough. His face was so deeply red that I was concerned for his blood pressure, and he clenched his fists and rolled his eyes skyward, so that the irises nearly disappeared. It was the kind of look he might have had if he were being boiled alive.

"You think she is a whore, do you? Isn't that what you said?"

"Yes, but I didn't mean it, Ramon. I really don't know why

I said it. You have to accept that—I just said something I did not mean."

This might have confused him, and I can understand why. It was an apology I personally might have accepted from someone, knowing as I do the vagaries of communication, the way you can feel so uncertain and groundless that explaining how you feel is beyond futile, and trying to do so often backfires. But Ramon would have nothing to do with these kind of abstractions. I imagine, like most country people the world over, that Ramon expected you to say what you meant and mean what you say. These straightforward people make it difficult on the rest of us.

With great purpose and deliberate thrashing, he stomped into the forest and came out with three rotting alligator pears, which were plentiful in Selvaroto. For a few seconds. he shuffled them in his hands, and then clenched his teeth.

He threw without a windup, just jerking himself into motion with a sudden whirl, launching one of the alligator pears at me, or so I thought. The thing exploded, just as I brought my hands to my face, at about the level of my head on the birch tree that stood about a yard to my left. The rotted shrapnel of the fruit, yellow and smelling like bile, flecked my face and hair, and the shattered pulp slid down the trunk. I watched it as it descended, thinking that maybe he wouldn't throw the next pear at me if I wasn't looking at him.

He did, though. The next one detonated at my feet, or on my left foot actually, the exact spot, I imagine, that he had been aiming at. The sting was terrific, unexpectedly sharp through the leather of my boots. The bulb bit into my instep and made me hop and curse.

The next one came immediately after, on my right foot, so that I had to hop again in a comical way, like a figure in a movie when a mobster starts shooting at his feet and commands him to dance.

Was this what he wanted, then, to just make me look stupid? I felt almost relieved when this seemed to be true. He could have my dignity; I would dance in the forest for an hour if he wanted; it was better than not knowing where his rage would end.

"Ramon! For God's sake, stop it!" I said, still hopping to play along with what I thought he wanted, but also because my feet still felt as though my socks had been lit on fire. "I am sorry Ramon, for God's sake. Now please, stop this. We need to keep moving." I spoke sternly, now thinking that an indignant tone, coupled with my dance of supplication, might appease him, or snap him out of this strange haze that my words had cast over him.

But now he screamed, as shrill as a child. "A whore! She is not a whore! I won't have you call her that! I will not!"

In time I would learn the source of this rage, but then I thought that it was just the most obvious—and most pressing— example of a character I did not think I would ever understand. Ramon, the great athlete, screaming at me in spite of what it might mean for our escape, simply because he wanted to scream at me. I was, at first, more perplexed than afraid. If you are a Cuban defector, travelling through the jungle to get to the motorboat, you do not start screaming—I had thought this would be understood, a given. Yet here he was, on a windless night, betraying our presence with an animal yell. My one hope was that his barely coherent screams would be mistaken for a jungle bird, or a boar in the midst of a slaughter.

"Holy shit, shut the fuck up!" I hissed in English. "Shut up! Listen to yourself!"

He screamed one more time, nothing I could make out, just

a long wail towards the sky that ended in a moan as he leveled his face at me again. His cheeks were sodden from tears and sweat, like he'd been slapped with a sponge. He stepped into the jungle again.

"Ramon, please, this has got to stop. I don't know what else I can say. Think. Use your head. We need to get to the boat."

But he was beyond my voice, even though he stood only about ten yards away. Thirty feet, about half the distance between home plate and the pitcher's mound. It had been a common drill in my career, in fact, to do something like this—to put on an extra chest protector and catch for a pitcher at about half the regular distance, in order to sharpen reflexes. But I didn't have any pads, and it was dark, and my last game with the Lansing Lugnuts suddenly seemed very far in the past. My hands stationed themselves valiantly in front of my crotch.

I probably should have run, of course, or hid behind a tree. But I really didn't know what he was going to do yet, and I also didn't quite feel that I had the moral prerogative to resist. Hadn't I called Rosa a whore, and didn't I deserve some sort of debasement because of it? I hoped, I suppose, that he would just make me dance again, or splatter my face with more avocado shrapnel, and I thought that perhaps this was his right.

Generous thoughts, it seemed, for the next one was aimed at my head. I barely saw the thing. I knew it had hit me when I closed my eyes, my head jostled, and the darkness became spangled. The carcass of the fruit fell to the ground, but my face was coated in juice that felt like rubber cement.

The pain registered only as the next throw was being released. In the brief, precious moments of stillness, opening my eyes against the stickiness and not yet feeling the burst of agony in my head, I saw Ramon in his windup. It was a strange but graceful thing, exactly as it had been described in the scouting report. His arm began low behind him, and then he paused and held it high behind his head, so that he looked like a matador poised over a bull. His leg lunged a full yard forward and then his long arm jolted past his head, brushing his ear, and his face was perfectly uncontorted (I'd never seen that in a pitcher before) as still as if he were waiting in line at the bank. I was thrilled to recognize this, thrilled to connect the fat man's misspelled words with the image now before me. Yes, I was in danger, but he had turned this enormous weapon, this enormous gift, on *me*, and I found something grotesquely delightful in this fact.

But then the pain came, and reddened my sight, and the next pear landed, exactly where the first one had, a few inches above the bridge of my nose—just about where you would put a bullseye in a human face.

I felt my right temple meet soft earth, and then I was asleep.

CHAPTER FIVE

I'D BEEN KNOCKED OUT BEFORE, TWICE, BOTH TIMES BY WILD pitches to the face. I've found that waking up from unconsciousness feels much like slipping into it—there's a vague pain on the inside and outside of the head, a dreaminess, a strong desire to sleep. On this occasion, I woke because Ramon was slapping my cheeks. I opened my eyes. It was bright, much later than dawn.

Ramon had composed himself, although his face and eyes were the kind of rash-red people get when they've been crying for a long time. "If you ever call her that awful word again, you will be dead," he said.

I squinted against the light, and twitched my head around in all directions, mouth open, disbelieving the sun. "Ramon, what time is it?"

"Your watch says eight. You've been out for a long time."

I couldn't see out of my left eye. I touched it, yelped, and decided it would be best if I never touched it again. My watch did indeed say eight o'clock. I had been out for almost five hours. Ramon sat near me, on a mat of broad leaves that he had lain over the remains of the alligator pears. On the ground beside him, neatly set side-by-side, was a long row of cigarette butts.

My face, hair, and teeth were all coated with the sticky dried blood of the alligator pears. When I tried to sit up, the rumbling pain in my head knocked me flat—I eventually found a kind of comfort by lying on my side.

"I mean it," Ramon said. "Never ever should you say such things about Rosa. She is as pure as a child. In fact," he regarded me with clear disgust, as if my repulsive condition had been of my own device, "It's probably best if you don't mention her name again at all."

"Ramon, it's eight o'clock in the morning." When I spoke, my face hurt. I felt the tight ache of a black eye, the sting of a broken nose. "We're still three hours from the beach. We were supposed to meet up with the charter boat between noon and three."

"So we'll be late."

"No, Ramon, it doesn't work like that. They're posing as sport fisherman—they have a day license." I paused to wince and tried to sit up again. "They're going to wait until three, no longer. We are supposed to meet up with them sometime before that, get you into a storage compartment in the hull, and capsize the motorboat. That was the only plan. That was how we would get to Miami. For God's sakes, they even have a plane ticket for you, for tomorrow night."

Ramon squinted and trembled. He lit another cigarette. "Well, I didn't know that," he whimpered. "I didn't know. How was I supposed to know?"

"Well, how did you think we were going to make it out of Cuban waters in the sunlight, you big fucking doofus!" I said "you big fucking doofus" in English—there was no Spanish equivalent. "For Christ's sake, Ramon, the Cuban navy does practice maneuvers during the day out here! We might as well go enlist!"

"Well, I didn't know! It was you—you said those things about Rosa! What was I supposed to do? I meant to kill you—I wasn't thinking. How can I think about the navy? How can I think about those men in Florida, when you call my princess a whore!" He began to weep.

I took a cigarette from him. I opened the duffel bag and got out some cheese and we ate. I found myself disbelieving the situation, disbelieving my watch and the sunlight, and the inevitable image of the men from the organization turning the boat around and heading back to Miami to report us as no-shows. And then I found that I was honestly amused. With the sunlight, it no longer seemed as though there was any danger. It seemed as though if we waited long enough soldiers would come and catch us, and I would smile sheepishly and throw my hands up in the air. Ramon would plead and cry, but I would joke with the soldiers, admit my naughtiness, offer them some beef jerky, and go back home disappointed but not terribly surprised, like a runner caught stealing third. In the Cuban sunlight, it seemed as though I had done no wrong; all the foolishness and malice and ineptitude had existed during the night. Things had started again. I needed to go back to Mexico.

"We're done, Ramon," I said. "We'll go back to Rios. Maybe Dance can get me a ticket home. When you think about it, we haven't really done anything yet. Just took a midnight hike through the forest—no one can bust us for that."

His mouth was full, so he sounded casual when he spoke, but I sensed immobility and dread seriousness in him. "No. We'll go now. To the boat. It doesn't matter that it's daytime. It's a big ocean. I don't care about the navy. We'll get into Florida somehow—all we have to do is set foot on dry land,

Charlie told me that. How hard can it be? Besides, you're an American, that will help."

I limped a few yards into the forest to pee. While there, I dumped two packs of Ramon's cigarettes into the bush, out of spite. "Not good enough." I called him. "I mean, think about it, Ramon—it's summer time. Even besides the coast guard, there will be fisherman, sailboaters. Any one of them can bust us, radio the cops. The ocean will be painted with peril today," I said—Spanish sometimes brings out the poet in me. "The Cuban sea is a web with many spiders."

He didn't respond but, when I came back to the clearing, he stood, shouldering the duffel bag. "We can't go back to Rios, Dennis, you will have to trust me on that." He said this with an empty, merciless voice. If he had a gun, he would have been pointing it at me.

"What do you mean?"

"That bridge has been burned. People there will know. There are CDR people in the village who suspected. They come by every morning to check on me. They always have some excuse, they say they want to borrow some rice or talk about the Toronados, but really they're just checking to see if I'm still there."

That people associated with the CDR—Comités de Defensia de la Revolución—might have had Ramon under surveillence was certainly a sinister and realistic prospect. I'd been told several times that in Cuba you couldn't swing a cat without hitting an informer, but for some reason it didn't quite ring true to me. "Bullshit. You're full of bullshit. If they suspected you, you'd be in Matanzas already, in a work program or something. They sure as hell wouldn't have made it so easy for you to get out."

He shook his head, wore the self-satisfied, thin-smiled

expression of a paranoid. "They want me to try to escape. Because they want to catch me. It would prove them right about me. They would have their excuse for not putting me with the all-stars and letting me tour. They would show me around as an enemy of the people. I'm much better to them as that than I am now—what am I now? I'm a local hero, no one understands why I didn't play in Atlanta. It's the way with people from Matanzas, we're always mistreated—Havanans are wildly jealous. When one of us becomes great, like I have, they say he's disloyal."

"You *are* disloyal, Ramon."

"They couldn't know that."

"What about Bulgaria?"

"That was a long time ago."

I almost forgot what we were talking about. I was still very weary. I recovered. "You're full of bullshit. I'll walk you back up to Rios, no one will notice you're gone."

"You will see Dennis. They can be slow here. It will take a while for the CDR people to figure it out, and then for the right people in Matanzas to hear about it. An investigator will come talk to my family, and then the FAR troops will be sent out. It will take a while, but it's certain that it will happen in this way. Best to continue on. I would dare the bay now much sooner than I would dare Rios again."

The fact is, I am quite often a groundless man. My touchstones are few, my sense of right and wrong frequently skewed; I am subject to the insistent advice of others. As such, it is difficult for me to make judgments. Although I felt that I knew a good deal about Ramon, there was no instinct in me regarding whether or not he was telling the truth. I could find no resources, no clues; whether to believe him or not would have to be an arbitrary decision. Ramon certainly had reason to tell me if in fact the Fuerzas Armadas Revolucionarias would soon know of our escape, but then again he had reason to tell me this even if it were false—for whatever reason, Ramon needed, more than anything else, to be rid of Cuba. He needed to founder on the ocean, or be arrested in Florida, or be torpedoed by the navy, or become a major league baseball player, much, much more than he needed to go back to Rios, even if it meant being safe.

I recognized my lack of understanding, and made an immediate decision. In the forest and the waters, I still possessed a semblance of control. Maybe I would prove expert at driving the boat, at splitting the blockade, at darting through the flats of the Gulf of Mexico—then again, maybe I would not. But if we turned back, this was all I had: either Ramon lied or he didn't. I didn't like it that he had this power over my fate—it was supposed to be the other way around.

Continuing the mission was a practical decision, then, but there may have been something else behind it. I was afraid, yes, more than I had been at any point in my life, but I can't discount the fact that going back to Rios had become equally unthinkable to me as it was for Ramon. It would have certainly meant the end of my association with Ramon and his promise, the end of whatever hope I still had. I would have had to throw the napkin from El Refugio and the scouting report in the trash, I would have had to go back to Mexico and resume my job of trying to figure out if the Culiacan Tomateros were corking their bats. If this notion did in fact influence my decision, then it was the first time my need to attach myself to Ramon and his greatness overcame my fear. "Fuck. Fuck. Fuck. Let's go," I said, and Ramon followed me along the stream. I could feel his smile burn in my back.

In spite of the extravagant smoking habit he'd bragged about, Ramon ran very well. With his boots clomping along the hardening mud of the stream bed, he kept pace with me as we sloped downhill along the stream valley, and passed me as the land began to rise again. I wheezed out that I should always stay ahead, since I had the maps, but he whooped and said that he wouldn't go too fast, and he would stay with the stream, and besides he had made this trip a thousand times; as a boy he came down to throw rocks as far as he could into the ocean.

As the stream widened, an equally wide stream of emptiness was created through the treetops, and sunlight came through and we could see very well in the valley. Ramon expanded his lead and began to run joyfully, weaving around saplings, leaping to grab at high leaves. He sometimes turned his body and ran backwards, waving me towards him playfully, but I was not ashamed at my pace. I was almost ten years older, and as I moved I cringed from the fresh welts of alligator pears.

I paid close attention to the strange jungle around me. The idea that the Cuban *guardia* might be pursuing us had taken firm hold, and I wanted to get my bearings. There was no path to speak of—we ran on a strip of soft dirt that acted as a border between the growth of forest and the slippery rocks of the stream bank. On either side of us the forest extended in layers— a density of tall grass bordered the stream bed, behind the grass sticker bushes stood taller than Ramon, and finally there were thick stretches of high trees with tapering trunks the color of sand. Noises traveled from the inner forest, from animals I couldn't see as I passed their voices at a jog; I heard the song of insects mostly, but also many birds, and sometimes scattering rodents. In the interior, I caught glimpses of many clear patches where I could hide if necessary, where the ground was open enough for sleeping on, so long as there weren't too many ants. It was darker there in the forest, and the trees and vines were thick, but not impenetrable, nothing like the jungles I imagined one encountered in Asia or the Amazon. The forest was dense, but not disconcerting. Here you did not expect to find the venomous toads or man-eating swallows or warthog-size tarantulas that the nature shows were always showing you of the exotic jungles. If we heard shots or dogs behind us, I told myself, it would not be so bad or so frightening to escape through the forest to one of these clearings and wait things out in there, eating yellow berries. And it would be easy enough to do, provided Ramon did not join me—he did not seem adept at lying low.

Ramon kept his lead, but never by more than a dozen yards. After twenty minutes of jogging, he no longer swerved off the path, but he still ran confidently. The fabric of his pants swished together as he ran, making a noise like the churning of a machine. He kept good posture. From behind he looked very much like an athlete.

I knew then that this was how I would always imagine Ramon, no matter what became of him. I knew that this would be the central image of a good story that I would have forever. I saw myself five years in the future, sitting in a Mexican cantina to watch the All-Star game, seeing Ramon grin and spit and stretch out his long arms to prepare for his first pitch, and this version of me remembers this sweaty view of him from behind, as he chugged his way along and outpaced me in his exuberance, after having defeated me for insulting his lady. Before he was even a free man, before the major leagues made him even more free than anyone else. I might nudge the drunk next to me and brag about my accomplishment. *Yo lo tome fuera de Cuba*, I would say. I got him out of Cuba.

I ran through a cloud of smoke and thus realized that Ramon had lit up in mid-run. The cigarette didn't slow him down much, but I noticed that it affected a change in his stride. He held his arms out wider and lower and he stopped kicking up his knees, apparently to conserve energy that his lungs couldn't spare. As we ran, I noticed his body make these adjustments periodically, either in response to different terrain, or to his smoking habit, or simply to his mood swings—like all great athletes, his body was like a car with a finely calibrated automatic transmission, which did its own thinking and made a thousand minute adjustments that its owner was not even aware of. It's one of the things I've learned to watch for in evaluating talent, these bodies that work entirely on their own, on a higher level than ever could be achieved from simply taking commandments from the brain. I kept my eyes fixed on Ramon's back just has his girlfriend had kept her hand there, as if not to lose him.

Earlier I had admitted to myself that Ramon's greatness could have just been another of Charlie Dance's delusions. But at that moment it all seemed clearly presented to me, it seemed that Ramon had already shown me every bit of himself that mattered, and whatever I didn't know wasn't being hidden or protected, it just wasn't relevant. All I needed to do was watch him run, watch him thrown, watch him allow his body to act of its own accord. Charlie Dance, I thought, might very well have been telling the truth.

I immediately wondered if this mattered at all. Ramon Sagasta would probably have to be beyond great for me to leave a legacy through him. There would need to be room in his story—in the back pages of *Sports Illustrated*, in the display case at Cooperstown—to tell of his escape and the man who rescued him. And besides all this, we were still a very long way from Florida.

When we came out of the trees, we had to jump from an eight-foot precipice that abruptly ended the forest and began the beach. I saw that the weather had darkened—clouds varying from pale gray to soft black blocked the sky entirely. Ramon didn't seem to notice. He stood on the beach, turning his head to scan the water. He nodded and clapped his hands together once, and he began to sing under his breath.

I took him to where the boat was stashed, and we cleared it of the fronds and heaved it onto the sand. Ramon cleaned the leaves and sticks and insects from the inside while I wiped clean and inspected the propeller blades and engine casing, pretending to know what I was looking at. The engine sparkled because it had been coated with a glittery, purple-blue paint, and on both sides it read "Evinrude" in silver cursive. It looked silly attached to the purely functional, army-green skiff, like a satellite dish attached to a trailer home.

Without speaking, we rolled up our pant legs, lifted the boat—I had the engine-heavy stern and Ramon took the nearly weightless bow, naturally—and we walked into the water, which was colder than I'd expected, and jumped in the boat when we were deep enough.

CHAPTER SIX

THUS WAS OUR LAUNCH RATHER ANTICLIMACTIC, I THOUGHT AT the time. It was a very simple matter of putting the thing in the water, getting into it, yanking the cord on the motor, and steering away from the land mass. It must have seemed this way to Ramon as well, because after we'd gone about a hundred yards he turned his back to the spray, grinned at me, and called out "We're off!" as if this had just occurred to him.

How far is it from the beach near Matanzas to the southernmost edge of Florida? That is a very good question, and one I can answer now in detail, having recently looked it up in an atlas—I had not done this at the time of our escape, but had relied on Charlie Dance's vague but emphatic guess of "one hundred miles and change." The maps would tell us as well, but we had not consulted these yet, because I was so utterly puzzled by the whole thing and Ramon was so utterly convinced that he simply didn't have to worry about it.

At that point, aiming for somewhere around Key Largo would have been our best bet. Since the charter boat would be vacating the coordinates 24°4'/81°1' in about four hours, we no longer needed to go so far west, but could take a mostly northern route. Other keys may have been closer, but Largo is big, hard to miss, and we wouldn't want to accidentally pull up below one of the long highways that connect the smaller islands—I'm not sure if setting your foot on American pavement will get you asylum. 145 nautical miles separate the beach near Rios to a spot just above the John Pennekamp Coral Reef State Park in Key Largo. A fifteen-horsepower motorboat, carrying approximately 500 pounds of gear and passengers, travels on a moderate ocean at about twenty miles per hour if you go at just under full-throttle. Stopping every once in while to pee, to check the maps, to change drivers, this trip should take no more than eight hours, no less than six.

It took me an absurdly long time—ten minutes or so—before I realized that I possessed none of this information; while I had realized that the charter boat would no longer be waiting for us, thus freeing us to choose a closer spot in Florida, I simply did not know where we were going. We were going away from Cuba—this had seemed like enough for the time being.

I released the throttle and the boat stopped dead. A bit of wave water sloshed over the gunwales, and Ramon looked at his wet pant legs with an expression of concern.

"Where the fuck are we going?" I said.

Ramon shrugged.

"Get out the maps," I said, but the duffel bag was next to me, so I got them out, laid them on the middle seat, and Ramon and I both moved to the center of the skiff and studied them.

We spent the next few minutes bickering like a couple on a road trip trying to decide which turnpike to take. Ramon insisted on going to Key West anyway, because the charter boat people might still be around, even if they were back on land—it was, I admit, a sensible argument. I could easily imagine higher-ups in the organization milking a trip to Key West for all the Curzan rum it was worth. I, however, latched onto the idea that we needed to hit the mainland—the idea of landing on an island off Florida, even an American one, did not seem satisfactory. I could imagine there being technicalities, the kind of arbitrary laws islands often have that serve only to remind you that they are not the same place that you came from. An island, after all, is the prototypical metaphor for something that does not look to the rest of the world for its cues—it didn't make sense to claim asylum in such a place. In my imagination the Keys didn't seem like America, they seemed like a theme park based on the concept of what America would be like if it were located in the Caribbean.

We argued for quite a while, but didn't get very passionate about it. The truth is, I like to argue in Spanish—the language seems designed for arguing, with its lightning pace and powerful stresses and insistent rhythm, and I take pride in my fluency. I have to admit I became churlish—it went a bit like this:

RAMON: "Key West is where the people from the organization will be."

ME: "The people from the organization will have already turned in the boat. They will not want to see us even if they are there."

R: "They will have to help us, for my sake."

M: "If we find them, they will be drunk and stoned and too busy visiting Hemingway's house to worry about baseball."

R: "Don't be foolish. It's not a good time for foolishness. The mainland is too far, we are risking it as it is."

M: "I'm glad you realize that, Ramon. For a while I was convinced that you thought I was a tour guide."

R: "At this moment, I would have more faith in a tour guide."

M: "At this moment, I would like you to lick your own ass and tell me how it tastes."

Et cetera.

Eventually, I caved in, mostly because I was embarrassed by my sudden and inappropriate playfulness—where had that come from? From desperation, the mad rush of hopelessness? That didn't seem right. While I was certainly anxious and fearful, I had hope in spades—hope, rather than confidence, was nearly all I could depend on.

The decision to go to Key West did not affect my steering. Charlie Dance had told me, in a rare moment of helpfulness, that Cuban patrol waters extended out twelve miles, and I decided to drive in a straight line until we'd passed this boundary. I put Ramon to work trying to map out a course—he twisted and tapped the compass that was attached to the gas tank, and drew on the map with a colored pencil.

I throttled the engine again, and steered at an angle towards the waves, as Charlie had instructed; I now knew what he meant by that. The waves pushed us high and sunk us low with dramatic, stomach-tickling regularity, but the water stayed out of the boat, and the waves did not threaten. The wind pushed and sprayed the way you would expect it to this far from land—the Cuban coastline had diminished to the point that it could have been mistaken for a cloud. All told, I felt no anxiety about the weather—it seemed to be doing what it was supposed to do, as were we. We put the miles between us and shore, and it sporadically occurred to me that I had gone several minutes without worrying about being spotted by a ship—the ocean surface held nothing but us, and its emptiness was so affecting that after a while I could not imagine it holding anything but us; if we had seen a Cuban patrol boat I would have been more confused than frightened, at least at first.

It was not a comfortable trip. Sitting on the back plank, I had to twist my body to keep hold of the throttle, which required quite a bit of torque—my wrist ached and shook, and I began to change hands with frequency. My shoes and the cuffs of my pants marinated in the seawater that collected in the stern. With our speed and motor weight, the boat naturally tilted up, so Ramon perched on his bow seat a few feet above me, dry as a lizard.

We plowed on through the steely water. The spray, light though it was, eventually drenched us both, but the air was warm in spite of the dark sky, and so the mist was a comfort. Ramon clutched the gunwales and stared not at the horizon, but at the passing swatch of ocean directly below him—I found this to be in keeping with his character.

After thirty minutes I asked him, twice, if he wanted to switch. He pretended not to hear me. I cursed into the engine roar, and I spit out a sharp swear. He then turned around and said something. I couldn't hear, so he crawled towards the center, cupped his mouth and bawled out "Did you say something?" I then realized that he actually hadn't heard me.

"Do you want to switch places?" I said.

He stared at me, finally understood what I'd asked. "No, not really," he said, and replaced himself in the bow.

He turned back around and reassumed the bow plank, and I smiled. Ramon had answered me with grace and honesty, he had answered the way a great athlete was supposed to. His simple answer to my duplicitous question had been no, he did not want to switch places. Of course he didn't want to—in the bow he sat placid and relaxed, refreshingly wind-sprayed, his arms laid on his legs like a Buddhist's. I had been ungenerous with him—it was me, not Ramon, who would have pretended not to hear the question if our stations were reversed. There was a kind of triumph in this. I watched Ramon with the confused admiration of a chess master who has just been mated by a child.

Ramon hadn't been trying to trick me—his nature itself, his personality on autopilot, had triumphed here. He got out of steering the boat because he was guileless and self-involved to the point of idiocy, and I didn't know how to respond. I didn't know how I could get my point across any other way but the one I had tried. To simply tell him that it was time to switch would have, for a reason that is difficult for me now to explain, seemed cruel. Thus was Ramon undefeatable, and thus had his selfishness served him his entire life. It is often the way with great athletes—most people are so bemused by the great athlete's inability to identify any concerns outside their own that they give in to them, grant them their large privileges, assume that this self-concern is deserved and necessary.

And so I kept my place, and angled the boat into a new wave—the vibrations on the throttle were conducting through my body and rattling my teeth. Behind us, Cuba lay shrouded and distant, but also disturbingly present, like the remembrance of a dream.

We were not progressing now as we had in the shallows. The boat climbed over the waves unpredictably—each cresting required me to lighten the throttle and crank it again at the trough. I maneuvered the steering in spastic jerks because I felt that I should be handling the boat in some way. Some of the waves seemed to come faster and taller than others, and these waves pushed us back to Cuba, as I could not find the courage to accelerate into them.

We were, quite perceptibly, making no advance, though the boat whined and the water sloshed around us—it was as if we were tethered to the shore by an invisible rope.

Ramon said nothing of this, never even looked back. My sense of groundlessness attacked me. With the roar of motor and wind, and the empty and vague oceanscape, and the silent, faceless Ramon, I felt entirely without resources. I wondered what was going on in his head—what did he think of me, of our lack of progress now? Did he know we weren't gaining any ground? Did he realize that our escape had stalled again, was possibly hopeless from the start, or was this just what I felt, touched by fear and incompetence? In the voiceless noise I doubted my own perceptions. Everything that appeared true to me was unconfirmed by anyone else and therefore suspect—I had no faith in the way things appeared. Perhaps we were in fact making progress, perhaps it was in my imagination alone that Cuba loomed so large. Maybe getting out was not such a diffi-cult thing after all, perhaps it really was just a matter of tooling up to a Floridian beach and stepping on the sand. I could know nothing until Ramon spoke about these matters—it was not that I trusted his opinion, but I needed to hear him speak, if only so that I could discount what he said, decide that I was more grounded than him.

In short, at that moment in the boat, with Cuba (it seemed to me) growing larger rather than smaller, I wished that the noise that silenced Ramon would stop, and after several long minutes it did.

It was clear that we had run out of gas. I could hear the engine hack and gurgle as it drowned it its dryness. For a brief moment, I believed that this portended disaster—we were out of gas; Charlie hadn't put enough in the tank. But I remembered the reserve tanks even before Ramon reminded me, which he did in a hurry, bounding over to the middle plank. He drummed his hand on the plank, impatient, but did nothing to help. In truth, there wasn't much help to be had—I just had to lug the thing over to the engine—and at that point I would not have appreciated the gesture, not when he spoke as he did.

"Do you know what to do?" he asked. "The hose must connect to that nozzle somehow—you should hurry, Dennis. Not moving makes me feel nervous, like something might swallow us up." And then the jackass lit a cigarette. This time, I spoke directly, not asking "Would you mind putting that out?" (his answer would surely have been "yes, I do mind"), but instead shrieking "Throw that fucking thing in the water!" a bit shrilly. He tried to hold back a smile and threw his smoke away.

The hose from the engine to the empty plastic tank came off easily enough—there was a black guard around the nozzle, which I just turned until the hose came loose. The reserve tanks were different, however, made of metal, and this proved to be a problem. I couldn't figure out how to get the nozzle attached to the only opening that seemed a likely spot. It didn't fit. The opening also had a sort of guard that could be twisted and taken off entirely, but none of this helped secure the hose to it. I tried it every way I could, and even asked Ramon if he wanted to give it a shot. Impatient as he was—he had now moved back to the bow and was leaning towards the water so he could smoke—he refused, saying he was no good at mechanical things.

I tried the other tank, but it was of identical construction. After twenty minutes, I found myself whimpering, frustrated to the point of hysteria. I sat and stared at the damn tank, unsure even of whom I should be cursing—Charlie or myself or maybe Ramon. In the end I realized that I just needed to pour the gas from the plastic tank into the metal one, and I wondered exactly how obvious this solution should have been. Ramon hadn't thought of it, but that didn't mean anything—he had greatness in baseball, he didn't even need to have minimum competence at anything else. As for myself, a meager practitioner of the game, a meager practitioner of many things, I should have done better, was expected to do better. It was the practicality of the thing that derailed me. As a word problem, a theoretical dilemma, I would have handled the problem with the gas tanks just fine (I did pretty well on the SATs, in fact, good enough to get into Stanford even before they recruited me). It was when a problem faced me in a practical situation, in a desperate situation, that my reasoning ability was shaken and shorn, precluded and sabotaged by the knowledge that I am a groundless person, especially in crises.

I heaved up the metal tank and carefully poured its gasoline into the plastic one. I reattached the hose and started the engine. Ramon looked back when it screamed to life, his eyes so wide open I could see the red veins at the back of his eyeballs, but he didn't ask any questions. He collapsed onto the bow plank in a crooked posture, as if he'd just been commanded to get as low as he could.

Maybe it was something we would be able to laugh about in time, once I explained to him how I got the engine started again. We had both missed the obvious solution, after all—there was no blame to be assigned that wouldn't be shared equally. What left an aching in my throat and stomach, however, was not the fear that I would be blamed for anything, it was fear for my legacy. I had begun to look at us as a story again, as the story of Ramon Sagasta's escape from Cuba that would certainly be told someday. I could find little of the heroic in it. There was nothing heroic in my waiting past the appointed time—that was necessity, and thoughtlessness on Ramon's part. The run through the forest—what was that? Endurance? Fortitude? It had just been a run, a long and difficult one, but a run nonetheless. Seventy-year-old suburbanites do it every day. There had been comedy, perhaps, in Ramon welting me with the alligator pears, and in our inability to solve the problem of the gas tanks, although I assure you there was absolutely nothing funny about these events at the time, nor do I think there is now. In any case, I could find no heroism yet. This wasn't necessarily the end of it—my legacy would be to get Ramon out, and perhaps that wouldn't require any heroism. Perhaps they wouldn't ask at all what it required—they would be satisfied that it had been done. You don't get into Cooperstown by being heroic (heroism generally requires selflessness, a quality that most certainly doesn't get you into Cooperstown), you get in by doing what you're supposed to do with machine-like efficiency, and then every once in a while doing what no one could really have expected you to do. And maybe that's what would get me remembered. I would save Ramon by doing what I was supposed to do, and if that was already in jeopardy then I would simply make up for it by doing something else. This was a vague way to think, I realize. The problem was that I could see the story already, see myself as an actor in it, and what I gave to this role would be all I would offer to baseball, and my one hope in this life was that baseball would welcome and celebrate my gift.

The storm came as I was thinking about Ramon's story, and my place in it. It came as a steady quickening of the wind, an increase in the spray—it was a slow, strange realization that what was wetting our faces was no longer saltwater skimming off the ocean but rainwater slanting from the sky. The pitch of the wind heightened; it pushed against my body and whined, as if frustrated that it could not knock me off the boat. The waves got taller, and I turned the throttle only in brief, tentative spurts, mostly because the noise comforted us, the one human noise against the ocean storm's many. There lasted less than a minute from the time I realized it had begun to rain to the moment I understood that this storm would push us back to Cuba, if it didn't kill us.

It was not that it was a violent storm, by any measure. All storms that far on the sea are violent, I suppose, if you're in a sixteen foot skiff, but it was the kind of storm that the locals on shore would probably not bother to mention unless they ran out of small talk. It might blow some driftwood onto the edge of the forest, drown some seagulls and refugees even more ill-equipped than us. The storm brought no lightning or thunder, just burly clouds and hard diagonal rain and the dazzling, reckless sound of strong wind.

The wind and the waves pushed us towards Cuba in great lurches. I abandoned the throttle and shouldered the duffel bag strap and clutched the gunwales the way Ramon did. He faced me now, but didn't look at me—he kept his eyes fixed on the middle plank, very clearly trying not to catch any sight of the sea, very clearly becoming nauseated. Water slurped into the boat, but as the waves pushed the stern upwards, almost vertical, most of it poured out past me. As the wave rolled under us, my end went skyward, though not as high or angled as the stern, and for a hovering moment I looked down towards Ramon, who seemed to be deep in the dark ocean—we were like children on a see-saw. We didn't speak or scream. Both of us chattered our teeth, but I couldn't have told you then if I was hot or cold. The one thing I remember thinking is that this would not be a good way to die, and feeling an honest curiosity about what would happen next.

Eventually we were simply pushed back to the shallows, where the sight of land gave me some courage and I revved the engine, as if now we were suddenly ready to get back in there. The motor whirred and I shot us towards the waves with some recklessness—the beach was twenty yards away at most; if we capsized the storm would hurl us onto the sand in a hurry, so Ramon's inability to swim didn't figure. The waves collapsed into our boat, we sunk lower, I twisted the engine throttle until it choked. One great wave got under us and heaved us towards land. When we jolted down I heard the propeller smack into the hard sand surfaced along with the hull, and the entire boat scooted sideways, parallel to the shoreline, and one final wave pushed us further up, almost to the tide line, and then, as it ebbed, Ramon and I simply sat in the grounded boat, like children playing makebelieve sailors.

CHAPTER SEVEN

THE BOAT WAS NOT WRECKED, BUT IT HAD CLEARLY BEEN OVER-matched by the sea, and it lay tilted and defeated on the beach. We abandoned it wordlessly, and lay on the sand next to it, wet and ponderous. On shore the rain came down as a soft shower, almost mocking us with its gentleness. My legs and arms were heavy, and I realized that my head still ached from the last night's concussion. My hand was sore from turning the throttle. Ramon had folded his hands across his chest, and he squinted at the mass of clouds overhead.

We didn't speak, and I hoped we would not for a while—I appreciated being groundless for the moment. I did not wish just then to discuss on what might happen next, or to understand with too much clarity what kind of trouble we were now in. I was breathing hard, but I understood that my exhaustion was mostly a result of anxiety. It was much the same in baseball—the game demands little physical exertion, but at the end of a close one I was always ready to collapse, even if I hadn't played much. I could feel a frightened grimace on my face, and I knew it must look ridiculous.

I regarded Ramon's posture—the long, reposing body, the

twined hands—with sudden and forceful spite. His placidity contrasted in an embarrassing way to my own figure of exhaustion and despair. Ramon had the aspect of someone who believed that the sky he regarded and the situation in which we found ourselves were equally curious and benign things—things that had been put into his life to make it more interesting and strange and spectacular. The fear I had seen jump into his face so readily at other times—in the forest after I came to, on the boat as the storm kicked in—was a powerful but ephemeral thing. He could sustain it no longer than Charlie Dance could sustain a smile, because it wasn't in Ramon to be afraid the way the rest of us can be afraid—indefinitely, even permanently. He did not remind himself that there are no mechanisms to keep our lives safe and ordered; I imagine he has never acknowledged this fact at all.

He possessed a kind of faith, I think, one that would have been encouraged in Cuba as much as in America: The great athlete wins, and the rest of his life is set up to ensure that victories continue. This faith makes people like Ramon dense in the face of loss and disaster. The great athlete cannot believe the troubles that so obviously loom, he can't believe he deserves them, and so he ignores them when they come; he suffers through them with continued disbelief; and when they are past, he forgets easily that they ever occurred.

It was that way with me, long ago; I had had that faith. In high school, I made exactly one error in four varsity seasons. My senior year I hit forty points higher than anyone else in the Round Pound School District. I once hit a foul ball so hard it went through a sheet-metal billboard. It's not that I got worse, it's just that there are a lot of school districts out there, and in every one of them is someone who's better than everyone else. By the end of my junior year at Stanford, I began to feel guilty for taking advantage of the third-tier groupies who hung around in case any of us got drafted. I threw away the souvenir program from my freshman year, the cover of which featured me glowering in full gear and read *Who is that Masked Man? Dennis Birch, Stanford's Backstop of the Future.* I stopped reading the daily reports that told us what our batting averages were. When I got drafted in the 22nd round, based on a late season comeback and an inexplicably good tryout in Baseball City, Florida, I waited two weeks before cashing my bonus check, certain that they would ask for it back once they took another look at my college stats.

I pondered the irony of my birth compared to Ramon's: The cruelest fact of Ramon's life was that he and his gift had been born in Cuba, a country that could and did decide on a whim that he couldn't play baseball, which is what he should have been doing all day long; while I had been born in America, a country that would actually pay someone of even my small ability to play the game, a game I should probably never have played at all.

This thought created no pity in me, however. In fact, I found myself furious at Ramon, in part because of his posture, his body's reflection of his failure to be concerned. He looked like he was sunbathing. I was convinced that a soldier would shortly stumble upon us and shoot us both in the temple, and my posture reflected this belief.

But mostly, of course, I was simply envious. He looked so much like a great player now, even more than he did when he was throwing the alligator pears at me. He looked like a dark-skinned Nolan Ryan—lean and self-absorbed, cockiness virtually emanating from his pores—reclining in the clubhouse after a complete game. I would have lived there, gladly, to have an ounce of this ability that seemed to seep from his skin. I could never know the discomforts and fear that must come with living in Castro's Cuba, of course, but I still believed this was the case, that

I would have made that trade in a second if some indulgent god had allowed us both to start over. While it was true that I couldn't imagine what it was like to grow up here, to suffer here, I also didn't know what it was like to never experience loss, or to forget about it the moment it came. This was the only thing I wanted to know in the world, because to know this would be to achieve greatness. As it was, all I could do was try to find a greatness to attach myself to, and that is no great destiny to have.

"What do we do now?" Ramon finally asked. He had not been thinking this question over, waiting for the right time to speak. The question had simply just occurred to him.

I sat up, tired of comparing our two bodies. "The boat won't make it. I have no idea what we do next, Ramon." I sounded tired, even more defeated than I felt.

For the first time in a while—even though I had been staring straight up for several minutes—I noticed the sky, its contours of giant clouds and blackness, patched randomly now with azure. Some of the clouds lumbered noticeably back toward the sea, some seemed close enough to touch, close enough to reach into and feel the wells of black rainwater. It might rain very soon, I thought, torrentially, but it seemed equally possible that it would just stay cool and threatening like it was now. It did not seem to matter much.

We lugged the boat back to the forest—the beach here wasn't much different from where we'd launched, but the terrain behind it was more like jungle, and it climbed. We slipped together on mossy logs and rotting roots as we hauled the boat. The land rose with patience, and did not culminate in a sharp peak, or in any kind of apex at all; it seemed; from the beach we had seen that it elevated consistently, impressively, but at a certain point, perhaps a thousand feet above the shore, the curvature of the hill hid whatever was above it from view.

The earth's slope made us drag the boat further than that I would have liked. Whenever we rested the thing, thinking we had placed it out of view, it would slide back towards the daylight. Finally we wedged the boat snugly between two birch tree trunks, and came out of the forest and sat together at the beginning of the sand, now wetter and more exhausted than we had been after the beaching.

I remembered to take the duffel bag. It was as heavy as before; although we'd eaten most of the food and drunk the gallon jugs, everything was now weighted with saltwater. On the beach, I pawed through the contents, shaking out puddles, checking for damage.

"What do you think, Ramon? Does this place look familiar at all?" I said.

He stood at the edge of the water, and swiveled his head in both directions. "I don't think so. No—I don't recognize any of it. I was never much of a beachgoer."

He was clearly unsatisfied with his own answer. "It doesn't look like anyone comes here, though. I don't see any fishing nets. I don't see anything. There are some beaches that are off-limits."

"Does that signify anything?" I felt like Sinbad when he discovered that his new island was a sleeping whale. I was certain Ramon was about to reveal something horrible—perhaps we were on the Young Communist training beach, or an area that had been quarantined from a reactor leak— since his tone never gave clues as to what kind of news he was about to give, I just had to anticipate the worst.

"Not really," he said, sounding bored. He was starting to pay more attention to the water as it rose to touch his feet. "I'm just not sure where we are."

"What about the hill? It's pretty big—what hills are around Rios?"

He shrugged. "Lots. I don't know. How far did we go?"

"No more than fifty miles," I said. I felt so uncertain about this figure it would not have surprised me if Ramon had laughed and told me it was impossible. Ramon's next question occurred to me before it was asked.

"What direction did we go?"

I didn't know, but I recognized this was of some importance. Havana, with its myriad dangers, was to the northwest. However, there wasn't really anything in terms of civilization to the south or the east, and so we probably wouldn't want to have gone there either. Perhaps it didn't matter after all.

What did I know? Key West was north—I had the latitude more than memorized, I didn't think I would ever forget those numbers. Cuba was south. To think about east and west, northeast and southwest, had been inconceivable—it would only have meant thinking about more Cuba, about Havana being over there, and Santa Clara over there, and everywhere green-jacketed soldiers who did not want me to take Ramon. There was north or there was nothing.

"Fuck," I said.

It would have to be the forest. There was no path here, but it was, if we used our imaginations, passable. There were areas where a fallen tree had cleared the vegetation, or rather, had created rot and fungus that could be clambered over. At least it looked this way from what we had seen of it—I did not want to think of what the jungle might look like at its heart, or what creatures might live there.

All of this quickly became irrelevant, for while I was reorganizing the duffel bag and Ramon was tracing shapes into the sand with the toe of his boot, we began to hear the distant rhythmic whirl of helicopter blades. It's a sinister sound in the best of times, and it chilled me so profoundly I stood paralyzed until Ramon swiped at me and waved at me to follow him into the forest.

We followed the weak path we had created with the boat. Once in the forest, we did not have to worry as much about the chopper, since there was no chance that they would see us through the foliage. Ramon told me, almost cheerfully, that a similar jungle cover is what had protected Fidel and his revolutionaries in Granma province, back when they were eluding Batista's air forces. It didn't comfort me much. Even on the beach, I hadn't really thought of the helicopter as an immediate danger; it was more symbolic. It grounded me in a way, it was an outside confirmation that what we were doing was a very big deal. Cuba had decided to use a chopper from her precious and dwindling military stores in order to find the pitcher I'd stolen. Fidel Castro—or at least his brother Raul, who headed the FAR—knew about Ramon and me, and had told his minions to get us. This was a large fact. The noise of the whirling blades served as notification that my crime would not pass lightly, that the chase was on, and it would not be half-assed on their part.

Ramon led, humming. I watched the ground at my feet, and breathed the second hand smoke from a new cigarette; I could not imagine how he'd managed to keep the smokes dry, but it didn't surprise me that he had. I had to stop thinking about Ramon and his strangeness; from this point on, I decided to regard him as a phenomenon, as a magician. He was someone who could do things that no one else could do, and this should have been sufficient to explain everything else about him. He was easier to reckon with this way.

We scrambled through the jungle for hours. The floor kept its damp, and the air about us was dense with humidity, so that the saltwater that drenched our clothes was replaced with sweat in a seamless exchange. Occasionally we would find an outcropping of rock where we could stand and gauge the distance we'd come, but the peak of the hill remained hidden by its stubborn curvature—we had reached the point that, at the beach, had seemed to be the zenith, but in fact we were only at a midpoint, a point that afforded another view of another zenith, which may or may not have been false. I felt that this hill could very well encompass the entire island, and that when they finally conquered it we would be standing at the dead center of Cuba.

But for most of the march, we couldn't think about distance traveled or distance remaining in any but a theoretical way—the trees and fronds and the thickening air itself blocked from view everything but the jungle's interior and the shifting sky. We needed to create our own path for the most part, every clearing only presenting us with yet another wall of flora to penetrate. We began to alternate the lead every half hour, and then every twenty minutes. When Ramon led, he thrashed at the leaves and sticks with both arms, sometimes crying out in his efforts. He tried to defeat the bushes and trees before him, to thrash and conquer. My technique was to dart through them, so that Ramon needed to follow closely. When I led, he would get slapped by the branches closing behind me. At times, if there looked to be a sticker bush or sharp twigs ahead, I would hold out the duffel bag and push it through before me, followed by Ramon muscling through.

It was a strange march, much stranger than the one we'd taken from Rios. For one thing, we never spoke, not even to agree on switching leads or to point out some obstacle to look out for. Ramon and I rarely looked at each other, rarely thought about each other I suppose, but were quite confident in knowing what the other would do, and that it would be the right thing to do. It seemed a strange state to be in with him, since I was not on his level, and since I depended on him to be much

greater than I was. In fact, it made me uneasy that things were
going smoothly, but I was also pleased; this would be something
to describe, this jungle teamwork, to the reporters in America.

However, "smoothly" may not be the appropriate word,
since I don't think I've ever been in more physical discomfort in
my life than I was during that march up the hill. After the first
hour, my thighs had made that transition from ache to burning
to slackness to numbness, and now all four sensations were
there. I had sweated more in our first mile than I had ever
believed it possible to sweat, and I've perspired quite a bit in my
time. Some sort of creek traversed the mountain in parts—
though it was not direct or open enough to follow—and we
drank its tepid waters because we were terrified of dehydrating.
This was a very real fear. We filled up the empty gallon jugs
from the creek—an unfortunate thing, since the plastic allowed
us to see the sediments and insects floating in the water—and
drank them in single sittings. We were sweating so hard that,
after one enormous swallow, I was certain I could see the water
I'd just taken bead up on my arm—drinking the water seemed
futile, like filling up a gas tank that has a bullet hole in it.

We continued to hear the helicopter sporadically over the
next hour or so, as it meandered above the jungle and the coast.
Twilight came, and somewhere around then the chopper left.
The air cooled, the humidity lessened, and we stopped resting,
mostly because the rock outcroppings seemed to have ended. I
was limp, and so was Ramon, but not so bad as me.

My method of hacking through the forest had deteriorated
to simply falling against and into it, and if whatever was there
resisted, to push my way around it. It was like walking through
the long cotton fingers of an automated car wash. I came to the
point where it would have somehow been more exhausting to
stop than to continue. I forgot what we were even doing this for,

and then remembered, and became confused because being in police custody did not seem a bad thing at all just then, being shot did not even seem something I should dismiss out of hand. I should consider it, I thought, consider what it would be like to be captured compared to this, or compared to dying on the ocean, or compared to succeeding and becoming an anonymous figure in an interesting story about a great pitcher.

I heard my thoughts in my head, as if spoken in an internal megaphone, laid over the constant interior complaint of my body, but the thoughts seemed far away, miles away from being exposed to the open air by my tongue. I did not want to talk to Ramon anyway. I followed and led, followed and led. My legs felt hotter than the rest of me now. I walked on blistered feet, breathed air that felt like tepid water, as if I were again breathing the liquid of the womb.

At around nine o'clock, we heard the music. I dropped hard to the ground and lay there. By slapping at his ankles and hissing, I got Ramon to do the same. I realized soon enough that the music came from a cassette tape, and though I couldn't see anything but a drape of long green leaves, I could picture the drab silver Soviet-issue boom box that it probably came from—they were ubiquitous in Cuba, though I hadn't quite expected to run into one out here.

"It's music, Dennis," Ramon whispered, and by way of further explanation he closed his eyes and began moving his shoulders to the faint rhythm.

"So it is," I said.

In the stillness caused by the cessation of our march, and the gradual slowing of our breath, the music came clearly. It was salsa music, furiously energetic; they were sounds I would forever associate with Latin America, salsa being the only music I had ever heard in this part of the world. It was music that compelled motion. It was crowded and aggressive, garbled and encompassing, and so it matched well with our surroundings. I listened for several seconds before I realized that it may not have been a noise we wanted to hear at the moment.

That kind of music never did much for me. It seems too generic—I've spent at least thirty months of my life in Latin America, and I probably still can't tell any given salsa song apart from the next one. For a few moments as I lay there, I forgot about what seemed certain to be the collapse of my organs, and I was simply annoyed to be listening to salsa music. Ramon, lying so close I could feel the steam of his body, was somehow dancing. He continued to lie flat and quiet, but his body shivered to the music—he was like a big, spastic snake.

And then, in spite of what I've just said about the similarity of these songs, I recognized what I was listening to. I'd heard it before—just a few times, but I was certain of it.

The song was one that had been popular a couple years before in Puerto Rico, where I'd spent my last season in the winter leagues and the second to last season of my career (I lingered for six weeks with the Lansing Lugnuts the following spring). The song had appeared in my life at a great moment, one of the greatest moments I've had in baseball, although it did not come on the field. If such moments had arrived with greater frequency in my life, if I had somehow figured out a way to summon them or perhaps create them, then I would have been a great baseball player, a first-ballot inductee into the Hall of Fame. I realize that these are very big *if*s.

My great moment did not come in a game, which is fitting. It came at a street carnival, a kind of third-world 4-H fair in the suburbs of San Juan that I had stumbled upon one afternoon after a lackluster performance at the Estadio Orlando Cepeda. The carnival suffered quite a lot in comparison to the kind we have in the states—there were a few stands where you could knock down milk bottles, a few bored carnies trying to guess your weight. Even the little kids were bored. But somehow the organizers had gotten their hands on a dunk-tank, a pretty nice one actually, with a glass front and an obnoxious carny perched above a thousand gallons of water. It was clearly the centerpiece of the whole affair.

The line was long, of course, since PR is baseball-mad and there was nothing else of interest. The customers paid a quarter for three balls, and threw at a bull's-eye about fifteen yards away. The carny seemed to be getting soaked more often than not, but he didn't seem to mind—it was a pretty hot day, after all.

I was trying to stay away from the thing, since I don't throw well under pressure, but eventually someone recognized me, or at least put two and two together—Caucasians that far from the resort areas and surfing beaches tended to be either baseball players or sugar company executives. One guy insisted I use the balls he had just purchased, and when I refused the crowd around him began to insist in a kind of good-natured way. Then the carny caught on to what was happening.

"Hey, a Yankee! Come here, Yankee!" he yelled. "Why don't you dunk me! Come on, for the glory of the United States!"

Puerto Rico, as always, was in the middle of asking itself whether or not to become a state, which always stirred up some strange opinions and patriotism around PR, and so the carny started to get a reaction from the crowd.

"*Gracias*, no," I said, and grabbed my shoulder. "My arm's a bit sore."

"So it's true that you're one of the mighty Lobos? You're one of the players on that extraordinary team! My goodness, what are you doing here, then? Shouldn't you be at home, waiting for the Atlanta Braves to fly down and beg you to come back with them for the World Series?"

He went on like this for a while, until he became exasperated and vulgar. "You bastard American shit-cake!" he said. "Why do you pollute our country? You won't throw at me! You're that bad?" he said.

There didn't seem to be any way out, and though my arm had already begun to shake and I had begun to see double, I finally grabbed a ball from someone, which elicited a small, polite cheer from the people.

I chucked a ball very, very hard at the bull's-eye and missed by quite a bit, and everyone yelped even louder. The carny looked at me with a new disgust. He could not believe, after all that, that I wasn't even going to hit him. He smiled enormously, and reclined on his platform, and from the top of the dunk tank's rectangle he took a boom box, which I hadn't even noticed before. It had been turned low to accommodate the carny's insults, but now he cranked it and held it to his ear, eyes closed, smiling, his head rocking. The music burst forth from the dunk dank, the crowd began to shimmy. It was salsa music, the kind that dominated our clubhouse, the kind they played over the loudspeaker in all the parks whenever someone hit a home run. Then, as now, the music had always seemed the same to me, the songs interchangable, each one just a new way of organizing the instruments and the chirps and staccatos. But I remembered the song that came from the carny's boom box. It was as distinct as Beethoven's Fifth to me—I would never forget it. In a moment it had become my anthem—this same song that I later heard in the jungle with Ramon—and I suddenly envisioned what I would do, and decided that it was a very good idea, and there was no doubt that I would execute it. With the song wrapping itself around my body, I felt that I was being guided, that I was doing something that could not be done badly, and even if it had gone wrong I wouldn't have accepted it. It is what they all must feel, the great ones, all the time.

The great moment came with the second ball. The crowd now seemed to expect me to hit the bull's-eye—surely I would adjust my sights, surely this bastard with his boom box was too great a target for me miss.

I motioned for everyone to give me some room. I got into a traditional windup, rocked back on my heel as it shifted right, kicked out my left leg and lunged. My arm whipped forward like a snapped rubber band, and the baseball thundered where I had meant for it to go. It shattered the plate glass of the water tank and hit the carny in the face, knocking him off the platform. He landed hard as the last of the water carried the shattered glass out of the tank, and he lay crumpled against the tank's bottom, where some of the shards must have torn his ass and legs. The boom box fell with him, clanking in the tank and then following the water out the empty front, and although it jolted, the music didn't stop, the song kept celebrating my great act. The carny moaned and lay still.

A good memory, the best one in fact.

This all came to me in a moment, and not as a linear remembrance, but as visions and noises jumbled and glimpsed, as such memories come. I saw the box, wet yet intact among the broken glass on the ground, valiantly pumping out the song I listened to now. I saw myself running for my car after I'd sufficiently basked in the crowd's eventual admiration, and I saw the exaggerated sneer the carny had worn right before I'd set him on his ass.

And then, after these pictures came to me, as Ramon continued to writhe on the grass, no doubt waiting for me to tell him what we should do, the music trilled in a strange way, made room for a guitar solo, came back with a snare drum riff, and I realized that it was not the same song I knew at all. Perhaps it had begun the same, but it was now entirely different, no longer mistakable. With a lunging stomach I felt that the memory of my great moment had been invalidated—I'd had no real reason to summon it, since what triggered it was a misidentification, a mistake. I wondered if I had done this on purpose, to use the memory of that moment to find courage; if this was the case, I thought it a very pathetic thing to do, like when a coach uses the story of a dead friend to get his team riled up for the big game.

I motioned for Ramon to wait while I moved in for a better look at the source of the music. I could not imagine what it might be. Cops, farmers, thieves, drug runners—anyone might be listening to this music, anyone might find themselves in this patch of jungle. For all I knew the city of Matanzas itself lay on the other side of the frond wall.

CHAPTER EIGHT

SEEING WHO WAS THERE DIDN'T HELP, ALTHOUGH IT WAS CLEAR that they weren't cops, and also that we weren't in Matanzas. Whoever they were, they weren't really hiding out in the jungle, since the clumpy row of trees behind which I stood acted as a demarcation line between dense jungle and the sort of sparse forest that Ramon and I had traversed after leaving Rios. Peering through the trees, I could see that the slope continued, but that a short path pushed its way up the hill, and, off in the distance, the hill visibly crested.

At the cusp of the path's dead end, about a dozen yards from me, was an open shack—three walls and a roof, the open side facing me. The back wall stretched far, about the length of a dugout—in fact, the whole thing was rather like a dugout, only a bit deeper and taller, and not sunk into the earth. An assortment of patterned furniture that would have been welcome in Charlie Dance's apartment had been precisely set along the walls, which had been painted or rotted a kind of brown. The floor of the place melted seamlessly into the dirt of the forest. In America, a place like this would obviously have been a refuge for squatters—here, it might have been some kind of vacation home. The boom box sat in the middle of the floor, where a coffee table might have gone.

The kids lounging in the chairs and couches, or gyrating to the boom box, or tending to a tiny fire outside and to the right of the shack, did in fact look vaguely like squatters, although in Cuba many people looked like this to me. There were ten of them, a more or less equal mix of boys and girls. I call them kids because they obviously were, although the boys all wore budding mustaches, the girls who danced plunged their hips in and out like matronly Vegas hookers, and most of them drank from liquor bottles and some of them smoked cigars. They practiced these adult activities with sleepy expressions, pretending to be bored by their vices, the look children have when they're secretly thrilled by their badness. In any case, I watched with interest as it dawned on me we had simply stumbled upon the outpost of some teenagers who had snuck away to be naughty. This was not the most serendipitous landing we could have had—I thought back to my blissful teenage getaway, the basement of Andrew Neill's divorced father's house, which to me seemed as decadent as Caligula's palace—but then again, it was not the worst.

They were doubtless a benign bunch, in the sense that they wouldn't turn us in to anyone: Clearly, there would be a great reckoning if any adult found this place, and we could use that to our advantage. To a communist/Catholic teenage girl, the thought of her father discovering this den of iniquity would probably foster almost as much terror as the thought of being found by the police did to Ramon and me.

I observed them for a while, and then a bored and curious Ramon Sagasta scooted up beside me with a great thrashing, betraying our presence. The teenagers fell silent and scattered to the edges of the shack, like cockroaches when the lights come on. Ramon took it all in in a glance and began to laugh as he stepped out of the brush with his arms open wide.

"No, no, it is not your parents. And it is not Fidel come to punish you." He loped towards the lip of the dugout, sniffed one of the liquor bottles and shut his eyes, exaggerating its effect on him. "Whew! You kids are up to some mischief!"

They stayed still, and Ramon continued a slow patrol around the shack and the open ground before it. He knelt by the fire to light one of his smokes off it. He inspected a few more liquor bottles until he found one that he took a swig from. I watched all this from a spot I had chosen in front of the brush— exposed, but not participating—and was interested to realize that Ramon was acting like a cop, like a Cuban cop especially. The way he sauntered around the place confident that the teenagers would stay where they were, the way he made sport of their fear, reminded me very much of someone with too much authority and a willingness to explore how it can serve him. This was offset a bit by his physical appearance: his clothes were black with sweat and jungle muck, he stank like a mule, and there were leaves stuck to his hair.

I looked worse. My left eye was still swollen and purple, my shirt stuck to my chest in meager strips, my hair stood in great pointed shocks. I smelled like rotten avocado and several gallons of sweat.

That I looked ugly and foolish may seem irrelevant. I mention it only because it was what occurred to me at the time, and it occurred to me at the time because—God forgive me—I had begun to notice that the five teenage girls who huddled together on a plaid couch were beautiful, every single one of them. That was a rare thing, and difficult to ignore. They were beautiful in different ways, as all beauties are, but they all had that long black Cuban hair, straight as wire, and they all had the

dull and fluid skin, and seventeen-year-old-bodies. What more
is there to say? Except that, when confronted with beauty, I
have always become more jealous than lustful, because it is usually someone other than me who gets to enjoy it. I was not sure
who deserved to partake in the kind of beauty I witnessed at that
moment, the immature, restless kind, but it sure as hell wasn't
a seventeen-year-old boy with a bad mustache and cheap rum
breath.

I don't know if Ramon noticed them, except as an audience
for his bullying strut. He may have been getting bored now, as
he reclined in a folding chair outside of the shack and regarded
them. It was an awkward time—the girls, gorgeous beyond
measure even in their fear, had begun to hang their heads, and
the boys looked at each other, trying to communicate without
words. The salsa music continued, but no one heeded it.

The silence broke when one of the boys stood up, pointed,
and said, "Sweet God, you're Ramon Sagasta."

Ramon's reaction was to roll his head towards me and raise
his eyebrows, as if to say "Oh no, another fan." I've come to
learn that the great ones are not disingenuous in this, that they
quite often are actually annoyed and disconcerted by the adulation they receive, but also that if they were to go without it for
one day they would probably wither and die. Ramon's look said
all of this to me, and it also said that whatever space in his brain
had been consumed by concern for our escape had now been
filled by other thoughts, by whatever preparations are necessary
to become a god to people.

The other boys acknowledged him with gesticulations and
barks of joy, although I noticed that one of them—all I remember of him is an exaggerated set of buckteeth—had clearly recognized Ramon all along, but had been too afraid to speak; his
reaction was patently fake, but went unnoticed.

The boys approached Ramon, with twitchy, stop-and-start movements, the way a poodle approaches a mastiff. They chattered as they got close to him; eventually one brave boy shook his hand, the others followed. They reminded him of great moments in his career. They spoke about games they had watched him play. They were respectful of Ramon and each other—each had their story, each was given due attention by the others—which made them unique among fans, and made this moment less like the typical fans-mob-superstar scene and more like a handful of kids sitting around pestering Grandpa for candy. Eventually they coerced Ramon into the shack, gave him a cup to drink his rum out of, beckoned me to join them, and somehow interspersed the girls between them as they took spots on the couches. It was all very civilized, as if we had crashed a cocktail party given by generous hosts.

As we nestled into our spots, the tallest of the boys, the one with the thinnest moustache, continued a story:

"It was when Conchanza played for Cardenas, and he was having that tremendous year, with one home run for every two games. And Ramon Sagasta—" while in the beginning they had addressed him personally, they now spoke of him as if he wasn't there, as a sign of respect I suppose; it was obvious Ramon liked this, he must have known it was the way one speaks in the presence of a god "—Ramon Sagasta has a history with Conchanza, they played together as boys with the traveling under-sixteen Nationals." Ramon held his fingertips together at his lips, like a ponderous psychiatrist. He would know how this story would end, of course, would know that it would be told and embellished to flatter him to an extreme degree. What was he thinking then? Was he embarrassed, as I would have been? Not likely. Did he feel this was his due, looking upon the teenagers and their tales as Zeus must have looked upon a hundred head of sacrificed cattle?

The boy continued. "Conchanza, so large and meaty. His meaty hands and beefy face, with that lock of hair that used to dangle down between his eyes." The boys laughed, they loved that they remembered this. "The stories that the paper had been telling had to do with stories from when they were young, how Conchanza's girls all ended up falling for Ramon Sagasta. Conchanza was no gentleman—in all the towns they visited he would find at least one girl to meet him under the bleachers after the game, and he would try to have his way. And the story goes that Ramon would be sure to take extra pitching practice at the same time Conchanza was trying to get his way with the girls, and Ramon would always let a few pitches get away from him, and sail under the bleachers. After a while Conchanza couldn't risk it anymore, and he couldn't find another place as private as the bleachers, and he had to give up his womanizing. And this is when they were fifteen years old!" The boy squealed this last part, overcome, even though he had just begun his story. He took a gulp from the rum bottle, and passed it to one of the beautiful girls, who drank even more from it than he had—not one of the girls had spoken a word since I'd been there, but they'd all been drinking.

"And anyway," the boy continued, "Conchanza is going to face Ramon Sagasta for the first time, since before that season he'd been with Cienfuegos. There's all this talk, in the papers, on the radio. My grandfather got me a ticket for the game, and I was there four hours before it began. I saw Conchanza hit batting practice, and almost caught one of his fouls. I saw Ramon Sagasta warm up—just ten pitches, that's all he took to warm up.

"It was over before it started—you could see it in Conchanza's eyes. He was afraid of what Ramon Sagasta would do to him. Make him look like a fool, maybe put every pitch right by him, never let him swing. He wasn't even trying to hit homers, he just wanted to not look foolish, and that is the surest way to look like a fool." Warming to the telling, he reached out and pinched the cheek a girl who sat before him on the ground, leaning against the base of the couch, cradling a cup of rum between her legs. He winked at her. She nodded her head, waiting to hear the rest of the story. She put her hand onto the teller's knee. This is what he'd wanted her to do, perhaps it's one of the reasons he told the story. Sweet little girl, I thought, you don't even know what's happening to you—you're letting the kid seduce you with a name that isn't even his. It's such an easy thing.

"Ramon Sagasta dealt with Conchanza's first four at-bats with eighteen pitches," the boy closed his eyes to remember the stats, "Six balls and twelve strikes. The wood of Conchanza's bat never touched the baseball. Four strikeouts on eighteen pitches against the greatest hitter in the league." The crowd emitted gasps and smacks, some of the boys clapped their hands, but the story was not over. "Conchanza gets to bat again, in the ninth. The game has already been won—twelve to one, Matanzas was up, and so Ramon Sagasta got to have his fun. Everyone stood, expecting another strikeout—even Conchanza did, although he tried to look fierce." The boy stood and imitated a windup. "And Ramon Sagasta rears back and throws . . ." the boy gave a gentle look to Ramon, who remained still and thoughtful, "—and fires the ball right into Conchanza's backside! He smacks him on the ass, as if he were spanking him for having the insolence to come to the plate against him!" The whole room was laughing now, even me, although not very earnestly. The storyteller sprouted tears, his voice racheted up several octaves. "And Conchanza gets to take his base, but how does the inning end?" He swallowed, took a drink, and thundered out his last sentence in the somber baritone you hear from the narrators of documentaries. "Conchanza takes a small lead, and before the next batter had kicked the mud off his shoes Ramon Sagasta picks him off at first!" Tumult, uproar. Glory.

A little while later, as we peed in the dark bushes, Ramon and I had the following conversation:

"That story the boy told about you and Conchanza, was it true?"

"Which part?"

"Just in general."

"Not very. For one thing, it was me, not Conchanza, who took girls under the bleachers. It is true he didn't like me, but not for any reason like that. Sometimes people just don't like you—it doesn't mean you did anything to deserve it."

"But what about the game? The way the game went, with you striking him out?"

"He never got a hit, I remember that. I do remember hitting him on the ass, but I wouldn't have done that on purpose. And it happened early in the game, the first at-bat maybe. As for the rest, who knows? Probably not just like the boy said. I think he fouled out once, and maybe he also grounded out. It doesn't matter. It could have happened. I could have done that if I'd wanted to. But what's the point? He didn't get on base, and the boy remembers it the way he wants to."

This, I think, was the point of the story. That Ramon felt that he could have done what the boy had said he'd done if he'd wanted to. That Ramon assumed the boy, and the rest of the fans, would remember it how they wanted to. He understood what he was there to do—just what was expected of him, and perhaps a little more. That's all he needed to do to be great. The story the boy had told was the kind that might be described in an exhibit in Cooperstown one day—they might describe the story as "perhaps apocryphal" or "unsubstantiated," but when you saw that exhibit, studied his game jersey and one of the souvenirs from his defection—the scouting report, the bleary instructions scrawled on the napkin—you would believe the story, and you would repeat it to yourself over and over. That's all it would take for you to believe in the greatness of Ramon Diego Sagasta.

After the story and the uproar, as the others spat out the requisite expressions of admiration, one of the boys looked me over, turned back to Ramon, then back to me, and said, "Oh my God! You're defecting!"

I had assumed they knew all along, but of course they just hadn't thought about it. When you are confronted with a hero from your childhood, situations and circumstances—even fear—dissipate, and you live in some strange world comprised of the unbelievable heroics of the past, and the equally incredible moment in which you revisit them in the presence of the greatness. You don't think about the body in front of you except in the context of what it once did, a throw the arm once made, a slugger the eyes once stared down. It was like this with me, in Charlie Dance's apartment as I got lost in the image and memory of Don Sutton—it did not once occur to me that Sutton might still exist and might continue to exist anywhere but in the past—and that was just a photograph, I've never even seen the man in person.

"The helicopters! That's what they were for!" said one of the boys, rather unnecessarily. "They're looking for you pretty good, if they brought out the helicopters."

"Of course they are, *tonto*," said the boy who told the Conchanza story. "Why in the name of God would they let Ramon Sagasta go? They'll do everything they can to keep him." It was meant as a tribute to Ramon's greatness, but I could have done without the reminder.

The boys seemed to think the defection was a great thing, and the fact that El Maximo was dusting off the helicopters to look for us only made it more impressive. They told us that they had first heard the chopper around noon, when they were back in their village, about five miles to the northeast. They'd heard it again once or twice, but not for long stretches. They told us that Rios was about fifteen miles away, and then graciously added that the FAR would have no way of knowing which direction we'd gone in, and they would probably assume we were already on the water and stick to looking for us there.

Only one of them brought up his sadness at the prospect of losing Matanzas's greatest player (notice how they assumed the defection would succeed—how could Ramon Sagasta fail?), but they seemed earnestly happy for him.

"What team will you play for?"

"If you play for Florida, we will be able to hear you on the radio sometimes."

"You will win the World Series, it's certain! The World Series!"

They started to look at me now, wondering. It was clear enough that I was American, but I hadn't spoken—they might have assumed I didn't speak Spanish. One of the boys said "And this is the man who will get you to Florida?"

Ramon and I were both silent, both wanting to answer, "That is a very good question."

One of the girls, who had regarded me carefully and assumed correctly, touched Ramon on the leg and said, "What happened?"

He told the story, leaving out nothing, not even the incident with the alligator pears. I despaired. Ramon did not have the capacity to cover up the blemishes of our escape, even his own—he spent some time narrating his own blubbering breakdown in the forest. The story wounded me more than I can say. I would hear him telling it in Miami, hear him detailing it to a writer at

Sports Illustrated, to an anchor at ESPN. What would I become, when Ramon was safe in the States, thumbing his nose at the organization's gag order? I could only hope to be sent back to Mexico. I could hope that Sportcenter wouldn't get hold of the baseball card that was made when I was in Triple A—it has me crouching awkwardly and looking as if I am about to sneeze. They might get hold of this and put it as a still on TV, laying over it Ramon's guileless monologue about the incompetence of the scout who came to rescue him. The way the scout couldn't figure out the gas tanks, the way he brought upon Ramon's wrath in the forest and caused them to miss their boat, the way he didn't even really know in what direction to steer. As he narrated, I kept my eyelids low, watching my fingertips press together.

The kids, at least, did not seem unimpressed. On the contrary, they thought it a great adventure, and did not seem to pick up on my groundlessness. I attributed this to the fact that a teenager would probably have made many of the mistakes I had made, or could at least sympathize with them.

They offered no advice or solace, merely awe. Their response to the story was to toast it, to turn up the music and begin dancing to it, which Ramon did happily. They made a circle for him, and he grabbed one of the beautiful girls and draped her around his body like a scarf, and they wrangled and writhed to the yelping and applause of the surrounding teenagers. I went by the fire to have a smoke. In this way, the night progressed, almost imperceptibly. They drank and danced. Occasionally I left the fire to watch them, finding myself frozen into a strange posture—arms crossed, one foot planted across the other, a fixed smirk. I had three or four glasses of rum. The night grew colder and I put more logs on the fire.

I did not know what to do, not then, not in the future. A few times I mistook the wind in the treetops and the symphony of insects for the whirring of chopper blades, and I tensed and made ready to grab Ramon and bolt. It didn't make me feel better to realize my mistake—it only reminded me that when they did return, as they certainly must, I had no recourse but to run. At the moment I could only tend to the logs and wonder.

Someone turned on Christmas lights that were strung along the tops of the shack walls, and which provided exactly the kind of illumination they wanted—a smoky red glow, so that they could watch themselves.

I grew wistful and tipsy watching them, and I stayed by the fire, no longer wandering over to them. They danced and drank. This little boxlike dugout in the middle of some Cuban forest contained more concentrated grace and beauty than I have ever seen, I believe. Some of the boys were ratty and loud and abrasive in that teenage boy way, but they somehow atoned for this by the way they danced, by how they served to complement the snaky bodies of the girls, how they framed them with their hands and hips. They did this all under the smoky red light, and they left the center of the floor to Ramon, who as a dancer was more enthusiastic than graceful, but his features and his history and the story I'd just heard contained enough grace for one man, even for a great man. Though there would be times later when I supposed there was something uncanny about Ramon, at this moment I doubted his greatness not at all. Only a great athlete would come upon a gaggle of teenage beauty in the middle of such an escape as ours, and then spend the evening among them, being flattered, dancing, throwing off the titanic troubles of the day like a wet parka. Only a man like me would, given the same situation, sulk and smoke alone next to the rock-rimmed fire.

I crouched and sat and sometimes paced and continually nursed bad rum. At first I felt almost petulant for doing this, but over the course of the hours I began to feel them watch me, the boys and the girls, and I realized my mystery. As they danced, they would shoot me peripheral looks, then lower their heads and whisper something to a friend. I reorganized the duffel bag, took out the knife, and pretended to work on the binoculars. This is a hard man, they would think. The American sent to get Ramon Sagasta would not be one to waste an evening dancing. Ramon's chaperon, Ramon's guide, Ramon's savior—I had seen what they thought of Ramon, what must they think of me? They were afraid, the girls especially. I was not foolish to them, I was the serious part of a serious business—the story Ramon told hadn't affected them at all; they had simply told themselves new ones.

At one point, Ramon danced over and said that we could sleep here tonight. I told him I wasn't sure what good that would do us, and he told me he was drunk. He told me this with great somberness, as if he were confessing to some terrible crime, but he didn't seem drunk at all. I waved him off and told him that I needed to think about things. Mostly, I watched the beautiful girls.

From hearing my conversation with Ramon, they knew I spoke Spanish, and eventually, some of the boys approached me. We had difficulty keeping our conversations going long, mostly because I had decided to adopt a gruff, business-like manner, but from these conversations I learned at least where we were.

The shack had been built long ago by one of the boys' fathers as a place to conduct extramarital affairs. Several years later, the father had seen the Virgin in the face of a palm leaf, and decided to quit his adulterous ways and raze El Secreto, as he had at one point called the place. His tender memories, however, made the destruction a difficult chore for him—a month after making his vow he had only managed to take down one of the walls, and even this had apparently been a very wrenching thing. In any case, he then died in a car accident, and now no one remembered the place except a few old mistresses and maybe one or two of the father's drinking buddies. The teenagers came at least twice a month, depending on how much liquor they could get.

When they spoke of it back home to one another, the kids called it "going to the jungle," even though, as I've said, it was more like an open forest here. The path that ended at El Secreto sloped up to an unpaved road that connected Duarte, the town the kids lived in, and two or three of the other villages. If you drove along this road, you might see the opening of the path if you were paying close attention, but usually when the kids left they tried to cover it up. The path came down from the road about two hundred yards, straight and directly downhill, to the shack. Duarte was about half a mile down the road, and it was called a town because it had the Cuban version of the post office, but most of their parents worked at the tourist resorts in Varadero.

Matanzas, by their best guess, was thirty miles away, which meant that we had drifted to the southeast, away from the city, during our adventure in the sea. I did not see how knowing this helped me. But Charlie Dance was in Matanzas, and though I recognized the absurdity in thinking of him as a resource, we didn't have many other options.

There was little I could do but continue drinking. I period-ically lugged myself over to fill my cup, and they hardly seemed to notice—they continued to dance like coke-addled Eurotrash. On one of these visits, I was startled by the voice of a girl—she had been resting in a chair, hidden from the red light by shadows. She asked me why I didn't dance, I mumbled some-thing, and she told me to sit, speaking slowly to gauge how much Spanish I had. Perhaps it is needless to say that I began to wonder, in a detached kind of way, about the possibilities of sexual contact with this teenage girl, whose name was Teresa.

As it happened, I could have had any one of them, or at least whichever one Ramon did not choose. After a half hour or so, the music quieted, and two of them wedged themselves next to me on the grainy couch and asked me to tell them the story of how I got Ramon Sagasta out of Rios. One of them touched my eye and asked if the police had done this, and then quickly she put her hands on my lip. "No, I better not know. It's not safe to know things here." They were inexpert seductresses, alternately batting eyelashes and giggling to each other about a song on the radio, but of course they were pretty as pastries.

The truth of Ramon's earlier braggadocio presented itself to me in prurient epiphany. If he could arrange an encounter with Charlie Dance, I should easily have been able to ride Ramon's coattails into some girl's pants. Granted, these weren't hookers, but then again I wasn't Charlie Dance.

This brought to me the happy sensation I had already had once or twice in Ramon's presence, and which was becoming more frequent as our relationship wore on. I felt something very much like a wave of faith, as the truth of Ramon asserted itself. He was, by definition, an exaggeration, someone who could not be as good as touted, who could not be as real as his reports, and yet he continued to prove the truth of them. This was the promise of Ramon becoming manifest. I had heard of his overhand delivery and the rage of his velocity and I shrugged, and then I saw him throw and felt the speed crash into my forehead by the way of alligator pears and the truth was instantly asserted, transferred from mythology. He had told me how he was received in this part of the world and I had shrugged, and here were boys who remembered him the way Peter remembered Christ. He had told me of the power of his name alone to seduce the prostitutes of Matanzas, and I had called his girlfriend a whore. And now I sat alongside him, and these sweating, worshipful young girls would climb on top of me and violate their upbringing and their honor at a whisper from Ramon Sagasta. They would climb on top of me, and who was I? A Charlie Dance minus two and a half hundred pounds. My debasement simply highlighted Ramon's power.

I wouldn't have even had to ask. They would know that it was the will of Ramon if I suggested we slide out into the wet forest and find a patch of moss. Armed with this understanding, I chose.

I approached Teresa and took a knee by her side, grabbed her hand and fondled it. I called her the most beautiful girl I had ever seen, asked her how she got so beautiful, and she told me I was drunk and that it was none of my business how she got that way, but she laughed and it was not unreasonable for me to assume that this was the only work I would have to do. The rest was formality.

But we continued talking, perhaps out of habit, perhaps because nervousness never goes away, even with a sure thing. We walked up the slope behind the dugout, I laid out a blanket I'd found behind the couch, and we lay on our backs and talked.

"You're a baseball player too?" she said.

"I was a baseball player. Now I just find baseball players." It didn't come out as impressive or mysterious as I'd hoped. I found myself feeling as I always do around women I'd like to impress. I was more than groundless, I was floating on a lack of understanding, absolutely uncertain as to what the right thing to say might have been, and equally uncertain that if I knew what it was, I would be able to say it.

"An interesting job," she said, but sounded unconvinced.

I just nodded, wondering how to begin kissing her, worried about how it would make me feel—I was exactly twice as old as she was.

She said, "But now you're in trouble. What will you do?"

"Whatever I have to," I said, and here I swung my face around and kissed her on the mouth, and she kissed back, and we continued this for a long time, until my neck ached. As soon as we separated she said, "If I were American, I wouldn't come near this place. And I wouldn't do anything as dangerous as this. Ramon Sagasta, my God! You could get in a lot of trouble. I don't understand men. You seem to enjoy making things hard on yourselves. I don't think I understand Americans either."

"Ramon will do great things someday. It's worth the risk to me, the thought of him playing in the United States, and doing great things. It's hard to explain, I suppose. I will be very proud if I get him there."

"But you were a baseball player yourself. Aren't you done with baseball?"

"You never get done with it. At least, I won't." As to the truth of this, who can say?

We kissed again for long minutes, then began speaking some more. From her I found out more of what I've related about El Secreto and its sordid history, and I added to my stock of Sagasta legend as she told me about a depressed great-uncle who had regained his will to live while attending a game in which Ramon threw twenty strikeouts.

Lazily, leaning back and squinting her eyes at me, she said something that immediately made me shiver. "Dangerous business, this one you're in. A boy at school became a *contrabandista*, and everyone says he drowned somewhere."

The word threw me for a bit—I had imagined it being pronounced differently. The meaning came to me suddenly, after a few beats of silence.

I had heard about the *contrabandistas*, the professional smugglers, mostly from the few Cubans I'd played with in the minors. One of my teammates in Cedar Rapids had used them to get out of Cienfuegos, and he would talk about his defection if he was drunk and someone prodded him—the excursion seemed to have been a pretty significant experience in his life, but not one he recalled fondly. He had called them the *contrabandistas,* or sometimes the Miami Pirates. For an exorbitant price, they took refugees to Florida on the skiffs and water toys Charlie Dance had referred to. They had a middling success rate, and it was said that they were quick to shove refugees overboard if they were spotted, but it was also said that they knew who to bribe and that if they really wanted to—meaning if you paid them a lot and there was a chance you could pay them more—they knew how to get across. And I had money, more than most Cubans had ever seen.

I had forgotten all about them until then for a very simple reason: They were my competition. I had had to pretend that I was being sent to Cuba because I represented a better chance for Ramon Sagasta than the smugglers. I realized even then that this was a grave falsehood, and so I just pretended that they didn't exist. I had hoped that Ramon had never heard about them.

Now, I grilled Teresa for information. She didn't know much, and didn't want to talk about it. With her fingers she played with my lips. "What do you care about them?"

"I need information. How much do they cost, in particular. And where are they."

"How am I supposed to know that?" She had been fiddling with my buttons, and she stopped. She began to notice the insects, and squinted and slapped at her arms. I didn't have much time.

We kissed again. Teresa kissed with an open mouth, but hesitated to use her tongue. I put my hand up her shirt and she pulled it away, but after a few minutes she grabbed it and put it back. I felt both of her breasts, we parted, our faces wet, my mouth dry.

She said, "I've heard it's about a thousand dollars. The ones in Matanzas charge that, anyway. My uncle Rico got away last year."

I sat up at this. I begged her to tell me more about Rico. Where had he gone, with whom had he spoken. Was he alive, had he contacted them, what was the trip like. Most of these questions met with a shrug and a kiss, so it took a while to ask them all.

The information boiled down to this: Rico got in trouble playing poker—the fact is he was too good at it, something of a professional, and the authorities knew about it. He got word that they were either going to send him away or start milking him for a portion of his winnings, so he decided to leave, and eventually try to get to Atlantic City. He went to the outskirts of Matanzas, to an area called Cerrito where the smugglers have a kind of headquarters, and asked around. If they believed you weren't a snitch, it was a relatively easy thing to be put in touch with the right people, especially if you have dollars, she said. She knew Rico had had more than a thousand, but she didn't think he'd spent that much. Through another relative, they learned he'd made it to Miami, and was working at a club there.

She then told me that she liked me very much. "You got Ramon this far, that's very impressive," she said. Her syntax made it difficult to understand if she meant that it was impressive that I'd made it this far at all, or that I'd made it this far with Ramon Sagasta. I must admit that, as I thought about it then, I was impressed with myself on both counts. I felt I deserved her. She then told me that there was no way she would let me penetrate her (even in Spanish it's a horrifically unromantic phrase), but I could kiss her some more, and touch her where I wanted. I did as she asked, and after an hour or so, about the same time the volume of the music in the dugout softened, we fell asleep.

Yes, she was barely seventeen. Yes, I took advantage of her adulation of Ramon Sagasta, and her misinterpretation of me as some sort of soldier of fortune. I have little defense except to say this: she was a great comfort to me, and she was only this, and I don't think that is such a terrible thing to make of someone.

I slept with my head on her chest—I had not known softness since three days before, when I'd been sitting on Charlie Dance's couch. If I had not had softness at that moment, I don't know what would have happened to me.

When I awoke, the first thing I remembered was the information about the smugglers, and remembering what I'd learned from her gave me a sense of victory. One thousand dollars, perhaps a bit more. I had this, I had seventeen hundred, enough for one trip out but not two. It was early to be considering the financing of the trip, yes, but it gave me a thrill. I found myself thinking about this new escape as if it were foregone, as if the *contrabandistas* were waiting in the dugout for me, printing out a receipt.

There was no decision to be made. It would be Ramon. It's probably not necessary to say how much I wanted out of Cuba at the moment, if only for the fact that I'd never been in worse need of an American shower or a non-Hispanic meal, but I didn't even think about that much. Ramon needed out, or at least I needed him to get out. I needed him to play for me. Things could be arranged for me later; I hadn't been seen by anyone who mattered, could tuck myself away in one of Charlie's rooms until a new ticket could be arranged. It wasn't a pleasant week I imagined for myself, but this only made it more heroic. I was convinced there was heroism in this decision that I had not even needed to pause to make. I would get Ramon out this way.

It's not like taking a ferry, of course. The boats made infrequent runs out, Teresa had told me. But maybe Ramon's celebrity would help, maybe the extra seven hundred would help. It didn't matter; my great moment, in a way, had already come, or at least it had already been established. I had settled upon a great sacrifice. We would get to the outskirts of Matanzas, we would ask around. We would bribe a family to hide us or we would steal soldiers' uniforms—whatever we had to do to avoid the police. We would arrange a trip for Ramon with the smugglers and find a place for him to hole up until the time came.

It was no sure thing, I understood this, but I also understood better than anyone how foolish it had been for the organization not to do this in the first place, as if I would be more adept at smuggling simply because I was an American, and had played baseball, and had a new Evinrude. A certain kind of logic rules the atmosphere in an air-conditioned office, I guess.

We had no way to get to Matanzas, and we had every reason to believe a full scale manhunt was already in affect, but I felt damn near boisterous. I couldn't wait to wake up Ramon, wave the wad of cash from my money belt in front of his flat nose.

I skipped around the corner of the dugout and stopped where the earth met the floor. All four of the remaining girls sat squeezed together on one couch; the boys sat on the floor, most of them hugging their knees to their chests. Ramon sat on an easy chair, flanked on either side by men in soldier's uniforms. He looked a bit like a dictator about to give a press conference, except the soldier's weapons were held out, vaguely pointed at his direction and then at mine.

"Dennis," said Ramon, almost lightly, as if he were happy to see me. "We were just about to wake you up."

CHAPTER NINE

It was the short one, with the buckteeth, who had told on us—to this day I think I'm the only one who understands that. The other kids just seemed to think it was bad luck, preoccupied as they were with wondering if their hideaway would be taken from them. None of them wondered why the cops had driven down the useless side road, then decided to hike down the barely visible path that led to nowhere in the jungle.

But I noticed that the short bastard with buckteeth contained a fear that was coming from somewhere else; he wasn't afraid of the cops, he was afraid of his friends, of everyone understanding that he had snuck off when all of us had passed out and that he had run down the dirt road and summoned the police. He was the one who had recognized Ramon immediately, back when we broke through the brush and came upon them. I can't say what his reasons were—perhaps he was a budding ideologue, perhaps there were rewards for snitching, although I can't think any reward would match the great pleasure of that hideaway for a lustful teenager, and he had certainly put it in jeopardy. Now, at least, the police would know where to go to find drunk seventeen-year-old girls on a weekend night.

The short bastard with buckteeth had hiked his way back towards Cardenas in the middle of the night, reported the presence of Ramon Diego Sagasta and some American smuggler to this brace of restless country cops, and the cops had come and tapped everyone on the heads with their billy clubs. For some reason they'd all sat there and waited for me to wake up, a touching gesture I thought, a small deference to either my American citizenship or my great seventeen-year-old bounty.

Together they barked at me to sit in the empty chair—their words overlapped; it was difficult to tell what they said, or to gauge their anger. Their lips worked beneath brushlike black mustaches. Because of the placement of the chairs, I sat across from Ramon and we stared at each other, like two chess players about to square off. Ramon grinned. This might have been a reference to my naughtiness in corrupting the girl, or it might have been an acknowledgement of the strange folly of our situation, or it may have been, as I believe now, that Ramon just didn't understand the trouble we were in. For those seconds, as the cops fingered their batons, and the kids held their breath, and we all waited for the last of our party—Teresa—to join us, it came to me that Ramon just could not understand the significance of the police. The adulation of the previous evening had been so thorough and unquestionable that Ramon could not at this moment fathom malice. He must have thought they were just fans who happened to be cops, that word had gotten out somehow, and these two had come to get autographs, to talk about the season. Ramon was not ready to be afraid, or to receive hopelessness, as I was. Something about his grin spoke of a curiosity—he wanted to ask about that unwelcome sensation that came with the silence. I wanted to lean over and tell him what it was. "Ramon," I might say, "that thing you sense, that you can't give a name to, is this: You will never play baseball again. That's all. We may suffer for a while, we may even die—who can say? But the real dread you sense is that you've lost baseball."

But instead I closed my eyes, and waited for someone to speak, and tried to be forgotten. I heard my teenager traipse down the slope, mutter a choked-off word at the sight she encountered, and then join the other girls on the couch. One of the cops said Ramon's name. It was so quiet I could hear Ramon's shirt shift as he nodded.

"You both need to come with us."

"Where are we going?" said Ramon.

"That's not for you to know."

Matanzas, of course, we would go to Matanzas.

No one spoke again for some time. Ramon had begun to glance at me, trying to catch my eye, as if he could pass me some secret signal that would spring us both into motion, or make us disappear. I took care not to look at him.

The other cop was taller, had pock marks on his face all the way up to his temples, and stood with one foot crossed in front of the other. He ordered us up and we began marching towards the road. For some reason, all the teenagers followed, and the cops acted as if they'd expected this. Ramon and I hiked up the path first, single file, with the policemen huddled close to us. They kept their guns out, one pointed up to the sky, the other aimed at the ground.

The path met the road after about two hundred steep yards. The policemen's Jeep, parked diagonally across the dirty road, was greenish-brown, the same color as the jungle floor I'd been staring at for most of the past two days. Rust had eaten away the back bumper and been painted with primer. The exhaust pipe hovered just above the ground. I found myself thinking in a lazy way that I didn't look forward to riding on that piece of crap all the way to Matanzas; it was certain to be loud, and probably had bad shocks.

"You kids should get out of here as soon as you can," said the shorter cop, who had thick sideburns that were just like his mustache. He gazed down the path. "And I wouldn't come back here for a while. You never know what might come out of the jungle." He giggled, and no one joined him, and his short embarrassment spurred him into action. He moved forward to grab Ramon's arm, and in stepping forward he caused a great movement among the teenagers—they scooted to one side of the road and hunched on the ground, crouching together. It was an exaggerated gesture of supplication, and the cop was surprised but pleased. Instead of grabbing Ramon's arm, as I'm certain he had planned to do, he patted it twice. "The game is up, Ramon Sagasta. It's time to face the authorities in Matanzas. It does my heart no good to take you in." He stood as tall as he could in front of Ramon, looking him in the eyes in the melodramatic way of someone who wants to make it very clear they're looking you in the eyes. "You and I were on the same field together once."

The taller cop uncrossed his legs and lifted his head. He had a whiny voice, and spoke rapidly. The words he spoke explained this—he had almost missed his cue; it was his role to do his partner's bragging for him. "Raoul played for two seasons with Santa Clara. He was the stolen base leader in ninety-one. You kids may remember," he said to the cowering boys and girls. They didn't remember Raoul, I was certain of this, but they nodded with great seriousness, even the girls.

Raoul pursed his lips in a wistful manner. Ramon's eyebrows had lowered in confusion. Raoul said, "The one time we faced, however, you injured your finger in the fourth, before I was called in to pinch run. I never got to face you at the plate." He adopted a bluff, manly tone. "But I will tell my children some-day that I played on the field with Ramon Sagasta. I will not tell them about today, but it is my duty, after all."

When Ramon spoke we were all surprised, perhaps more by the fact that he could speak than by what he said. Since the van-ishing of his smile back at the dugout, it had seemed right and natural for him to be silent. He said to the cop with sideburns, "How do you think you would have done, Raoul Pena?"

Ramon would later admit to me that he knew the man's last name through the usual village gossip—Matanzas and its satel-lite villages isn't that big a place, and at some point Ramon had heard that Raoul, the Pena boy whose father worked with a neighbor at the sugar plant (or something like that) had become a policeman. Raoul, of course, in the egotistical way of failed athletes who actually care whether or not people pay attention to them—while those of Ramon's ilk simply know that people do—assumed that Ramon remembered him from the game, had considered him a worthy adversary and had done so much home-work on him that the name had stuck. Foolish of him, of course—I doubt Ramon could remember the name of his last manager—but it was no more outlandish than the notion that Ramon would remember the name of some local boy who had joined the police force. It's strange what we remember, Ramon told me later, and it must have been God's will that the name of Raoul Pena would stick in his brain. He knew as well as I that it wasn't in his nature to remember much of anything that didn't concern him directly. He also knew that he was blessed, and that at times this blessing seeped off the baseball field into real life.

Raoul Pena grinned. He must have hoped for this. Riding over in the Jeep, responding to the snitch's report, he must have wondered if the great Ramon Sagasta would recognize him. Just as quickly, he would have dismissed it as impossible—two years with Santa Clara? Even with a stolen base title, what distinction is in that to someone like Ramon? But he would have kept it his the back of his brain as a kernel of possibility.

Raoul Pena gulped and lowered his voice. "It's difficult to say, Ramon. We were both younger men. I could hit well to the opposite field in those days, and you still were working on your breaking pitches, if I remember."

"So you think you might have hit against me?" Ramon said this boyishly, beginning to grin again.

"I'm saying it's not out of the question."

"How would you have done it? Waited for an outside fast-ball? Perhaps waited for me to make a mistake on my curveball? You're right, I was struggling then."

Raoul Pena's fat mustache bobbed with his head. "Yes, I would have waited for an outside pitch, but if you had hung a curve you can believe I would have ripped it." His hands had come together in fists, as if he were gripping a bat. He hadn't meant to do this, as it kept his hands away from the holster, and I knew exactly how he felt. I do this with my hands all the time, unconsciously.

It was like they were having a grinning contest. Both men showed so much of their bad dentistry and stretched their lips so wide I found it odd that they could enunciate at all. Ramon said "But maybe I just would have gunned away on the inside. One, two, three! All at ninety-eight miles per hour."

"And maybe I would have timed you by then, and sent it away to San Juan!"

It was all very good-natured, or so I thought. I thought that Ramon was simply trying to befriend him, and was amazed at how willing the cop was to let him do this. It seemed ill-conceived to me, even as a last-ditch effort. Neither cop could have let us get away—the snitch was still there, after all, and would have told someone else eventually. No amount of charming and bantering could extricate us from this, and I grew quickly weary with Ramon's attempts—it made me dread all the more the moment that I thought was imminent, when Ramon, certain of their friendship, would ask for release and Raoul Pena, in obvious distress, would have to deny him. It would make for an awkward Jeep ride back to Matanzas.

The grinning and the banter had reached a crescendo when Ramon struck. Still smiling wide, he nodded along as Raoul simulated the crack of the bat that accompanied his hypothetical long ball off Ramon's hypothetical fastball, and then Ramon's face went still and blank, and he gurgled out the stunning words: "Bullshit, you shit farmer's son. You wouldn't have been able to hit those pitches with a tennis racket."

It certainly wasn't my turn to speak, but I said *"Que?"* in a raspy croak, as did two or three of the teenagers. No one heard us. Raoul Pena didn't need to ask Ramon to repeat what he'd said.

"Is that the case, Ramon? Well let me say this:" What he meant to say next was that Ramon wouldn't even be able to throw pitches after he had spent fifteen hours getting whooped on by the Revolutionary Police, but he was flustered, and he stuttered and mangled the words that had meant to cut Ramon. He tried to repeat himself, and again misspoke, this time so badly that one of the beautiful girls covered up a giggle. Eventually he just cursed and grabbed Ramon by the arm and walked him to the Jeep. He guided him over, the way he would a wounded comrade, or a blind person. Even in his rage and humiliation, Raoul Pena could not exorcise his regard for Ramon's legend—I wondered what it would take for Raoul to actually punch him. Maybe it would be the same at headquarters, no one able to bring themselves to touch their hero in anger. Perhaps they knew that the name of Ramon Sagasta was so substantial that it would be a sin to hurt the man. His American accomplice, however, they might not have trouble abusing. Don't think this didn't occur to me.

Raoul Pena got into the driver's seat, but the tall cop didn't move. I assumed it was his job to get me, but he just stood there biting the tissue of his lip and gazing at his boots some more. Raoul drummed his fingers on the dash, Ramon had nestled into the back and leaned his head to the left, as if trying to catch a nap. In a lame gesture I walked myself over to the Jeep and climbed in next to Ramon—what else could I do? Nothing, of course, but nevertheless it felt like the most unheroic act I have ever committed, worse than the time I slammed my finger in a car door so that I wouldn't have to bat against Peter Kaptzos, the Detroit Tigers' fireballer who had been sent to Double A to work on control problems.

"Arturo!" called Raoul Pena. "Arturo—come on, now!"

So the tall one's name was Arturo. He turned upon hearing his name, lifted his backside off the Jeep's frame but, instead of moving towards us, he settled his palms on the hood and shook his head slowly, ticking the quarter-sized bald spot at the top of his head from side to side like a mesmerist's watch. He took an enormous gulp of snot as he sniffled and raised his face to us. He was an ugly man, a face like a vulture's with the beak cut off. "I don't care who you are, Ramon Sagasta. I don't care at all. There is no man on the planet who speaks that way to Raoul in my presence. No man on God's earth."

Ramon lifted his head. He sat taller in the seat, and he pressed his hands together. I don't know if Ramon had ever felt fear the way that I had, or if he was feeling anything like it now, but I did feel him stiffen beside me in the way that is particular to a frightened body, the barely perceptible clenching of nerves and muscles that must be what animals detect when they are said to smell fear.

There are a thousand different varieties of fear, of course, and any honest culture would have a name for every one of them, the way the Eskimos have all those words for snow. What Ramon was feeling, I imagined, was the variation of fear I had felt when he began throwing alligator pears at me—fear touched with surprise, and darkened by the sudden acknowledgement that the anger which you fear has been justifiably provoked. Or perhaps it wasn't so complex for him, maybe it was something like fear mingled with confusion, the inability to understand the origin of that anger that you fear; this is often worse, I think, because when you don't know the cause of your fear, you cannot reasonably predict how far it will go. In the forest, I had realized too late that calling Ramon's girlfriend a whore had been a major offense. I knew he would enact some sort of vengeance, that he would be obliged to do so. I also knew that he probably wouldn't kill me for it (although, by his own admission, he had wanted to). Ramon couldn't take that for granted right now, not being able to even guess the extent or the source of Arturo's anger.

Mine was a special blend of fear, rare and unpredictable, a fear that strangely blended hope (I hadn't insulted Raoul, after all, and I was still somewhat certain they would hesitate killing an American) with a deeper dread than Ramon could have known, since I knew the source of Arturo's anger. He was Raoul's lover. It was there in the way he gripped the hood of the Jeep, as if he was squeezing Ramon's throat, and in the way he spoke Raoul's name, and in the exuberant veins of his neck, and in the way he clearly watched Raoul from the corner of his eye without moving the irises. It had been there when he recited Raoul's baseball accomplishments, and in the way he watched his feet during the exchange with Ramon, proud and happy for his lover but unable to watch, afraid to see the disappointment in Raoul's face if Sagasta did not remember him, or if—Dios forbid—he insulted him.

And Ramon, the great idiot, had done it, never once considering that the greatest threat came not from the man but from the lover of the man. Raoul, embarrassed, uncomfortable with sweat, anxious in front of the children and Arturo, was ready to zip back to Matanzas in silence and finish this experience, but Ramon had ensured something else. He had done it not in some effort to free us, not because he sought the inherent advantage of getting under his captor's skin, but simply because he could not fathom the arrogance of this farmer cop who seemed to think that at one point in the distant past he could have hit a Ramon Sagasta fastball, this small-time *guardia* who now made his living ticketing the farmers who didn't pay tax on the cane they sold at roadside stands. It was a notion so ludicrous it could not go unpunished. And so he served him a great and terrible insult, the way he might have served him a great and terrible pitch long ago.

Ramon might have seen this as a great moment, if he'd thought about it much, which he wouldn't have—many great baseball moments are often the ones like these, that come far away from the field, when you exhibit the will and courage and arrogance that serves you when you play. I thought it must have been very true that even in his youth Raoul could not have hit Ramon's pitches with a tennis racket, and the pain for both the policeman lovers must have come from this truth, and from the surreal image it conjured of Raoul taking the plate with a tennis racket cocked behind his head, and still managing to fan every pitch.

For both of us, the fear that all of this produced was intense, since it also happened to be the worst kind of fear, the fear that certainly deserves its own word in our language—the fear that you will very shortly be killed. The knowledge that Arturo may have wanted to kill us filled my body like a gas. Arturo was unavoidable death, and he had a pistol and a quiet, empty forest and a handful of teenage witnesses who could very easily be hushed. And he had seen his lover lose the one thing of importance to him—the memory of baseball, the way he had been able to tell himself that he was pretty good, that he might have even hit against Ramon Sagasta. By the time he had become an old man, the story would have mutated and grown, and he would be telling everyone at the cantina about the time he'd ripped a double off the wall on a hanging Sagasta curveball, and this story would be the most important thing in his life. Ramon had taken this away, this dream of a lifetime's glory; he might as well have robbed him of his pension. Raoul had been partly broken in the work of a minute, and Arturo knew all of this; you could see it in the veins of his neck.

If someone wants to kill you, and they have the weapon, and the opportunity, and the lack of compunction, what stops them? Certainly not you (or, at least, certainly not me). I honestly would like to know. For Arturo really did want to kill Ramon—I still haven't decided what he would've done with me—but, of course, he didn't. In our case, it was Raoul who stopped him, who shut off the engine immediately upon seeing the glaring fury of his partner, and came around the front of the Jeep and took his biceps in his hand and squeezed rhythmically, with another hand on his back, which he must have been rubbing. It didn't seem to soothe Arturo, but he looked away from Ramon and into the eyes of Raoul—yes, they were lovers, no doubt now, and even Ramon nudged me and gave me a look that said "Oh my God! Homos!"—and they spoke quietly to one another. Their voices became louder the longer they talked, and soon they were bickering, and eventually Raoul said "I can't talk to you then! You do what you want! Child!" and melodramatically stomped to the edge of the forest, squatted, and began ripping apart a leaf.

Arturo ignored him and summoned one of the teenagers, who listened with grave attention and then sprinted down the road towards Duarte. Arturo then approached us—we remained rigid in the Jeep's backseat—and looked us over. The fear was still with us, the worst of fears. It would not have surprised me if he had pulled out his pistol and simply shot us each in the temple. In fact, I found myself assuming he would do this—in spite of the obvious fact that if he were to kill us he would have taken us into the woods; you tend not to think of such things at such moments. I waited for the sound of the unsnapping of a button on Arturo's holster.

Instead he poked a finger in Ramon's chest. "You, Ramon Sagasta, get out of the car. You too," he said to me. "But don't think this gives you a chance for anything. We're still taking you in, and you don't want to try your American tough-guy stuff on us." The way he said this implied he didn't really think I was capable of any American tough-guy stuff, or perhaps he didn't even think that concept existed anymore. I wouldn't have argued either point. I followed Ramon out of the Jeep with my hands held up in a vague, apologetic way.

Raoul spoke from the edge of the forest. "This is just stupid, Arturo. A waste of time. I don't want you to think you're doing me any favors with this. You're embarrassing me, to tell the truth." Arturo didn't respond, and he finally unholstered his gun, but I no longer thought he was going to kill us. He pointed it at us, but without any kind of urgency or intensity. I had also been comforted by the whiny, exasperated tone Raoul had used in chiding Arturo, and also because the teenagers—who had heard Arturo's directive to their friend—seemed excited about something, sitting up on their knees and arranging themselves to get a good view of us.

Ramon wanted to ask what was going on. I could practically feel the question seeping out of his pores, but he was afraid to speak anymore, considering what had happened the last time he did. He blinked at me vacantly, and I realized he wanted me to figure things out. So I said it, breaking a silence I had held— with the exception of "*Que?*"—since I woke up. "Sir," I said, sounding even meeker than I'd intended, "Can I ask what you are planning for us?"

CHAPTER TEN

Arturo was proud to answer—there was no registry of my insolence in asking. "I have sent the boy home to get a ball and a bat. We're going to put this boastful peasant to the test." He stuck his finger into Ramon's chest again, causing him to take a step back and assume a wounded look. Only Ramon Sagasta could have been made indignant in this situation. "I'll give you a chance, you overrated cockroach, to prove your lies. You're going to pitch against Raoul. You'll be begging to go to Matanzas to forget your shame."

Ramon skipped over the moments of relief that began consuming me. As I listened to my heart and wondered how long it would take to stop its clamor, as I felt the dried sweat on my face reassume its liquid form, Ramon began to babble.

"What, in the name of God? You're going to have me pitch against him? For what purpose? What good can this do anyone?" he said, as if he could assume the cops intended to do some good to someone.

Arturo swung his arm around laterally, parallel to he ground, and whacked Ramon against the chin with the handle of his pistol. Ramon stood still for a moment, as the teenagers gasped, and then dropped to one knee and spit goopy blood on the ground. I bent next to him and watched, but couldn't think of any help to offer. I just watched, and he spit again. His eyes were shut tight. When he opened them again, they would become wide with disbelief, I knew this.

Raoul screeched something. Arturo walked away from us and away from Raoul, towards the teenagers. The teenagers were beginning to unnerve me, not that I had much nerve left. They were too much the witnesses, serving no purpose now except to wonder and react to what happened to us, and to remind me that I'd done something vaguely immoral with one of them, and that this entire thing could be interpreted by some as a reckoning for that. I tried to put them out of my mind, and tried to keep them out of view. I was all the witness I needed. However I now behaved, with courage or cowardice or indifference or incompetence, I did not want anyone around who didn't contribute to either our deliverance or our ruin. The teenagers had come to seem like some eerie Greek chorus that refused to speak. I wasn't thinking about how pretty the girls were anymore.

Being struck shut Ramon up for good, and he and I stayed on the ground until the boy returned with the equipment. Arturo stayed where he was, away from Raoul, who stayed where he was. It was not the least strange thing that we had become embroiled in a lovers' spat, and that we were at once the source of it and the possible resolution.

I found some toilet paper in the Jeep and helped Ramon clean his face—he had a cut on the inside of his bottom lip. The lip had already swollen, and would clearly become bigger, the kind of fat lip that would impair speech. But the bleeding had stopped, and he wouldn't have gotten stitches for it even if we'd been in the States. He didn't say anything, but he clearly considered it a near-fatal injury. He kept dabbing his lip and squinting at the results on the toilet paper, as if he could barely bring himself to look. I got off my knees and crouched, and he sat beside me, legs sprawled out before him.

I speculated. Ramon had a very tall order in front of him. It was up to him to resolve the conflict between the two lovers, and he had two options. If he chose to throw as he could and struck out Raoul, that certainly wouldn't settle things—it would embarrass them both, and later on Raoul was sure to blame Arturo for his obstinacy, just as Arturo was sure to blame Raoul for letting him down with the bat, though this would be an unspoken, festering blame. If Ramon let him hit, perhaps that would salvage some pride and repair relations ("I knew you would do it, *mi* Raoul!" I could hear Arturo gasp), but it would destroy the Sagasta legend at the exact moment when we most needed to trade in on it. I couldn't help wondering if Ramon's comment to Raoul hadn't in some way been exactly what they'd been expecting from the great hero; it was certainly what the teenagers had wanted. They would be telling that story until their grandchildren sent them away to the state home for the aged. To serve a meatball to this stout cop, five years removed from a mediocre career, would dispel Ramon's legend in that small company, and that legend was all that we had. It was the only reason we weren't on the way to Matanzas already. Then again, it was also the reason I wasn't at a breezy ballpark in Tampico, eating *flautas* and filling out a conditional inflation form.

I took comfort in knowing that these speculations were not occupying the head of Ramon Sagasta in the least. He was still feeling his lip with his tongue and wincing. When the ball came, he would pitch. He obviously had to, there was no arguing or escaping. They'd put the ball in his hand, he'd throw it as hard as he could, or as curvy or sinking as he could, and try to get it past the cop. That was all there was to it. No repercussions to anticipate, no feelings or options to consider. Throw the ball because they insist upon it, strike him out because you can. Is there any other way? No, or at least there should be no other way. There should not be so much speculation in life, we should all be as blind of the future as Ramon, but you have to be as good as Ramon to attain this blindness.

In the silence we heard the scuffling feet of the teenager who had sprinted, hung over, to the village and back. He handed Arturo a long, light wooden bat and a baseball, and then collapsed like Phidippides next to his friends. They had assumed their positions as spectators, the girls sitting cross-legged in a half ring and the boys kneeling behind them.

It wasn't as difficult a matter as I'd thought it would be to get Raoul to participate. His pouting stopped instantly, and he walked over to take the bat like a child accepting the toy he'd been throwing a tantrum over.

Arturo set a gym bag from the Jeep in front of Raoul. "This is home plate," he said. He began to count off the feet as he moved towards us. He put the heel of one foot directly in front of the toe of the other, and repeated this with agonizing patience until he'd marked off sixty feet, six inches. When he was finished he scuffed a line on the dirt road. "No rubber, no mound—so what? You're Ramon Sagasta! You throw lightning bolts! You fart perfume! You don't need a rubber to pitch against Raoul Pena! Am I right?"

"Yes, okay," said Ramon, who was still standing by the Jeep. He didn't acknowledge the sarcasm. Arturo was right. Ramon didn't need a rubber and a mound to strike out this man. He took the baseball, and said, almost as if he were talking just to me, "And if I get him out in three pitches, you let us go, okay?"

The three of us—Raoul, Arturo, and me—all said "*Que?!*" together, but for different reasons. Raoul, standing thirty yards away, just didn't hear him, while I was certain that my Spanish had left me for a moment, and Arturo was simply reacting with disbelief. Raoul began walking towards us, waving the bat like a baton in one loose hand. "What did you say?"

"I said that if I strike you out then you must let us go. It seems like a fair exchange—you seem confident I won't be able to, after all."

Arturo began protesting in stutters. The impossibility of Ramon's notion expressed itself in his inability to properly sound out his words. He was trying to cram ten expressions of outrage into each word, and he simply gurgled and sputtered.

"No, no, no," Raoul approached, shaking the bat from side to side in concert with his head. "Put that thought away, Ramon Sagasta. It's up. You're done, forget this being released business. We couldn't if we wanted to."

I now wondered if this was true. Could they have released us if they wanted to? They wouldn't have told anyone else what they were coming out here for—they probably doubted it themselves when the breathless bucktoothed bastard found them napping on the road to Cardenas and told them his fantastic story; perhaps they wouldn't have reported it. The teenagers were the only witnesses, and they couldn't count for much. The only reliable thing about them was their capacity for fear—they could be easily mastered by the softest of threats. Even if they did tell someone, bragging to a brother or sister under the covers in the room they shared, overheard by their neighbors the way all of Ramon's childhood secrets must have been overheard— even then, what of it? The stories of children are hard enough to believe, and it must have been common knowledge that any story involving Ramon Sagasta would carry the air of a fable, certainly not something to be acted upon in any literal way.

So perhaps this wasn't true, I decided. Perhaps if they

wanted to they could very easily let us slip back into the forest, or even give us a ride towards Matanzas. Besides, it seemed pretty certain that we'd be caught eventually anyway, so it wouldn't really be a betrayal of the motherland. The impossibility lay in the conjunction; it was a mighty large "if"—they could let us go *if* they wanted to. It was a fact as big and encompassing as the forest that they did not want to let us go; all germs of this desire had died when Ramon called Raoul a shit farmer's son. And it was unlikely that they would be more inclined towards mercy if in fact Ramon humiliated Raoul by burning him on three pitches thrown from level ground.

To say that I failed to understand what Ramon was thinking is not just an understatement, but it is also misleading. Certainly, I was at a loss, but this was no failure of mine—no one could have known what function in his mind caused him to say such things. It may have been cunning, it may have been innocence, it may have been the simple desire to make things interesting, it may have been fearful desperation. No one should ever know what is going on in the mind of a great pitcher—this is a truth, but there is more to it than that. In regards to a truly great pitcher, one should not only fail to understand his mind's movements, one should immediately recognize the lunacy in even pretending to believe that knowing him is possible.

I am now wary of drawing analogies between life and baseball, although I often give in to the temptation. The extrapolation of the graces and failures of the game onto the larger stages of the world virtually never works, in my experience. When a political candidate tells you his party hit a home run in dealing with health care reform, for example, you must never believe him. Hitting a home run is a strange and wonderful and somehow merciless thing. It is a process of near-total elimination. When you hit a home run in a professional game, there is suddenly no pitcher, no runners, no crowd, no meaningful population at all on the earth. You have killed them all by doing the one great thing that moment can afford. The world has been reduced to one great act, and the multitudes exist only to observe. At night, when I'm just about to fade off into sleep, I sometimes realize that my mind has generated this superlative experience, I see the image of the immense ballpark and I feel the honey-smooth vibration of the connected wood along my arms and nerves. My body shivers at the moment of imagined contact. This happens to me almost every night, involuntarily, so powerful were the eight dozen instances in my professional career when I hit one for real. There is, quite literally, nothing in the world like it.

No experience in life is truly analogous to anything that happens in baseball, at its best and at its worst, just as there is probably no experience in life that can truthfully be compared to another. And so I don't mean to say that Ramon's inscrutability was akin to the way he kept a poker face on the mound; I mean to say it was the same thing. I was coming to accept Ramon's greatness as a truth, I think it is fair to say. After all, the world seemed to be conspiring to make me accept it. Charlie Dance, I could have discounted easily enough, but the legends the children talked themselves into believing, the honored and grave expression on Raoul Pena's face before he received the insult, the anguish on it afterwards, the sad aspect of Arturo as he defended his lover against a force he clearly reckoned to be godlike—this was strong testimony. And yet this did not do it, not quite. This was simply the kind of hype people like to tell themselves about athletes, the interior fabrications that invariably lead people to tell the athlete that they are shorter in real life than they thought they'd be, or that they look almost normal when they're not in uniform. The average fan is convinced that greatness seeps out of the great ones like a natural musk. Stories can be embellished and repeated to friends and amplified over beers because there is no one on earth who can contradict them, no one who does not want this to be true. I have seen it before, and I am an expert; I have searched a lifetime for the source of this absurd power. How is it that one casts this spell? The answer is in people like Ramon Sagasta, and you could observe them and interview them and study their motions and movements and techniques and biographies for decades and you will still never figure it out. I won't, at least.

The testimony of children, the fact that he impressed cops and teenagers and fat American scouts could not be enough, not for me at that stage, especially when it didn't matter at all if I was sold on Ramon's greatness or not. It wasn't a decision I had to make. But what brought up the question at all, and gradually leaned me towards favoring Ramon, were these various aspects of his personality that came across not as analogous to success in baseball, but as the baseball player personified. Ramon acted the way great baseball players act. Period. This might have been enough for me, but what happened next eradicated my doubt so thoroughly that afterwards it became difficult for me to believe it had ever existed.

"You can let us go if you want, Raoul, don't give me that," Ramon said.

Raoul waved a hand over the heads of the children. For a few seconds he was too outraged to speak, and so I did my part. "They won't tell anyone," I said, with a casual murmur, as if I was bored by the whole thing and wanted to get to the Matanzas prison so I could catch a nap. "They were smoking and drinking all night in a jungle hideaway—you think they want anyone to know what they were doing out here? And you know, Raoul," I said quietly, pretending that I didn't want Ramon to hear, "we're going to get caught anyway. Someone else will get us, and when that happens we certainly won't be stupid to tell anyone about you two."

Now Arturo spoke, and he was as adamant as Raoul. "Impossible. I don't even know why we're talking about this. Just shut up and throw, Ramon."

"I don't throw unless we have an arrangement."

Now Arturo pulled out his gun and pointed. It took him several seconds to unlatch his holster, heft the piece comfortably in his hand, and steady it in the air, but this didn't mitigate its menace. "You throw when I fucking tell you to throw."

Arturo's was not a credible threat. He was not going to shoot Ramon for not throwing, we all knew that. Yet the pointed gun was a sinister thing, there was no denying this, and it implied something—not imminent death, perhaps, but certainly it indicated some kind of iron resolve. Arturo had determined that Ramon would throw.

Ramon was undaunted. "How about you let us go if I throw him six strikes? Six in a row."

"Throw the baseball."

Raoul began to speak, in a voice that faltered, which frightened me as much as the gun—if Raoul was worried about what Arturo might do, then certainly we should be. He called out "This is stupid, Arturo. Stupid! We take them to Matanzas. Now!"

Arturo ignored him. "Hurry up, damn you!" he said to Ramon.

"I tell you, Arturo, I'm not throwing just like this. I throw three strikes, embarrass Raoul, and then we all drive to Matanzas? What is that? What's the point? Why don't you just take us there now?"

"Here, Ramon, where we are now—it's not you who's in charge. It's me. I may decide to shoot you even after Raoul has hit your pitches. I haven't decided yet. But I'll most definitely shoot you if you don't throw to him."

Arturo was starting to piss off Raoul, and this may have saved us. Raoul was starting to feel patronized. He said "I don't know who you think you are, Arturo. Who asked you to do any of this? Did I say I wanted this?"

This threw Arturo for a bit—he creased his forehead and watched Raoul stomp off to the edge of the forest, but he kept the gun level.

Ramon saw his advantage. "I know! I know! Listen to me, all of you, I have an idea." A deep swallow, a straightening of his posture, and a squinting of his eyes. "I will pitch from here. If I get three strikes by him from here, where I'm standing now, you let me go. How can you deny me that?"

In the end, they couldn't. Ramon stood about a hundred and ten feet from the bag that served as home plate—nearly twice the standard distance from the mound to home. Or, as it immediately occurred to me, Ramon had agreed to throw from a distance that was very nearly equal to the distance between home plate and second base. It was a ridiculous distance to pitch from, a ridiculous proposal altogether. Arturo didn't really agree to it, he just nodded a little and holstered the gun and asked Raoul if he was ready. Raoul struck the ground with the bat and cursed, and not just because it was a waste of time or because of Arturo's obstinacy—he was afraid he'd strike out, this was clear to me.

The distance was one that I, as a former catcher, was comfortable with. To throw out a stealing base runner, the catcher must make an immediate throw—no time to grip the seams—that travels 120 feet with little arc, covers this territory in less than 2.5 seconds (for most base runners) and strikes an area that is perhaps a bit larger than the strike zone. This area is calibrated and positioned by the body of the second baseman—or where the body of the second baseman will be, once he gets set. If the ball arrives in this general area, an agile second baseman can catch it and swipe it down to tag the incoming ankle in a deft motion. The tagging of a stealing base runner, when done correctly, looks like it has been precisely choreographed. The throw is, of course, the hardest part, and no catcher is blamed too much if it is off, or arrives too late. If you throw out half the runners who try to steal on you in a season, you are better than everyone else. If you get a quarter of them, you are average.

In the summer of 1987, which I spent with the Quad City River Bandits, I threw out forty-four percent of the base runners who tried to steal on me. This was easily the highest percentage I ever put up, easily the highest percentage in the Midwest League that season. I'm not sure what happened—it wasn't as if anything suddenly clicked, as if somehow my body finally understood something new. I just started getting them out.

Throughout this unlikely streak of near-greatness, I continued to understand too well how difficult, how unlikely a thing it was to throw out a runner who gets a jump and tries to steal second. How your timing must be superb, the situation ideal, all events conspiring towards the out. There simply seemed to be too many factors for success to be conceivable. For example:

If the pitcher has thrown a breaking ball or a change 80 percent of the time, your odds of getting the runner decrease radically, because the ball simply won't get to you very quickly, plus the movement on the ball might cause it to land strangely in your mitt, or even hit the dirt.

If the runner swings, this creates a slight blur that somehow stays in the air, or at least in your eye, at the precise moment you're trying to align the target, which isn't even an object, but empty space that will soon be occupied by the body of the second baseman. Add to this the fact that you are still wearing the catcher's mask, and the sudden jolting of your body has likely caused the mask to shift, so that your vision is obstructed by the bars of the mask. This is especially true on a hot day, when sweat has lubricated the mask's rubber grips.

Sometimes the random grip you've been forced to take puts unneeded and unwanted spin on the ball, so that it curves, or breaks, or bounces in front of the second baseman.

Add to this the fact that throwing a baseball accurately 120 feet in the air in less than 2.5 seconds is simply a very hard thing to do.

These truths sent me, during the 1987 season, into what I can only now think of as a kind of depression. The acknowledgment of this truth, that throwing out base runners was something that no one had any right doing with any degree of success, was like finding out that there is no God.

I had no control over this kind of event. I could try as hard as I might, do drills and lift weights, but if the out was not meant to be made there was nothing I could do. I generally did not take such a mystical approach to the game, but there was no other way to accept my success during the 1987 season except by saying that it was willed by the almost organic energy of the game, and it quickly died, as I knew it would all along. And because I could not understand the origins of my unlikely streak, when it died there was no way to summon it.

This is all by way of saying that the throws Ramon had arranged for himself—three pitches at 110 feet each—were extremely difficult to make with accuracy and medium velocity. Someone standing with a baseball bat at second base would have been able to hit any of my throws right back at me as easily as if they'd been whacking at a T-ball stand. And I mean anyone, not even a ball player. After 110 feet, the throw that I had channeled all the energy of a moment into had slowed exponentially. What might have left my hand at eighty-five miles per hour, and glazed by the pitcher at sixty, slid into the second baseman's glove with barely a smack of leather. Ramon had guaranteed that he could make Raoul Pena miss on three straight pitches from this distance. If he did, it we could go free.

CHAPTER ELEVEN

THE POINT WAS MOOT FOR A COUPLE REASONS. IN THE FIRST place, it was not possible that Ramon would do it. One hundred ten feet, no mound, no rubber, no catcher's mitt to throw to. Raoul was certainly nervous, and this would work for Ramon, but not so nervous that he couldn't tattoo something coming at him from thirty-five yards away. And I also doubted that Ramon would be able to find the strike zone from that distance, with no target. The one negative in the scouting report had been a slight problem with accuracy, and although he'd found my forehead easily enough in the forest, that had been from thirty feet or so, and those alligator pears had been big as softballs.

But the main thing was that they weren't going to let us go even if he did it. That was clear enough. They didn't have to let us go, so they wouldn't. If Ramon somehow managed to strike out Raoul, the poor cop would experience a disgrace beyond salvation, Arturo would immediately gauge the enormity of the shame and ruin he'd brought upon his lover, and they would take us to Matanzas reflexively. It did not stand to reason that they would feel charitable towards us if this thing should come to pass, or that they might feel obliged to keep their word. It was not much of a word to begin with; no solemn vow had been made, it had been more of a nodding of the head to get things moving. I thought we all understood this, but it was impossible to say what Ramon understood.

Arturo placed himself slightly to the left of left-handed Raoul, a spot where he would be safe from most foul balls. He put his palms flat on his thighs and leaned forward. He was stationed in front of the forgotten teenagers, and when one of them shifted and snapped a stick he turned slowly and regarded them, puzzled. He then snapped his fingers at a skinny boy and directed him to stand several meters behind Raoul to chase down any balls that went astray. The girls sat in a row in front of the boys, smiling as for an inspection—smooth of skin, wearing light-colored, modest dresses, but skirted by the sleazy, sexual presence of the dark boys behind them, they seemed pure and soiled at once, like hookers dressed up as virgin schoolgirls, waiting to be selected. They certainly wanted to please Arturo, curry favor with him; they did not seem to know he was homosexual, and so they gave him those faces, offering them like sacrifices, unsure of how to smile but certain that they should give it their best. He disregarded them, and they looked at each other, terrified. I tried not to look at Teresa, but once she caught my eye, and gave a surreptitious wave, and I blushed.

Ramon asked if he could warm up, and it was decided after some negotiation that he could throw to me a few times if he needed to. I don't know what this was for. I didn't have a mitt, and I didn't move any farther beyond the thirty feet that separated Ramon and me. I simply didn't want to leave him. We had clearly chosen sides—the policemen/lovers whispering strategy far down the road, the refugee outlaws bedraggled and sullen at the makeshift pitching mound, the children watching with the inherent neutrality of adolescence. He tossed me the ball and I tossed it back, pleased, as I always was, to receive a toss. Being thrown a ball has been, throughout my life, the universal sign of being needed. Many things are spoken in the soft toss of a ball—trust, for the most part, or at least the belief that the receiver is capable of catching it, the understanding that he will give the attention to your actions that you give to his. It is the beginning of a connection that can be silent or laid over with chatter, that can last until the tiring of the muscles. It is better than a conversation, better than any overt display of trust or affection—it is the best connection I know of, the connection this inanimate spheroid has the power to make between two humans.

He looked at me intently as we threw, as if trying to communicate something. I wondered if he had concocted some means of escape, and meant to indicate this with his gaze. Perhaps he had thought of a plan to commandeer the Jeep, or wanted us to burst into the forest and run back to our defeated boat at the shoreline—it would have been better than this. Whatever it was he meant to impart to me, it was a hopeless thing. Hopeless because I had been thinking about these possibilities since the cops had settled us into the Jeep, and these thoughts had come to nothing. Hopeless as well, because I am not the kind of man who is easily made to understand things except by the most thorough explanation; a winking of the eye, a focussing of the gaze, a slight nodding of the head—these would never suffice to clue me in to even the most obvious scheme. Hopeless, finally, because the thought mechanisms that controlled Ramon Sagasta's mind were the processes of the great athlete, and though I had come to recognize and even predict the end results of these processes, I could never have any intuitive access to them; whatever Ramon's thoughts were, I was sure they would have surprised me had he spoken them.

He caught a toss and didn't throw it back—instead he

began bouncing lightly on his feet, getting warm. With me, it was always the other man who stopped playing catch, who caught the ball and didn't return the throw. I was incapable of ending a game of catch.

He nodded to Raoul, who nodded to Arturo, who nodded back to both of them and told the teenager to get ready. I moved close to the teenager, in position to call the pitches.

Ramon said it one more time. "Okay, then. If I strike him out, then you let us go. You drive back to Matanzas like nothing happened, and maybe you even give us some dry clothes, heh?"

"I don't know about that," said Arturo. He walked over to Raoul and placed a hand on his shoulder, squeezed it in a gesture of comfort, the way a father does with a very young son. Raoul looked down and tapped his shoes with the barrel of the bat. He seemed reluctant to look at Arturo, who gazed at him like he was trying to remember his face. Arturo said to Ramon, "But you can have your freedom. If you strike him out—which you won't—you can have your freedom."

There was no wavering in his voice, no exaggerated bravado, no shaking hesitation—it was not his voice that told me he lied. He sold it very well, in fact. He sounded earnest, sincere, even a little afraid, as if he was indeed concerned about the prospect that he might have to let us go and cover up his discovery.

And yet for all this I knew he lied; I was more certain of this than I was of the fact that Ramon could not strike out anyone at over one hundred feet. If it somehow happened, if Ramon was truly a great one and could do this thing that could not be done by anyone, this thing that would be both testament to and proof of a greatness that perhaps I could give my life over to— then it would still all be worth nothing. We would still go to Matanzas. I would get lost somewhere in the rural legend this would become—I would be reduced to a bit part in the story these teenagers would eventually pass on to their generations about Ramon Sagasta and the impossible strikeout in the forest. This would be my legacy, this and an empty room in Wichita that will forever have posters of all-stars tacked to the wall. The rest of my life would be a cell in Matanzas.

It was not his voice, nor any winking indication he gave to his lover, nor any instinctive sense of dishonesty about the man. I simply knew. He would be unable to let us go, unwilling to let us go. He would not let us go. He would not. It hurt me when I realized this, it hurt me physically, a tightening in the muscles of my stomach. Then I realized I hurt not because I had dismissed all hope, but because I was coming to believe that Ramon might do this glorious thing, and I would have to be present at the aftermath, when the triumph came to nothing as Arturo and Raoul reneged on their promise. I could not predict what Ramon might do at such a moment—perhaps that would break him for good, perhaps he would no longer be a great athlete after this moment. Maybe at this moment everything he had would be taken away from him. I didn't want to be there for that.

Ramon waved his hand to clear Arturo from the batter's area. Arturo scuffled off towards the teenagers and knelt. "When you're ready, Ramon," he said.

Ramon pitched. As in the forest, he kicked his leg out slowly, as if pushing it through water. His upper torso then twisted and thrust forward with a speed I'd never seen in a human body—torso followed legs with a force and accuracy that was machine-like. I couldn't even see the ball until it was halfway towards us. I watched it drop, but I noticed the spin of the seams and saw that it was a change-up; it didn't drop because its velocity was dying, it dropped because Ramon had meant for it to. Even so, it was fast, probably as fast a pitch as

Raoul had ever seen. A change-up. The fastest pitch he had ever seen, and he had been a professional, sort of.

His swing was so late I could hear the whish of his bat and arms at the same moment I heard the ball hit the ground—if someone had been catching, the smack of the mitt would have preceded the sound of the swing. The ball skidded between the boy and me, and after directing a hollow glance first at me, then at Arturo, the boy chased after it down the road.

"Strike one!" Ramon called, bouncing. He clapped his hands twice and kicked at the ground where the pitching rubber should have been.

I looked at Arturo, who pretended to pull at a loose stitch on his sleeve. Raoul stood cursing, rubbing his hands. He squeezed the bat handle. He unbuttoned his green shirt. Arturo told him quietly to relax, Raoul said he was relaxed, he just hadn't timed the pitches yet.

I now felt eyes upon me. I thought perhaps they might be one of the girls', but all the teenagers were chatting with each other behind concealing hands about what they'd just seen. The boys fidgeted behind the girls, rising taller on their knees as if their views had been obstructed, using hand gestures as they speculated about what kind of pitch it was, and looking very serious.

Ramon watched me. They were his eyes that I felt. He was somber now, and he stood still in the middle of the road. He had no baseball and no glove. He held a good posture, and kept his arms by his side; he looked to me like a man waiting for a firing squad, and for this reason it occurred to me that he hadn't had a cigarette in a long while, and must have wanted one badly. I wanted to bring him one, I wanted to light it for him. I realized what the look told me now, the same one he'd given me during our game of catch.

Ramon was going to bean Raoul Pena with the next pitch. He had waited until he had thrown the first; he had been timing and pacing it as much as Raoul had. He knew he could hit the spot he wanted to, even at this distance, and with the appropriate speed. He would hurl the ball towards the unsuspecting policeman's wide, sweaty head, smash the baseball into his face, stun him or even knock him out. I knew this as clearly as if Ramon had spoken it, I absorbed it all from his stare, and I remembered our silent teamwork in the forest, the way we had taken for granted our knowledge of each other.

I stood eight feet from Arturo. He had put the gun back in the holster, but he had not snapped the strap back over it. The situation favored us. The loose gun, the fact that they had put Ramon in a position to neutralize one of them. The happenstance that had presented us with homosexual lovers—if something happened to Raoul, Arturo would instinctively rush over to him, kneel over him, not thinking about the exposed weapon protruding from his hip.

It wouldn't even require courage. I didn't know what a gun felt like, but I surely could not fail to slip it from Arturo's holster if Ramon managed to peg Raoul. And if the opportunity was not there, it was easily excused—Ramon was 110 feet away, after all; you couldn't fault him for throwing wild.

So had Ramon realized, after all, that they were not going to release us after he'd done this wonderful thing? He must have, because he certainly knew now that the strikeout—this impossible, god-creating thing—was his for the taking.

The boy had retrieved the ball from the forest and had begun sprinting back to us. When he got near me, I motioned him to slow down.

"Are you ready for that outside pitch you wanted?" Ramon yelled to Raoul. "You said you would have waited for that. Or for a mistake on my change-up. I don't think you should wait for that one. So get ready for the outside." There was no doubt anymore. Ramon was setting him up; waiting for the high outside fastball, Raoul wouldn't be able to react in time.

There was no injustice like this—Ramon would not be able to finish this sublime thing he'd begun. He would have to waste his next pitch on a beanball. He would not be able to bring this great act into the world.

What I wanted, more than anything, was to watch him finish. I wanted to see him strike out Raoul Pena on three pitches from 110 feet with no rubber or mound or target. This was all the legacy I needed—to be the shadow on the road, the one who had played catch with Ramon to warm him up for this moment. Now I could not have it—he would sacrifice his moment for our freedom. It is true that there was a lot at stake for us, but this seemed a hollow rationalization. If you could do this thing, strike out a man at 110 feet, you needed to do it.

I took the baseball from the skinny boy, pretending to look it over for scratches and dents.

I felt a kind of outrage that was like a raging virus, spreading through my nerves. I could not fathom the malice and fear and lowliness that existed in these men who would spoil such a moment of greatness. Ramon could do this, if only he wasn't convinced that the strikeout would earn us nothing but a quiet ride to Matanzas. They were ruining this for me. Ramon was one of the great ones. It is not something to be said or believed lightly: Ramon Sagasta was a great pitcher, and I was the witness to this. I need this to be acknowledged. I expected Raoul at least to understand: you must let the great be great. You must put them in a position to create their legends, and never ask them to use their greatness for anything else.

Arturo continued to watch Ramon, who was stretching his

arms by reaching towards the sky, and Raoul, standing ten yards in front of me, took a practice cut.

When I saw that Arturo's back was to me I assumed a pitcher's stance, then leaned back in a graceless motion, not even trying to imitate Ramon, and threw the baseball at Raoul Pena's head. It hit him with the nauseating thud of hide on bone, slamming against the area of his skull above and behind the right ear, the spot I imagined you might put a bullet if you weren't quite sure where to shoot someone.

He didn't drop, as I'd assumed he would, but instead half-yelled and half-moaned, flung his bat towards the forest, surrounded his head with his hands without touching it, and doubled over. No one knew what had happened, except for Ramon and me and the teenager, who took several steps back and clearly wished he hadn't seen it.

As Raoul did not drop to the ground, Arturo did not kneel over him, and thus the gun wasn't as exposed as I'd hoped. He had, however, completely forgotten his role as captor and rushed to see what was happening to his lover. He placed a hand on Raoul's back and another softly on his chest and bent his head low to look at Raoul's face. "What is it? What is it?" he repeated, and Raoul just moaned. I don't know why he didn't fall down.

This took about five seconds. Unfortunately, in his pain Raoul kept turning around, his feet scratching on the ground as they groped and stumbled. Arturo pivoted with him, and it was impossible to approach them—the gun presented itself, but then the two spun again, and then again, and I couldn't take the chance of moving in and startling Arturo.

After these five seconds, Raoul dropped to a knee, quieting down as he did so, and Arturo went down with him. Their backs faced me. I strode with great purpose towards Arturo's backside, grabbed the exposed handle and tried to lift the pistol, but it was snug in the holster. He felt the tugging, and slapped his hand on top of mine. I clicked back the safety, which I felt under my finger, then pulled the trigger.

Arturo made an entirely different kind of noise than Raoul had. Something rumbled in his throat. It sounded like he was about to throw up, and was trying to keep it in. His body immediately went static—rigid but unresisting. I stood up and scrambled several steps back, the gun having kicked out of the holster with the report. From my new position, I regarded the two policemen I had overcome.

The bullet had gone through the holster and bloodied Arturo's thigh. Raoul didn't seem to notice what had happened—his eyes stayed closed and his hands hovered around his temples, as if restricted from touching his head by a magnetic field. He was on his knees now, sitting back on his heels.

Arturo fell to his side, making the rumbling noise—a noise of great pain suppressed. He squinted and kicked up dust and held onto his thigh a few inches above the knee. He winced and groaned, and the blood stain spread slowly and imbued his pants leg. I left them there and walked towards Ramon.

Ramon held his arms up. His nose was scrunched, his face protesting the decision I'd made—he looked as if he were about to complain to an umpire who had prematurely called a game because of rain.

"Get in the car right now," I said, and opened the driver's side door. "Right now, Ramon."

He did it quickly enough—I still had the gun, and had shot someone, and even if he didn't fear me I certainly made him curious enough to shut up and do what I told him.

I unhitched my money belt and forced it into his hands. "Ramon," I said, "You need to go to Cerrito. Don't tell anyone who you are." His reaction to this was predictable, and I cut him off. "Yes, I know, everyone knows who you are. What I mean is you have to do your best to be inconspicuous. Find someone who can hide you away. Go to one of the cane farms and latch onto an old couple or something like that, people who couldn't possibly be CDR. You can spend about five hundred dollars for bribes, so it shouldn't be hard. Just don't talk to anyone you don't have to talk to. Don't let it get out that you're there. Find people you think you can trust, and ask about the *contrabandistas*, have them set it up while you hide. You have enough money. Lay low there, lay very low, until they can get you out."

"I don't understand. We'll deal with this later. Come on, we need to go, now. We could be in serious trouble for this. For what you did."

I began walking away, backwards, slowly. "No, Ramon. I stay here. I can't kill the cops, and if we leave them here they'll start a chase. I need to stay and cover them."

"What is this? What do you mean?" he said. "Stop that shit! Come on—just knock them out or something. We're going to get chased no matter what! Let's go."

I kept walking backwards. "No, Ramon. I'll stay and cover them. Just get to America. Please get there. Become a major-league baseball player, Ramon. Please."

He gaped, and made protest sounds, but then I turned my back to him and walked to the fallen cops. The teenagers stayed where they were. On the spot, I decided that I would take everyone back down to the dugout, and we would wait until it got dark. I didn't think to wonder what would happen after that—it seemed like a long way off. Maybe I could tie them all up somehow, and run off to Varadaro to throw myself upon the mercy of some rich Canadian tourists. Or maybe I would just wait and wait until I was certain Ramon's lead was large enough, then hand the weapons back to Arturo and Raoul and hope they took me to prison. By then, enough time would have passed, Ramon would have either found a place to hide or else he would have given himself away. At least he would not be chased now, at least not by these two, as he took the road to Matanzas. I had considered this, and realized that it was the only thing I could give to him.

The engine hummed, which I took as his decision to accept my proposal and abandon me. The engine made several more sounds that were grating and harsh, but the kind you would expect to come from a Cuban army vehicle.

When I reached the policemen the engine noises stopped, and I turned to see Ramon climbing out of the Jeep. "Dennis," he whined. "I don't know how to drive this."

Yes, it was to be expected.

I can't say I was overly saddened. We would be chased now, for we had no means of tying up all the witnesses, and I wouldn't know how to begin knocking them all unconscious, but at least I would still be a fugitive, rather than someone simply waiting passively for capture. The sacrifice had been offered; it wasn't my fault that the stupid oaf couldn't drive a stick.

I do not need to say, I think, that our destination was unknown. I simply drove in the direction the boy had gone in to get the baseball. The beaning and shooting of two policemen was too recent in my body's memory for me to think very well.

"Why did you do that?" Ramon said after a while—we'd just passed the turnoff to what must have been Duarte.

"I want you to get to America, Ramon. In a way, it's the most important thing in the world for me right now."

"No, not that. I mean why'd you hit that cop with the ball?"

"Well. It was either you or me. I was closer. I didn't mind doing it."

"What?"

"You were going to bean him on the next pitch. That was our plan. Right? Ramon? You were going to hit him in the head on the next pitch. Right?"

Ramon found and lit a cigarette very suddenly, as if he had just remembered that he smoked and needed to get one down. He waited until he had exhaled his first breath before he spoke, the way smokers do. "I don't know about that. He was a long way away after all, and he had a little head. Plus, you saw me out there—I could have struck him out. I was going to, Dennis, I was going to get him. And if I'd struck him out they would have let us go—weren't you listening?"

I nodded my head as if nodding along to slow music, and I began chewing my lip the way Arturo had when he'd leaned against the hood of the Jeep. I saw blood specks on my hand, which was gripping the top of the steering wheel hard because of the loose steering and bad suspension.

"Oh well," Ramon said, slumping low in his seat. "At least now we have a Jeep."

CHAPTER TWELVE

Yes, we had a Jeep. We also had a bottle of rum, some comic books, a box of crackers, and a large tin of green chiles— evidently Raoul and Arturo had been planning a picnic. Ramon mangled the tin with the Swiss Army knife, spewing runny chile goop all over his pants, and eventually he threw it out and we ate the crackers.

I didn't talk anymore about what had happened with the cops. I didn't think I could explain it to him, how I had been so certain of what our mutual plan had been. As if I could ever understand what he was thinking by a glance at his face.

I eventually decided that my course of action had been the correct one. Ramon had been planning on striking out Raoul, never doubting this would earn us our freedom, and so I had spared myself the sight of his disappointment. I had spared him the debasement of exhibiting his skills in vain. This was a good role for me; I would make sure that Ramon Sagasta would only reveal his greatness when it mattered.

I felt vaguely sorry for Raoul Pena and his lover Arturo, although they should have known better, and they had gotten and would get what they deserved. They would be relegated to playing the clownish antagonists in our story, they would be the shortsighted, desperately jealous peasant cops who served as our first human obstacle. I understood the ache of mediocrity that had made them want to defeat Ramon, I understood the panic that must have set in when they realized Raoul would not hit his pitches. Nevertheless, it is fitting that they be remembered only in order to highlight their own foolishness, and Ramon's greatness, and possibly my sacrifice. The story told in America, perhaps on the placard in the Hall of Fame, would do us all justice.

While Ramon had been stalling out the engine and murdering the clutch, I had retrieved the baseball that had ricocheted off Raoul's head, and before we drove away I nestled the ball in the duffel bag. It was just a baseball, scuffed and yellowed and now splotched with blood, and if I hadn't grabbed it maybe one of the teenagers would have retrieved it, or maybe they would have left it in the forest. But it was an artifact now. If we made it out I would take it with us to the States and it would be, in itself, the symbol of this great story—in this future world that seemed so clear to me, this baseball would someday be auctioned off, then donated and mounted under glass in Cooperstown, New York. Two million people every year would read of the story, read the placard explaining the baseball's significance to the history of their beloved game. They would read my name—they would quickly forget it, among the mass of names celebrated at Cooperstown, but they would read it and say it to themselves and this would be my legacy. Then they would stare at the baseball in its glass cube, slack-bodied, slack-faced, just standing still and gazing at this scuffed and yellowed relic, standing still as if they absorbed something from it, as if it radiated something.

The forest gave way after twenty minutes. The copses

thinned and the trees shortened. We wound our way up a hill, then into a meadow of tall grass, much like the meadow of Rios only the grass was taller and butter yellow. Ramon whistled, played with the air and spit in his mouth, hummed along with the engine, but we didn't speak, and I was glad of it. Ramon had finished with what he had to do—he was a gift now, a body containing an exquisite gift, and it didn't concern me what he said or thought. I had become absolutely convinced of his greatness, and needed him only to carry on with me, to continue this strange and unfounded trust he seemed to have in me.

At a fork in the path, I arbitrarily steered left, and we found ourselves on a dark brown road that was wide enough for three Jeeps. It cut uphill through a noisy and humid forest, and the clicking of insects and the ever-narrowing stripe of sky worked me into a nervousness I hadn't felt since that moment I'd been crouching at the edge of the meadow in Rios. The fear came not from the jungle but from a simple fact that seemed to be screaming itself into my ears along with the cicadas: We didn't know in what direction capture lay. One could, naturally, take this as a sign of being very far ahead, yet I'm here to say this is pretty much impossible to believe, at least in Cuba when you're traveling with someone like Ramon Sagasta, when you've stolen a national treasure and a military Jeep, when you've shot and maimed policemen in the process, and when you have little stomach for this kind of thing in the first place. What you become certain of is this: When you hear no noise behind you, it is just as likely that you're running towards your captors as away from them.

As always, I was groundless, with no way to tell my directions or my position. All I knew was that beside me sat a justification for all of this, and while it did not cancel out my fear, perhaps it made it more palatable.

I drove on. The road leveled off as it outlined the forest. That is to say, the jungle remained tall and reeking on our left, but to the right, at the edge of the road, the earth just dropped off, and all there was to see from where I sat was the water. As the road meandered and dipped I could see that we were, in fact, quite a ways from the beach—the sharp drop of earth became a broad decline a few hundred feet below us, and the land became forest again as it evened and blended with the shore. At the edge of the road, the view must have been magnificent if you had the leisure for gazing. In America, there would have been scenic rest stops along a road like this, where legions of SUVs would gather at sunset. All I could think about was the precipice, the fact that it would be very easy, given my sweaty hands and the knobby road and the shaky steering of the Jeep, to snag a wheel on the road edge and plunge down and die in that beauty.

The forest and the plateau ended simultaneously. The trees shortened and became high grass, and we seemed to be on a plain with nothing discernible in the distance except a few black tree trunks, the remnants of slash-and-burn. Ramon said something. I asked him to repeat it, having nearly forgotten he could speak.

"We're on the road to Matanzas. I recognize this field. I don't know how we got here, because I've never even seen that place we just went through, but I recognize this place. I've stared out at it a thousand times from the bus, on the way to games."

This information meant very little to me. It seemed irrelevant to think about where we were going. Cuba is an island—was there any place on this island that was any less treacherous for us than any other? At this point we were simply expending energy and gasoline, wandering around in a stolen army Jeep until the inevitable moment when they would catch us. We were like base runners caught in a rundown, knowing that escape was too silly and hopeless to even consider, but running until the last possible minute because that is what is expected of you, and that is what your body simply does on its own.

Of course, that is a ludicrous thing to say. We were nothing like base runners caught in a rundown; there is no truth, as I have already said, to baseball analogies. It is nothing like life, expect when you are actually there playing it. Baseball does not work theoretically, because baseball is the opposite of theory. It is simple physical action, in spite of all of the strategy and tactics attached to it; each game is the story of what men do with their physical beings, their reflexes and power and nerve. Every experience it offers is a unique thing, one that can be felt and remembered in the body, and sometimes the skills it teaches can be taken off the field and shown in other arenas of life—I did it at the carnival in Puerto Rico, Ramon did it on that dusty road outside Duarte, but these skills must invariably be returned to the baseball diamond, and locked away and kept there and never extrapolated to what it is actually like to live in the world. Ramon, once we were caught, would never find anything that remotely resembled throwing a baseball against an opponent in a professional game in the United States. Being caught by the Revolutionary Police would not be like being a runner tagged out at second. Sacrificing myself for the sake of Ramon Diego Sagasta would not be like laying down a bunt to advance a runner to third, or like stepping into an inside pitch so you can get your team a runner on first. It would be a unique thing, as unique as Ramon himself, to give up my freedom for him. I had already tried it, but my efforts had been frustrated because of a manual transmission.

I did not know, at that moment, how the next sacrifice

would come about, but I suppose it had been decided for some time. In our last moments of relative silence, gliding along the meadow road, I explained to him in detail everything I knew about the smugglers, everything he would have to do if I managed to set him free. I told him not to pay any of the fee until he had seen some of their gear, and that he should under no circumstances let them know how much money he had. I told him the kind of people he might want to look for to lie up with—preferably an older farm couple, maybe a widow. He absorbed it all, listening with the fear and attention of a child hearing a ghost story. He didn't ask me what I would do. He may not have believed this was something that would ever come to pass. He might have believed by then that we would certainly be taken together, the money confiscated, the smugglers in Cerrito immediately becoming a dream, a story we tell each other for the rest of our incarcerated lives about what might have happened to us.

The military police cars in Cuba don't have sirens, I don't think. At least, they didn't use them for us; they just started shooting. They came as a terrific disappointment, just as I'd begun to get comfortable with the silence; two Jeeps spewed side by side out of a trail that cut through the plain—apparently they had been lurking there, for some reason feeling the need to ambush us rather than simply block the road. Perhaps Arturo and Raoul hadn't been specific enough when they radioed in. But they mistimed it, and came out of the tall grass together several hundred feet behind us, so that we didn't even notice them until the bullets pinged against the metal. After my initial groundlessness (I actually wondered, for a stupid second, if it had started to hail), I felt a flashing, furious aching, not fear or panic, but a kind of remorse that settled into a determination. As long as there was gas in the tank, and I was not dead, there was a chance that Ramon Diego Sagasta would someday find his place in American baseball. Even when a bullet cracked the side mirror, a bare two feet from my head, I thought of nothing but the rectangular structure in Cooperstown, and the possibility of what might someday rest inside it—a muddied hat and the blood-red name on the jersey, and a weathered glove and a blood-splotched baseball—because of what I did at this moment.

"How far?" I said, and swallowed some bugs. Ramon shrugged. Who knows what he thought I meant.

"How far to Matanzas?" I said.

"Oh, to Matanzas." He filled his cheeks with air and squinted. "Oh, I'd say two miles, maybe. To the outskirts anyway. Matanzas isn't very large, but it has some suburbs."

"Do you know your way around? Could you get to Charlie's apartment?"

"No," he said immediately, almost before I finished speaking. "I wouldn't be able to find it. No." He adjusted himself in his seat to turn and look at me, and then he spoke softly, as gently as he could while still being heard above the engine and the wind and the occasional gunfire. "What is this about, Dennis? How do you figure we could make it to Matanzas? I like it that you aren't giving up, but really—the police have radios, you know. They'll lead us into the city, and more will be waiting for us, don't you think? That's if those behind us don't catch us first."

He made good points. They weren't gaining on us, and it seemed to me at times that we were building a bit of a lead, probably because I was risking faster turns and tighter corners than they were (eventually they would have to answer for their Jeeps, after all). Yet this could only be taken to mean that they had resolved to funnel us into Matanzas, where there was certainly some sort of blockade. They fired less now.

One way out might have been to turn up one of the connecting side roads that began appearing. Almost every quarter mile a dirt road, narrower but not much rockier than the one that we followed, would intersect with our path and wind away, either into the gradual slopes to the left of us or downward towards the sea to the right. Some of these roads cut through short forests, or through strange juts in the landscape, so that it wouldn't take long to disappear into them, but only if we'd been granted a larger lead—they would hear the buzzing engine of the Jeep even if we veered off unseen. I asked Ramon twice where those roads went, and he said he didn't know, and when I asked him a third time, he became irritated.

"I don't know, Dennis! For God's sake, haven't I already said that?"

"Just guess, Ramon. If we turned up one of those roads, where would we come out? In Matanzas?"

"No, Dennis, that's the thing, I don't know if we would come out anywhere. They stop after a while, I think. I don't know. They don't even get used by cars, really. They're for mules and bicycles. They just lead to shanties. They'll lead up to the villages of people who work in the cane fields. Why would you want to go there?"

The answer to that was so obvious that I was sure Ramon had realized it the moment he'd said it, but I didn't get the sense, judging from his expression, that he did. "You know, Ramon, you're right—there will be some sort of blockade in Matanzas. If you could make it into one of these villages, you could hide out for a while, don't you think?"

"I suppose," he said lazily. He seemed to be disappointed in me for suggesting this. He was disinterested and sullen, as if I'd just woken him from a nice nap. I wondered if this was him giving up on me, preparing to accuse me of betrayal and incompe-

tence as soon as our capture became incontrovertible. I squinted so as to avoid seeing him from the corner of my eye. If
Ramon's faith in me had run out, I did not want to know.

After a minute Ramon spoke again. "That smoke is from the
refining plant, about a twenty-minute walk from the center of
the city." Again he spoke with lassitude, sounding like a tour
guide towards the end of a long shift. "We'll be there soon,"
he said.

"You could make your way to Charlie Dance's if you had
to," I said.

"No, that will never happen."

"No, listen to me. I mean if you had to. If these cops weren't
on you like this. If you got hold of a bike or something, after hiding away for a few days. Remember, you've got all that money.
If you hide away in some shanty town for a week, and then come
back into the city, you could get to Charlie's, couldn't you? And
then he could put you in touch with a *contrabandista*."

"No, I couldn't get to Charlie's. It's a long story."

I didn't know what to make of this. I imagined they'd had
some sort of falling out the last time they'd talked, and it would
have been just like a Latin American to throw away his chance
of escape for the sake of a petty grudge. When I played for
Lansing, a Dominican pitcher once threw a ball straight into my
hip, thus walking in the winning run and ruining a shut-out, just
because I'd refused to loan him my car when we were teammates in Dover. I did not in any way respect this kind of hyper-
sensitivity to wounded honor, but I had come to understand
that there wasn't much you could do about it.

"For fuck's sake, Ramon! I'm being serious here!" I shouted
with the exasperation of someone who simply wants to shout.
"Charlie Dance can help you. *Could you get to him?*"

"Charlie Dance can't help me anymore, Dennis. The police

might have gotten him already. Besides, I wouldn't go to him if I could."

"But you could get into Matanzas? You think you could? You could hole up somewhere? And then find someone to get you out?" I was nearly screeching, almost crying in desperation.

"Up there, next to the smoke, is the water tower. We're getting close to the stadium."

"You were listening to me, right? You can do this, can't you Ramon? Yes, I know you can. I know how badly you need this."

He turned to look at me. I couldn't look back, because the road had narrowed and become twisty—my hands gripped the steering wheel so tightly I could feel the strain in my wrist. Ramon's eyes became a physical presence on my face; it was like he was painting my cheek with his stare. "Charlie said you would be safer than the smugglers. Besides, the organization wouldn't pay for it, and Charlie said if they sent someone down it would be safer that way, because you would be American, and clever, and that I could trust you with my life."

Nothing in his tone told me that my actions had disproved this, and for this small kindness I was thankful. Ramon could trust me with his life, that was true, but what came of that blind trust was not something anyone could have predicted. As for being clever, perhaps that was still to come.

I said, "Pay them half up front—don't show them where you're taking the money from—and don't pay any more than six hundred at first. After that they'll give you some sort of ticket, or mark you in some way. Don't trust anyone who wants all your money, or who doesn't mark you. With as much money as you have, you'll be okay. Maybe you can't trust them the way you trust me, but it's a business to them, and it's in their interest to get you across, to get the rest of your money. Try to get a life-jacket from somewhere."

He leaned back and looked up at the sky. "Yes, Dennis. I'll do as you say."

He spit, and watched his gob career through the air. "I kept telling Charlie it would be easier in the first place to work with the *contrabandistas*. He kept saying the organization had to do it their way. First he said it would be cheaper, then he said it made them feel better to use their own people. Other days he said other things. Sometimes I think he didn't really want me gone. I kept offering things to him, I kept trying to squeeze it out of him. I kept saying, 'Charlie, without me you wouldn't have been laid in a year. Don't you think it's time to pay me back?' But of course that's the point, Charlie can't get laid without me. He got used to having me around. I don't think he wanted me gone as badly as he said. But he kept sending the reports anyway. He didn't think anyone would listen. And then you came."

Over the course of the next few miles, I taught Ramon how to drive a stick shift. Sensing the dread panic of my voice, he listened to me closely. Still hurtling down the road, we switched places, which somehow didn't slow us down much. I told him not to shift and to keep his foot pressed to the floor. I showed him how to brake and how to start the engine again if it stalled. I told him that if he had to slow to make a turn, to just floor it again until we got back up to speed—there's no way he could have handled the concept of second gear. Then I borrowed Ramon's lighter, which took some convincing, since he understood that he wouldn't get it back. I paused to stuff the baseball into the pocket of Ramon's pants, telling him to take good care of it—"You'll want a souvenir, right?" I said—and then crouched in the back, where I unlatched a plastic reserve gas tank, and waited.

I had sketched out the plan (though it seems a bit generous

to call it a plan) shortly after I starting noticing the side roads. At this point, the main road had narrowed somewhat. Before Ramon and I switched places, I had begun to swerve around felled trees and piles of brush that had tumbled into our path. It had slowed us a bit, and done the same to our pursuers, and at times we had to duck as we plowed through the dense foliage that hovered over the sides of the path like threatening rain clouds. The obstacles in the road had made me simultaneously fear and hope that the path could be easily blocked off altogether.

What I was waiting for was another partial blockage. I instructed Ramon what to do with the greatest shouts I could produce; now that we had reentered forested terrain the noise and echo of our modified Jeep engine was substantial. He took it all in with typical imperturbability—or perhaps it was plain ingratitude. He turned back to me now and then as I shouted, nodding his head gravely, wrinkling his forehead. When I was finished, I made him repeat it back to me. "Slow down at the next fallen tree," he shouted over his shoulder. "Wait until you jump out, then put the pedal on the floor again. At the next path that goes up the slope, check for the cops, if I don't see or hear them, drive to a shanty town. Ditch the Jeep in the trees. Find someone to help me."

He had absorbed the important parts of the plan, although he'd left out those of my phrases that emphasized the dramatic nature of my sacrifice. It's just as well. I didn't want to confuse him with any sort of notion that my sacrifice was something that he didn't absolutely deserve and shouldn't have expected. Somewhere not so far in the back of his mind, Ramon probably wondered why it had taken me so long. This did not bother me, so long as he remembered my plan long enough to escape from pursuit, long enough to remember me to the Hall of Fame.

We came upon a fallen jaguey tree. Its trunk had slipped its mooring in the wet earth beside the road and it now lay at the right shoulder, its roots flowing out like catfish whiskers. The short fat trunk and the stocky branches extended to the middle of the road.

Ramon swerved towards the left side without slowing; I thought he had forgotten, and I was ready to shout to him, but then I heard the engine bellow as he pressed the brake and accelerator at the same time, and the Jeep chugged and slowed. Ramon looked back, waiting to step on the gas. I grabbed the gas tank and hugged the duffel bag, thinking that it might break my fall, and jumped out of the Jeep towards the left shoulder, where there seemed to be something like a ditch. The world spun in whirling green and brown, and when I stopped rolling I was so far from the tree I thought it must have been a different one. I scrambled up and scurried with the tank to the jaguey tree. The engine gurgled as Ramon floored the accelerator in third gear, and eventually it responded and he shot off down the dark corridor.

I hadn't reckoned how much time I would have before the police Jeeps came. A matter of seconds, certainly. It was not much of an issue; either I had enough time or I didn't.

Some of the brush near the ditch was loose, so I hauled armfuls of it into the section of the road next to the fallen tree, trying to drape the width of the road. After only a few seconds I could hear the engines in the distance, so I stashed the duffel bag among the brush and soaked the entire barrier—jaguey tree, brush, and the remnants of Charlie Dance's army service—with the reserves from the gas tank. They fired once or twice when they saw me, and shredded some of the leaves high above my head, and I knelt beside the fronds of the fallen tree to flick the lighter. The gas-soaked leaves of the tree caught, as did some of the brush, but not as impressively as I'd hoped, until I lit a fourth section of the tree and a whoosh of expanding flame burst from my hand, and the thing was done. I patted myself furiously and rolled into the ditch, but my clothes had only been singed a little.

The yellow and blue fire swept up the tree and the brush in a spiraling sweep, and it rose to its height at just the moment the cops would have been passing through it if they had they kept their speed, which they didn't. They could have shot me now, easily—in the first Jeep, a rifleman still sat up on the headrest of his seat, sighting a weapon that rested on the top of the windshield. But they didn't even seem to notice me. It wasn't that they were distracted by their foiled pursuit, at least not yet—they just seemed to be in awe of the fire. Indeed, it was spectacular. I don't know if it's true of jaguey trees in general, but this one shot red sparks and ashes into the sky of such iridescence and beauty that it seemed I had lit off fireworks. The flames roared a dozen yards into the air and seemed to be stretching themselves to go higher, to ignite the tops of the trees that hovered above and shaded the path. It was a contained fire, but terrible and ambitious and garish. It burned the tree and brush a radioactive orange, and at its height it was a whitish yellow, the color you see when you stare at the sun for too long. The Jeeps laid marks where they stopped, I could just hear the screeches over the fire's clamor. The men got out of their vehicles, keeping an eye on the thing and holding their guns, as if they would soon be given the order to shoot it and were afraid that this would piss it off.

The driver of the last Jeep, embarrassed at somehow falling so far behind the others, did not stop to admire the thing. He decided to go through it.

I must admit I don't know the science of such things, but I

would hazard to say that this wasn't as dumb a decision as it may have appeared. As I said, the fire was awesome, but hardly substantial. Half of the wall of flames was founded on nothing, a simple stretch of brush, a duffel bag, and a pool of gasoline that would be consumed in an instant. It had looked fierce at the moment the others had arrived, but it was not an impassable barrier. The men in the final Jeep hardly even checked at it. They slowed enough to maneuver around the gaping soldiers and myself, and they ducked low and pulled their jackets up over their heads, and because even the driver did this they entered the fire three feet too far on the right side, and clipped the jaguey tree. The Jeep toppled onto the driver's side, and it carried the blazing tree with it. When they had stopped skidding, they came to rest with the orange trunk of the jaguey tree inverted and leaning against the exposed underside of the Jeep, its roots dripping lumps of fire onto the passengers. They screamed.

The others made a great production of rescuing them, as they certainly recognized this to be their only possible chance of gaining credit from this little adventure. The entire batch scampered to the fallen Jeep and began tugging at the men inside. There was no organization, no attempt to move the lava-dripping tree or to right the Jeep, no ascertainment of consciousness or injury—they just started yanking at their comrades, and eventually they got them out this way. The wounded were herded together on the ground at the shoulder of the road, and the others knelt beside them offering cigarettes.

It seemed a bit uncanny that no one had yet captured me; I was standing ten paces away from the closest soldier, and I didn't have any weapons. The only noise was the crinkling death of the fire and the murmuring of the wounded. They seemed to accept with animal dumbness that they had lost

Ramon—there were no instructions from the commander, no one jumped past the smoldering tree to see if his Jeep had left tracks. No one got on the radio, and no one cursed and kicked and threw their hats on the ground the way frustrated pursuers do in the movies. It did not appear that they had lost anything, though I had to believe there would be hell to pay for this; they should have captured us, after all, and I was still there for the taking, and they didn't seem to want me. It didn't seem like a good idea to overthink my situation, so I went into the jungle.

Of course, I hadn't really thought to escape from this—I hadn't even thought to try. I had assumed that when I got my bearings back after tumbling into the shoulder ditch, I would find a Cuban cop standing over me pushing a muzzle on my forehead. I hadn't anticipated more flight, and I wasn't too excited about it, although after the stillness of the roadside it felt right to be thrashing along in the foliage again. The soldiers erupted in a tumult of voices that faded as I plowed deeper into the wet trees, and then I heard them enter behind me, and I tried to run. After two dozen yards, I realized I had fled into one of the slopes that stretch from the road to the sea—those yards drop terrifically, and soon there was nowhere for my shoes to grip, and I was on my back and ass hurling down the decline, slowed by contact with trees and roots and rocks. My vision became a streaky, jolting view of green and brown. I didn't worry about the soldiers anymore, although at one point, as I slid down a smooth muddy stretch, I saw one of them bounce past me, flailing and groaning, looking much more helpless than I felt. He hurtled ahead of me and was suddenly inert, splayed against the trunk of a thin tree, and unconscious.

Since my body was now rigid and clenched in on itself, I was able to control my movements somewhat, and I came to a stop by plowing my feet, like an upended skier. I didn't think to take the soldier's handgun from him, and he didn't seem to have anything else that might have been of use, and I certainly wasn't going to kill him. I figured when the other Cubans found him it would give them an excuse to stop their second pursuit and haul him back up top.

So now I stood on the slope with one foot jammed into the base of a tree to keep me stationary, probably pursued by others, but not feeling as endangered as I once had. It was hard to wallow in this, however, since it probably hadn't been more than a minute since the Jeep crashed.

There was no way to flee horizontally along the slope, and though I ached from the bumps and had been certain during my long slide that one of the rocks or roots would split my head open in short order, I had to take to the muddy incline again. I put my rear back on the ground, aimed my body for a relatively clear path, and leaned back like a six-year-old on a Fearless Flyer.

When I played in Lowell, outside of Boston, the Transportation Department released a report naming Massachusetts the safest place to drive in the country, a notion that assaults the practical experience and common sense of everyone who has ever been there. The explanation for this, of course, was that the safety index was based on the number of drivers killed per 100,000, and because of the traffic in Boston no one can ever drive at a speed that will kill them in an accident. This is the idea behind my unlikely survival of the slope outside of Matanzas that by all rights should have shorn me in half—because of my virtually constant contact with rocks, roots, trees, bushes, even animals (once or twice), I was never going fast enough for the contact to kill me. A few times I met with an obstacle that halted my progress entirely, and I had to whimper and rest and then throw myself down again, certain of more contact. I can't vouch for the health of my internal organs, since they took quite a pounding, but a full twenty-five minutes after I leaped into the trees to escape the Cuban cops, the slope leveled and I was still conscious, and I probably hadn't covered more than a half-mile of terrain. I bled from my forehead, my wrist, both knees, both calves, and from somewhere on my back, and my clothes were comically shredded, so that I looked like one of the guys Zorro humiliates by initialing his shirt, but I could walk. I know this only because I tried it out briefly—pacing ten feet or so before finding a blanket of moss and stretching out and sleeping without discontent or fear, just a faraway worry about how sore I'd be when I woke up.

CHAPTER THIRTEEN

THERE ARE TIMES WHEN THINGS ARE MORE SIMPLE THAN YOU HAVE any right to expect them to be, when something that by all rights should pose a challenge turns out to be something you can walk and whistle your way through. They should be fantastic, gilded moments, seen as evidence of a benevolent God, or good karma, or whatever. They have always made me uncomfortable, for the simple fact that I expect very little in my life to be easy, and when these moments come upon me I feel certain that I am missing something. It is this discomfort with blessed fortune that marked my uneasiness with baseball—from my earliest days in the game, baseball was something that came too easily for me, and so the game, even at its most glorious, was married in my mind with discomfort.

I began playing at twelve—my father had never bothered to negotiate the forms and carpool schedules involved with little league, and so I didn't join a team until middle school. I went to the tryouts because I liked the uniforms I'd seen on the eighth graders. Because of a March ice storm, they had borrowed a pitching machine and corridor net from the high school and held tryouts in the gym. I showed up a half hour early on the first day, and asked someone to show me how to swing. An hour later, having sent four line drives through the fabric of the corridor net, I was sent by a fat coach in tight shorts to the other side of the gym to work out with the eighth graders.

My feet echoed against the hardwood, and it was the only noise in the gym until I heard my name whispered. I heard the fat coach—in that strange, dripping accent possessed only by fat men in the Midwest—tell someone that he ain't never seen no damn thing like it. I could only assume I had done something terribly wrong, that my gross lack of understanding or pathological technique was so outrageous I needed to be diagnosed by the head coach. The hits had felt good—solid, true, violent; I had never done anything as satisfying—yet I couldn't believe that I had already found the purpose and method of this game, that it should be so easy. Baseball was a significant thing, excellence in it should not have come naturally to someone like me. I walked across the gym floor with perhaps a vague inkling that I had tasted something that would change my life, but all I allowed myself to assume was that I had missed something enormous—in some way I had to be cheating, the fat coach had to be mistaken.

As it happened, I had missed nothing—baseball was that easy for me, at least until Stanford, and I never once fully accepted or enjoyed this. Even in high school, when my name was in the paper every other week in the spring, when my dad had to get a post office box to deal with the recruiting letters, I was sure there was something I wasn't quite doing right, an unfair advantage I was enjoying that I didn't even know about. Something would derail my greatness, and it was there all along, I could feel it like a ghost, or a virus.

That thing, of course, turned out to be the major league curveball, and the major league fastball, and the major league game configurations, and in general everything about the major leagues, and not even that, but the watered-down version of the major league game that you get in Triple A. It was much more than I was equipped to handle. It had been there all along, waiting for me as I'd expected all along, and it came just as I began to assume that perhaps it was possible for something to be as easy as it seemed.

And so, you might understand the trepidation with which I met the fact that I had apparently eluded the entire military search machine that Fidel Castro had sent after me.

After my protracted tumble down the hill, I had the presence of mind to choose an isolated spot in which to pass out. I settled on a particular stretch of moss because it looked comfortable, and because I couldn't have made it much farther, but I also recognized that it provided a thick cover. The ground there was wedged into the hillside a bit at the base of a tree that had been uprooted. I covered myself with fronds and snuggled up next to the hard-shelled insects that fed on the rot of the tree. The moss smelled like canned spinach, and it tickled my face.

Throughout the night I was awoken by various noises, at times the typical jungle sounds, but also the sound of men, two or three times, who were looking for me. I stayed still, trying not to drift back to sleep and thereby give myself away by snoring. They spoke loudly to each other and stomped hard on the layers of green, annoyed by the jungle and the unlikelihood of finding me there. Once they came so close their clomping boots vibrated the ground under me, but they never saw me, and they passed by.

I left the spot fifteen hours after I'd found it. I reasoned that the search must certainly have moved elsewhere by then, and since I wasn't sleeping I couldn't deal with the bugs anymore.

Stinking, wounded, grubby beyond repair, I walked as a fugitive through the Cuban countryside. I never again saw my pursuers from the forest road.

I walked away from the sunrise, along a flat road that sometimes meandered back into the forest but rarely sloped. In time I came to the industrial docks that ring the harbor of Matanzas, and I entered the city through the corridors of concrete and drab government buildings where the shipping business is conducted. I co-opted a sort of poncho from a dockside shack, and because it had begun to drizzle I managed to disguise my tattered clothes and body without being conspicuous. I trudged along the gridded streets of the city, passing residential houses that were the size of my old garage, a few sad tourist spots, a multitude of newstands where the last thing you could get was a newspaper. None of it looked familiar, though Matanzas isn't a large city, and I'd covered a good bit of it trying to find El Refugio several days earlier. A loafer trying to nap up against a gutted refrigerator told me how to get to Salamanca Street, but he was dead wrong, and I ambled through the streets for another ninety minutes, nervous and weary. Twice I passed near policemen, but they didn't seem to be on any kind of high alert, and I was able to shuffle past them. I made sure to say something within earshot of them so they could hear my fluent Spanish, and not think to suspect me of being the American fugitive their radio had probably told them to be on the lookout for. They certainly weren't going to mistake me for Ramon, anyway.

I wandered around the central part of the city for nearly two hours, until I recognized, of all things, a red vintage Lincoln that I had walked past with Charlie Dance and which had not been moved since that time. I stood by the car and traced the path with deliberation back to El Refugio, and from there I managed to find my way to the battered apartment building where he lived.

I may have wondered what Charlie Dance could do for me, how I could convince him to find me a ticket home, how long I would have to hole up in his stained, stuffy apartment, eating his tuna and hot dogs and listening to him complain about me. I also may have worried about what Ramon had implied, that the FAR or the NRP or whoever the hell was in charge of the search might have taken Charlie away, or camped out in his house to lay in wait for Ramon and me, in case we were stupid enough to go to him. If I did wonder these things, such thoughts were superceded by Charlie Dance's attachment in my mind with a place to eat and shower. It was all I needed in the world. But the notion that overwhelmed me as I thudded my palm against his door, as I heard him wheeze and shuffle and whisper something to someone, was that Charlie Dance would be in a position to learn, some days hence, what had become of Ramon.

The instant he saw me, he began shaking his head slowly and painfully, as if it were encased in a gel. His hair was mussed and shiny. He wore enormous boxer shorts and an even bigger gray T-shirt and white socks pulled up around his calves—I had woken him up.

Charlie Dance squinted at me, then pushed both hands against the door frame as if to steady himself, as if he might faint like a Victorian heroine. "God damn it all," he said, then he shut the door again.

It seemed to me that he expected me to take a clear lesson from this—he had shut the door with no great speed, not at all as if he expected me to force my way in, and indeed I didn't. I stood still outside his door, and then I heard his fat body drop itself into one of his recliners—I could actually hear, across twenty yards of space and through the thick cedar door, the whoosh of air expelled from the cushions by his great mass—and I grew indignant. It bothered me that Charlie had plopped

into his chair, as if he had just dismissed a vacuum cleaner sales-
man. I opened the door and walked into his house, and he didn't
seem surprised.

"So you fucked up," he said.

"Not really." I stayed by the door.

"Oh, so you didn't fuck up. So you're in Miami right
now, not in my living room. You're a fucking figment of my
imagination."

If I haven't already, I need to make a very simple point
about Charlie Dance. About half of what he said was virtually
impossible to respond to, by dint of either his tone or his body
language or the words themselves. I have never met anyone who
made me think harder about what the next appropriate thing to
say was. At this moment, I couldn't think of anything.

He put his palms to his eyes, then moved his fingers
through his hair until he was pulling at the ends. "I knew you
would fuck it up. I really did. They didn't tell me nothing I
didn't know."

I caught on. "They've been here?" He didn't say anything.
"Who was it?" I said.

"They're all the fucking same. Yeah, they came here. They
know I go to the games. They don't know why, but they know I
watch a lot of baseball and ask a lot of questions."

"So why didn't they take you away?"

He shrugged, as if it didn't matter, but I think he was acting this time, I think this was something he actually did care
about. "I'm an American national, kid. And I haven't done anything, not the way you have. I didn't tell them shit, didn't know
what the fuck they were talking about, I said. They left. What
the hell else could they do? There's lots of us that watch baseball down here. Ain't a crime. The bottom line is, I sold it to
them. They really don't think I had anything to do with it." He

turned to me now, tilted his head to the side and squinted at me. "And it better fucking stay that way."

Very quickly, as if he suddenly realized I wouldn't have the guts to rat on him, he brightened, and said, "Oh man, did I sell it to those idiots. 'You mean Ramon Sagasta *defected?*' I said to them. 'The Toronados pitcher? Holy fuck! *Dios mio!*' Oh man, did I sell those commie flunkies." He started to drink from a can and grumble, ". . . fucking bother me in my own house, sit your mangy asses on my couch . . . fucking third world security guards . . ."

Then he stood up, which surprised me. "Where is he now? Is he outside? Or did he get caught?"

I told him that Ramon was hiding away somewhere in the outskirts if we were lucky, and that he had money and would try to find the smugglers. I told him about the cops and the chase. I told him the skiff was a piece of crap, which he scoffed at, and I told him we had gotten help from some peasants and hitch-hiked to Cerrito. I didn't tell him about Raoul and Arturo, or about the children in the forest, and I didn't tell him about my sacrifices. This, all of this, belonged to me; just now Charlie Dance didn't get to hear about the legacy I would leave.

"So he's not coming here?" This was the first thing he said, and he said it quickly, almost interrupting me as I finished my story.

"No, not unless he really fucks up. He got away yesterday, and I told him to hole up with a local and not let anyone know who he is."

"And you think Ramon Sagasta can do that?" he said.

"Actually, yes I do. He wants it so bad. You must know that. I think he'll get out. He's stupid and reckless, but he'll either get out soon or die; I don't see him accepting anything else."

Charlie pondered this, swishing air in his cheeks and picking at a blemish under his chin. "You know what—you may be right about that. He may just do that." He didn't sound convinced, but he allowed it as a possibility.

The difficult thing to understand was the fear that was so evident in Charlie Dance. His was the kind of fear that I suppose we call anxiety, although this doesn't seem quite accurate. It is the kind of fear that does everything it can to hide itself to others, and in so doing turns the face red and makes the stomach gurgle and tighten. It's the kind of fear you get when you are pulled over by a state trooper when you have a bag of dope in your glove compartment; you need to do everything you can to appear unafraid—it is fear blended with the hope that your life will return to the way it was before, dreary as that may have been.

Perhaps I am speculating too much in retrospect. I know now that is the kind of fear that gripped him, but I believe even at the time I recognized a strange anxiety in him. He delivered his standard caustic words with too much speed and emphasis; before, in cursing me and the organization and Ramon and Cuba and the world in general, there had been a kind of apathy about him, as if he didn't really care if the universe wanted to be as generally shoddy as he deemed it. But now he was too invested in the moment, he cared too much about things. He tensed the muscles of his face over and over, scowling and squinting and licking his teeth and chewing on the inside of his cheek. He did the Charlie Dance equivalent of pacing, which meant that he circled the coffee table once or twice. He refused to look at me for more than a moment, and when I went to the kitchen to get some water (it came out brown from the tap, so I drank a Polar) he made no comment, and I returned to find him hunched forward on the chair, staring at the floor, with one fist gripped in his other hand.

As I watched him fret, something came to my senses in a wave, like a burst of sound. It was a smell, in fact, not terribly pungent, but among the typical stenches of Charlie Dance and his apartment it came forcefully, with a push of wind from a window somewhere, I guess, and it washed over me and I noticed it. I don't pretend to have any kind of ability in discerning aromas; the perfume could have come from a duchess or a whore or a nun, for all I knew, but I did know that it was the smell of a woman.

It still didn't follow. Charlie Dance was scared, he wasn't nervous or embarrassed about having a girl. Besides, he wouldn't have felt concern about me discovering this; he had tried to get me to serve as his pimp, after all (that was another thing—he hadn't demanded his hooker money back yet, which was one of the first things I'd expected him to do). And besides all this, he'd made it clear in his inadvertent way that it wasn't me that caused his alarm—it had been Ramon, and the prospect of a visit from Ramon, that concentrated his face and put a tiny shake in his hands.

"Who's back there, Charlie?" I said.

"Fuck off. Get out of my house."

"Where would you have me go, Charlie?"

This got him out of his chair. "That's what you think? You think you'll stick around here?" He went to the door. "Oh-ho-ho, son you are mistaken. If you had any thoughts about laying up here, well you can flush those down the toilet. I did my job. You fucked up yours. You got the FAR bastards on my ass—you've done quite enough already, you puke. I'm not going down with you just because you couldn't get out. Now leave." He opened the door and spit out into the hallway. It was a great meaty gob of spit, he must have been saving it for a while.

"Who's the girl, Charlie?" I stood up, and I walked towards

his room, where I assumed the woman must be. It is difficult to say why I did this; in spite of our antagonism, I quite obviously had no business looking into his private rooms, and even at the time I was aware of the tackiness of doing so. I must have had my reasons, however, since I remember being propelled, as if involuntarily, towards the door, and equally propelled into teasing him. "Who's the girl, Charlie," I said. "Is she cute, Charlie?"

When I said that, I realized what curiosity I needed to satisfy. I had asked if she was cute as a joke, but in that lightning way the brain has I immediately wondered if she was in fact a pretty woman, which led me to wonder how much Charlie would have to pay her, which led me to remember what Ramon had told me soon after our first encounter, that Charlie was unable to get hookers for himself. I don't suppose I had completely believed Ramon at the time, but I didn't know him then, had thought him prone to self-aggrandizing exaggeration. Now I had to believe him simply because I believed *in* him. I completely accepted it now; Charlie Dance couldn't get hookers because the experience was so miserable they considered it beyond price. So it couldn't have been a hooker in Charlie's room, this would have meant that Ramon was untruthful. I needed to see who it was.

He tried to stop me, first by shrieking out in that strangely womanish voice he assumed when he had lost control of his anger, then by lumbering towards the door, but neither of these slowed me. I almost didn't hear Charlie Dance anymore. I had fixated on the light plywood door, the panoply it might conceal.

I saw her in the first moment, because there was nothing else in the room to divert my attention. No décor, no carpet or dresser or television. A square bed with no frame or headboard—just a mattress on a box spring—next to it a bedside table speckled with pill bottles and a lamp, and, on the middle of the square mattress, a girl, a woman, wearing pajama bottoms streaked from the moisture of her legs and the room, and other than this nothing but a crucifix hanging from a chain around her neck.

With the opening of the door the girl jerked and turned her head to me, but then her head relaxed back onto the pillow, and I was interested to see that she didn't try to cover herself. In fact, as I gaped at her she moved her hands, which had been laying by her sides, in back of her head, thus thrusting her chest out a few inches. There was nothing sexual or coquettish about this, however—she just seemed to disregard in an instant that I was there.

I noted them for a remarkable set of breasts, from her slight movements they showed themselves to be as firm as footballs, much like the pair I had encountered about thirty-six hours earlier. They were the breasts of a developed teenager, though I had yet to otherwise determine how old she might be.

Her skin was the color of sand, but it was marked in places with red welts, not in such abundance that I could say she'd been deliberately beaten, but more of the kind that might come from general rough handling, from wrestling or hiking through a jungle. It seemed so incongruous, however, on the voluptuous figure that reclined in an ambiguous stillness—she could have been waiting for someone to feed her grapes or for a warden to administer a lethal injection—that I stared without compunction. I stared at her and I wondered. Some of the smaller marks, the redder ones, I noticed to be teeth marks. There were vaguely concentric circles of them around her nipples, and her breasts in general seemed more abused than the rest of her, as if she'd been nursing a fanged baby. I noticed a cluster of hickeys at the waistband of her pajama bottoms.

I had identified her in a few moments as a managed whore

or a hostage, as a woman who had been here for long days, who had been penetrated and gnawed upon by the fat beast more than she thought she could bear. I thought of all the things that must have changed about her—what she understood about men, the way she dreamed at night, her knowledge of how to exist only within herself—in the slow torture of Charlie Dance's bedroom. He had lain on her until his smell had become hers, until his fluids seeping into her, like acid in a well, had corroded everything about her. The woman he had done this to was Rosa, Ramon Diego Sagasta's Rosa.

CHAPTER FOURTEEN

I HAD BEEN FORBIDDEN TO SPEAK OF HER, YOU'LL REMEMBER, forbidden to say her name because I had once surmised out loud that she must be a fantastic lay. This is the first thing I thought about—that I wasn't supposed to say her name.

Simply put, I could not work my brain into enough contortions to figure out what she was doing there. The idea that Charlie Dance had stolen her shortly after I'd taken away her boyfriend was a notion of such outsized proportions that I couldn't really consider it. I didn't know Charlie Dance well enough to dismiss the idea, perhaps, and what I did know of him certainly didn't preclude gross and even criminal immorality, but it just seemed out of the question. For one thing, he was too fat to have gone out and kidnapped her. Even if he'd had someone else do it, she would have been able to escape easily enough, I should think. There was, however, something of the prisoner in her aspect. She wasn't handcuffed or restrained in any way, but the way she held her body seemed to indicate that she couldn't possibly have moved off that spot. It was as if her body had suddenly become dense, or her muscles impotent. She may have been drugged—I didn't try to read the labels of the pill bottles—but her eyes were clear and wide open. I didn't believe that she was a prisoner in the most literal sense, but that instead something inside of her kept her there. Here again, I have the advantage of retrospect.

She continued to stare up at the ceiling, until finally my stillness confused her, she turned her eyes towards me and then the muscles of her stomach and arms clenched and she shivered. She was preparing herself for something. I understood that she believed I had come to sleep with her; I understood that Charlie had the power to give her to other men if he wished.

Throughout all these thoughts of mine—which comprised maybe a minute or so—Charlie Dance stayed behind me, mumbling things and trying to maneuver his body into some position that might have physical authority over the scene. He tried to squeeze himself past me in the door jamb, which I wouldn't let him do, and then he looked over my shoulder and babbled things, and then he took a few steps back, as if he didn't care what I saw, and cursed, and I stayed for another minute and stared and held my breath.

I finally shut the door to Charlie's room with an extreme gentleness, as if it were made of thin glass. I did this in part to block her out, to erase her, but also because it seemed the respectful thing to do, it had the feel of placing a jacket over the face of a dead man.

In the kitchen, where we went next, and where I had expected Charlie Dance to start off with "I can explain," he instead said this:

"Yeah, it's fucking her. You figured it out. Congratulations. Are you happy now?"

I, of course, had figured out nothing. I hadn't even thought there had been anything to figure out. I'd come to his house from desperation, not curiosity. Any port in a storm. I'd heard a noise when I first arrived, and the smell of a woman reminded me of it and I went to look. That was all. What had he thought I'd been investigating?

"What are you going to do with her now?" I said.

"What's that mean? What am I going to do with her?" he said, as if the question were absurd, as if I'd asked him when he planned to lose some weight. "Fucking keep her, you mope. She's mine. Fuck off, you. I know you ain't going to tell anybody." I should mention that, throughout this, Charlie was making a sandwich. He made it carefully, laying lettuce, white cheese, some kind of bologna, pickle, in a delicate pattern. It was a very pretty sandwich, the kind you see in commercials for luncheon meat. He cut it in half and put it on a plate. In this activity I saw none of the glutton I knew Charlie Dance to be—I just saw a section of his life, the way he made a sandwich with food he must have selected at the local bodega. Charlie Dance lived down here, had done so for more than a year. He shopped down here, made sandwiches down here, this was the life of Charlie Dance. And he had, for all I could tell, a sex-slave in his bedroom.

"You've lost your goddamn mind," I said. "I'm taking her back to Rios."

He knew I couldn't do this, but he didn't insult me. He chewed and nodded his head, wandered into the living room and sat on one of the sofas. I followed him but didn't sit down.

"How you think you're going to do that, big man?"

"I'll figure it out. It can't be any harder than it was getting from Rios to here," I said, and I was pleased with myself, because it was very true.

"That's a hell of a point, " he said. He didn't know what else to say. I'd never seen him like this. I don't know if he believed me or not, but he was confused. He didn't want the girl to leave but he didn't know how to keep her—I think it was as simple as that for him. He was worried in the most selfish way possible. Worried not for his own safety or life, but for his simple desire. He wanted the girl naked in his bedroom, and that is all.

Finally he shook off his pondering and said "Just get the fuck out. Go back home. You're so fucking lucky you're not dead you don't even know it. You're alive because those dumbass yokel cops didn't want to kill Ramon Sagasta, and because they're even more incompetent than you are, which is hard to imagine. In any case, you best just cut your losses and get back home. Hitchhike to Havana. You'll be able to get a plane out somehow. Maybe a boat—that'd be a fucking hoot, if you got a boat to Miami. For all I care you can call the State Department and have them come rescue you. But from this day on, you don't mention what you saw in there. You don't talk about that chick ever again."

"Well, that's all very helpful Charlie, but I don't know if I'm the one you should worry about. What about Ramon—whether he makes it to Florida or not, what happens if he finds out?"

"Finds out what? What the hell are you talking about?"

I don't know from what recesses of my understanding it came—the clues he had given me, now that I think about them, would not have added up if I'd sat down and tried to make sense of them—but some part of me had become illuminated, I understood something that my mind had not yet put into words. Solemn as a rabbi, speaking without realizing what I was about to say, and without even acknowledging that I planned to speak at all, I said "He gave Rosa to you. He gave Rosa to you so that you'd write that report."

"*That* report? Fuck it all, it wasn't just one. I wrote a dozen reports, and you know how long it took those bastards to even write me back? I honestly don't even know why they keep me on.

If I say I've found a guy like that, and I have to tell them about him twelve times? What's the fucking use?"

Silence followed this, during which Charlie suddenly understood that I had suddenly understood, that I had not known until just then. For ten seconds, he didn't blink or breathe, until finally: "Wait a fucking minute. You didn't know?" He closed his eyes and genuflected—it was the unholiest thing I've ever seen. "I thought that's what you'd come here for. I thought you'd figured it out."

He thought I'd figured it out. As if there were something to figure out, as if this mystery had been right before me all this time, and I just hadn't thought about it hard enough, hadn't asked the right questions.

He might have been right, perhaps I was simply too groundless a person to ask the most important questions about Ramon's defection. It had never occurred to me that I would have to look beneath the surface, play detective. Actually, it probably wasn't all that hidden—there was only one question I had ever needed to ask: How was Ramon paying for this?

The scouting reports, the motorboat, Charlie Dance's guardianship, the provisions, the charter boat in the Florida Keys, even myself—these were valuable things to someone who wanted out of Cuba. I had not wondered why he merited them simply because I thought that question had been answered long ago, at the time of Ramon's birth, when the same forces that had blessed me with mediocrity bestowed greatness upon him. To me it had been a closed book. Ramon Diego Sagasta was a great baseball player; it was the lot of people like me and Charlie to serve people like Ramon.

But Charlie Dance did not think this way. From the very beginning, I should have recognized this fact and wondered what was in it for him, keeping in mind that he didn't given discounts to immortals.

"He gave you Rosa," I said. "That was the only thing he could give you that you needed. Because you can't get whores for yourself."

"Now hold off—that's Ramon shooting off about crap he doesn't know. I got a strange relationship with some of the hookers. We disagree sometimes. I wanted one that wouldn't do all that griping. Rosa over there, that *chica*'s quiet as a mouse. And you saw her, she's a tight little piece, that's sure."

"He gave you Rosa. He just gave her to you, like a bribe. To tell the organization about him."

"Stop saying that! Did you turn retarded? Jesus, snap out of it. Or are you trying to make me feel bad? If that's it, then trust me, you can save it."

"It's not that," I said. "I'm just curious . . . Dammit, Charlie, it wasn't enough that he can throw a baseball like that? That's not enough for you? You needed him to give you his fucking girlfriend?"

He rolled his eyes—it seemed I had a singular ability to disgust Charlie Dance with my ignorance. "There's nothing free here, you sad mope. Nothing free anywhere. If you want something, you pay for it. I didn't make that shit up. Ramon knew the rules good enough, and so did she. She knew the rules better than he did, even. She ain't tied up, you know. She could walk out right now if she wanted, but she won't, because she knows you gotta pay for things."

The implication was that I, as usual, was the only one who didn't know the rules, and I suppose I can't argue with that.

"*Jesus* goddamn *Cristo*," he said. "I can't believe you didn't fucking know. Bad luck. I guess I should have fixed the lock on that bedroom door."

I couldn't do anything except sit on the ugly couch and gape. It occurred to me that I should have laughed it off, shored up my position with some cynicism, as if I had always suspected something was going on. I wanted to do this so that Dance wouldn't have the huge advantage over me he now had, this knowledge that he had wounded me. But I couldn't fake my reaction.

"He told me he was going to come back to get her," I said, remembering this fact suddenly, hopefully. "He seemed pretty insistent about it. I guess it makes sense now. I just thought he meant he was going to get her out of Rios. But he meant he was going to come get her from you."

"Oh yeah," Charlie almost laughed, his eyes brightened. "He made no bones about that. He kept saying that this was temporary." In imitation of Ramon, Charlie began speaking with a Cuban-American accent, which didn't really make sense, as Ramon spoke no English. "*When I am big star in the States, I send expensive men to come take her from you, bring her to me. You only get her for a little while, Charlie, a year tops.* The poor little puke actually believed it too. It made him feel better I guess. He just doesn't get it."

"What doesn't he get?"

"Shit, kid, you've been there, what do you think? First of all, he may not make it. The chase is on, right? Those smugglers may not want to risk taking him, assuming he even figures out how to get in touch with them. But let's say that works out, and he gets across and the organization is so damn happy they put him right into the starting rotation of the Triple A club. Then what?"

I confessed I had not thought that far ahead.

"You can't even imagine. You never even saw him throw."

"I *did* see him throw," I said urgently. "From 110 feet. He was about to strike out Raoul Pena, who used to play for Santa Clara. And I caught for him, when he threw some alligator pears."

This gave him pause. He sneered in confusion, then waved

my words away. "Whatever, kid. Try to stay focused, I'm talking here. Ramon gets to Triple A, he starts striking people out, and right away they talk about calling him up. You met the dumb bastard—when that happens, do you think there's any way he's going to remember that *puta* in there?" He jerked a thumb toward his bedroom. "I'd bet my nuts he doesn't remember the name of his hometown once he's played in Yankee Stadium."

"You don't know what's going to happen, Charlie," I said. "You don't know what he'll do." I didn't mean it as a threat, just as a salient point.

He chewed on the inside of his cheek. "Yep, you're right. I guess I'll just have to wait until a commando squad on the Sagasta payroll breaks down my door and takes her away. Then you can say 'I told you so.'"

True enough, the speculation was worthless; if I stayed in Cuba it was possible that I'd never even know if he'd gotten out, or what had happened to his career if he had, since it was unlikely Castro would allow it to become common knowledge that Ramon—who had already tried to defect before—had become a major leaguer in America. And still, the question was unavoidable. Would Ramon remember Rosa and her sacrifice? What about me, and mine? Granted, it had not been as total (facing machine gun fire pales in comparison with letting Charlie Dance slobber over one's naked body), but it would not have cost him as much. I asked only for remembrance, not rescue.

And of course I never, in a decade of speculation, could know what he would do. I allowed that perhaps I had done a great thing, if Ramon did indeed get across. I allowed that there was a chance he would remember me, repeat my name and my story when he had some distance, allow me to share in his greatness. And yet I still can have no access to the thought processes of the truly great, even if my name is someday among theirs in Cooperstown. They are great all the time, while perhaps I have it in me to be great in moments. We all have our moments, after all, and it is folly to say that those who are truly great simply have more of them than most; that is not it at all. The great are great all the time, even in suffering, even in defeat. We are separated from them by a wall of comprehension and grace that I still do not understand, but which is almost the only thing I still believe in.

I stood up and asked Charlie for some money. I was conscious of him owing me a great deal. From his perspective, which did not assign any value to Ramon's greatness, I had simply been sent to Cuba so that he could have a live-in whore. This was his response:

"How about this—I'll forget about the two hundred you owe me from before."

This was all I got from him, but in fairness, I believe he considered it some kind of gift, if he even knew what that word meant.

I didn't ask what he planned to do with Rosa. He would keep her, of course, and I didn't see what I could do about it. I was a fugitive in Matanzas now, and even though my deep tan and fluency might help me remain one, I couldn't go to the police. Besides, he was right—she wasn't technically a prisoner. She had gone willingly because she loved Ramon Sagasta, and believed in him and his word; he would send for her when he became a star, she knew this, it would not be long now. With her hands cradling the back of her neck, her body ravished red and raw, staring at the spackled ceiling of Charlie Dance's bedroom—Rosa would wait and wait, until she lost faith. I hoped that one day Charlie Dance would indeed be woken from his cynical stupor by a band of commandos Ramon had hired with his first big league paycheck. I hoped they would rough him up on their way to the bedroom, where they would gingerly lift her, tell her to hush, that it would be okay. I hoped that they would take her across the Straits in a steady boat, completely grounded in their competence.

But this was too ambitious, too ornate a fantasy to be harbored by anyone but Rosa herself. Acknowledging the unknowable nature of the great athlete, in the end I simply hoped that Charlie Dance would tell her someday about the circumstances under which her beloved had abandoned her, the enormous distractions that would meet him in America. The way he would be treated in that league where the balls are thrown like bullets that change trajectory in mid-air, where the batters can hit things most people can't see. She must try to understand, or at least recognize the futility in understanding, what would happen to someone like Ramon when this new world accepted him.

I walked out of Charlie Dance's apartment, nodding my head at his offer to forget the two hundred. On Salamanca Street, in blazing sunlight, I realized that I had left simply because I couldn't be around him anymore. I had nowhere to go, no money, no identification. I spent the night underneath a bridge close to the docks.

I was back at Charlie Dance's house two days later, vaguely thankful not to have been incarcerated, but otherwise a woeful man. In those two days, I had come to appreciate the difficulty of getting to Havana, where I might have somehow contacted the organization. On the first day I'd tried to walk the fifty miles, but after two hours I passed out by the side of the road (I hadn't been eating well in Cuba). The next day, I walked to a suburb of Matanzas and found some garbage to eat, which I quickly threw up. I slept on a mud flat near the beach. The next morning I walked back to Charlie Dance's apartment and pounded on the door, bloody in places, footsore, so filthy I almost felt bad about entering a house.

He cussed me out, then shut the door on me, but I fell asleep in the hallway and a little while later he told me to get the fuck off the landing or the neighbors would call the police. I took this as an invitation, and after more cussing he let me take a shower in his bathroom. I spent most of that afternoon listening to him abuse me—he was serious about getting me to leave, it wasn't his usual stream of casual insults, which at times seemed almost like banter. He really wanted me out of the house. But I was weak and mute as a turtle, and eventually he began to soften. He loaned me pants and a belt and a button-down shirt (it was like trying to wear a sail), then, as dusk came, I realized he would let me sleep on the couch for the night. He gave me fifty dollars and told me he'd take it back if I wasn't gone by morning.

I'm not sure how I managed to get so much from him—my only guess is that I hit some sort of heretofore inaccessible vein of pity or guilt in Charlie Dance, for he had to have understood his role in my current condition, and I was truly pathetic. I had dropped at least ten pounds since he'd seen me last. I bled in copious trickles, and my formerly dashing black turtleneck had been reduced to a collar and half a sleeve. As I had walked through Matanzas on the way to his apartment, an old street vendor had asked if there had been a bus crash in the mountains, and was I the only survivor?

I smelled her throughout the night. She would certainly still be on the bed, still bruised and sweaty, gazing at the ceiling, waiting for Ramon Sagasta to sign a big-league contract. I didn't hear her cry out, I never heard the mattress squeal as he buried her in it. In my head, I did not hear Ramon's pained description of what he knew the experience was like for one of Charlie Dance's hookers, the monologue he'd weighed me down with in the forest, brief hours after we'd met, although I still hear it sometimes now. Sometimes, when I think of Ramon, it's what I remember.

Just before dawn on that night of refuge, Charlie Dance went to the bathroom, and I woke. I heard the porcelain shift in the floor as he settled himself on the can. I sat up on the couch, gathered a few things I planned to steal in a blanket. I crept into his room and lifted Rosa, slung her across my shoulder. She was naked to the pajama bottoms, but there was no time to dress her—a rumbling in the bathroom told me that the worst of Charlie's business was over. Her muscles were rigid, but her expression was blank and sleepy. She was awake, but apathetic; it was her body that remained terrified, her mind had been somewhere else for a long while. When we got outside I set her down, wrapped her arms around her chest to hide her boobs, and jogged her down Salamanca. Every few steps she stumbled and I had to balance her back on her feet. Eventually we hid behind a bus stop and I dressed her in one of Charlie's T-shirts. At this point, she snapped out of her dreamy malaise, and began to protest in the distinctive whine of the newly-woken, and I snapped fiercely at her to shut up. I made her sit down with me, draped the blanket around her, and when it got light I told her to sit still and wait until I got back.

I found a room to rent for the day at a motel for prostitutes and johns. I'd passed by it the day before on the way to Charlie's; it was more of a ruined two-story apartment building than a real business, but there was a discreet sign that listed the hourly prices in dollars. I paid for three days in advance, then went back to get Rosa.

After we checked in, we both slept some more, then she woke me up and insisted that I return her to Charlie Dance. I had not really heard her speak clearly until then. Her voice was surprisingly loud and confident, and I noticed that she shared some of Ramon's inflections and pronunciations.

"Get me back there," she said the moment I opened my eyes. "I need to go back there. You shouldn't have taken me."

The first thing that occurred to me was that she didn't know who I was. "Rosa, I'm Dennis Birch. I'm a friend of Ramon's."

"I know who you are. You're the American. It's good that you got him out, but you shouldn't have come back for me. That wasn't part of it."

"Ramon knows you're with me," I said, lying with rare conviction. She started shaking her head right away, and kept shaking it as I spoke. It was disconcerting, but I continued. "He paid me extra to come get you. I'm going to take you back to Rios, and you'll wait for him there. It's so much better that way, don't you see?"

"No, that wasn't the arrangement at all."

"Fuck that!" I said in English. "Forget the arrangement! The arrangement made you a whore, and it was ridiculous in the first place. Ramon deserves to be in America, that's where he belongs—he doesn't have to pay for Charlie's reports. You don't have to pay for them. The reports were the truth! Why can't you people see that? Goddammit, it was Charlie's fucking duty to write the reports, just like it was my duty to come get Ramon."

She wasn't buying any of this. She kept shaking her head, like she had Tourette's Syndrome. I kept arguing, she kept resisting, and eventually she touched me on the hand and said, "So he's in America now? You got him out okay?"

I summed up the final leg of the defection (starting with Arturo and Raoul), and she absurdly took the story as proof that Ramon was already safe in Miami. It comforted me to see how firmly she believed he had made it. "Ramon will be fine, then," she said, with somber finality. "He knows enough people, and with that much money . . . yes, he's made it across. Good."

"Then it's ridiculous for you to not go home. He'll come and get you at home."

With a small shrug of her shoulders, almost casually, she said "No, no. I can't go back to Rios," and I understood that she had made this a fact, that I would never get her there.

I assumed at first that a return to Rios frightened her because she couldn't explain herself to them—I assumed she had just run off, and that she now refused to return because she couldn't explain this, or the fact that she'd so clearly been abused. But I now remembered the glimpse I'd had of the village, the tableau I'd witnessed of the family's farewell to Ramon, and I came to believe that it was a different kind of shame she worried about. I thought about the boisterousness of the men, the way they clearly wanted to avoid the dread that a silence would bring. I thought of the mother's excessive petitions to the Lord, and I understood that they were prayers of contrition as well as protection.

"Oh," I said, almost sheepishly. "They knew about it too. Ramon's family—they knew about the arrangement."

She didn't say anything, just looked straight into my eyes with a kind of defiance that suggested I drop the subject altogether. And so I did. I could offer no more arguments. Rosa couldn't go back to Rios because she feared the shame that came with having escaped Charlie Dance; to the family, the fact that she was no longer with him would reveal a weakness in her, a lack of faith, an indication that she had not been prepared to fully sacrifice herself for Ramon Sagasta. Like Ramon and Rosa herself, the family had considered her enslavement an exorbitant but necessary price for Ramon's freedom, and she had welched by allowing herself to be rescued.

"Jesus," I said. "Am I the only one who didn't know about this?"

She shrugged her shoulders, as if to indicate that I probably was.

I went out and got some food, and when I got back I told her that I wouldn't take her to Rios. After that she put herself in my hands, without much gratitude but also without much griping.

With Charlie Dance's money and clothes, I managed to set us up into a sort of life—fifty dollars went a long way in the beginning. After a few days in the hooker motel, I used ten bucks to rent us a shanty house on the outskirts of the city and tried to develop a nest egg for us. Matanzas is a pretty town, and the clear waters and the beaches to the south attract a good number of Canadian and German tourists, so now I get some work doing freelance translation for tour groups. Sometimes I make money playing a game called four corners, with the fishermen who loaf on the beach. We take turns trying to hit balls of duct tape over each other's heads with a thin birch branch, and the winner takes a dollar a game. I win most of the time—I still have my old swing, which is good enough for this place.

Rosa watches and listens for Ramon. I bought her a radio, and she fidgets with the dial once or twice an hour, trying to pick up a station from Miami or the Keys. When the Florida Marlins are playing, she hikes up a hill near the beach, where the reception is better. I tell her that there was no way he'd be in the majors this quickly, even if he'd made it across, and besides, he wouldn't be playing in the National League, but she doesn't seem to hear me when I give advice that goes even slightly contrary to her hope. Still I remind her, almost every day, all the reasons she should put him out of her mind. *You don't even know for sure he made it across*, I tell her. *Even if he did make it, the organization might not give him a look right away. Even if they did, they certainly wouldn't pay him very much at first, and he would be too busy to orchestrate your defection.* I never tell her that he might simply have forgotten about her, that's the one thing I never say.

In the mornings, she goes out in search of a newspaper, and if she's successful, she spreads it out and reads the sports section with furious intensity. The paper sometimes has articles and scores from American baseball, but this is another futile thing. The last time I checked, there were seven major league teams with Cuban players on the roster, and not coincidentally those seven teams never seem to show up on the box score page of the newspaper. We will not hear about Ramon that way.

But still she sits gravely at the table after we drink coffee together and she reads the rosters and box scores. She found an R. Sagatano once, playing for Pittsburgh, and an R. Sagerstra, who had just joined the Mariners, but neither of them was a pitcher.

One day, as I was reminding her again that she shouldn't get her hopes up, she uncharacteristically slapped the paper on the table and glared at me. "Do you put him out of your head, then, Dennis? Do you not think about Ramon anymore?"

"Yes, I think about Ramon. Of course. It's hard not to—he's why I'm down here. I just mean that I've managed not to count on him too much. He may not even be there, you know. I told you that."

"But you don't believe that. You believe he's over there, and that he's pitching. You believe it just like I do."

"Yes, but that's only because I like believing it."

"Then keep believing it," she said, and reopened the paper. "And leave me alone or take me back to that fat man's house."

Maybe I should have. Everyone else was willing enough to hand her over for the cause. I had some money then, I might have been able to get back to America. I weighed these facts sometimes, thought about the logistics, but I never felt that I was close to leaving. I became conditioned to waiting in the dark with her, speculating and hoping while recognizing the improbability of it all. Matanzas is an easy place to wait—every Cuban

I saw down there seemed to be doing just that, loafing in the sun, chatting listlessly, waiting for something to happen. The weather is nice, the sea is a different kind of gorgeous than any I've ever seen before, and it became hard for me to remember what there was for me in America. Maybe staying in Cuba had something to do with a mission not quite fulfilled, maybe it has something to do with why I took Rosa away from Charlie in the first place, the way I tried to have another great moment by rescuing her. I cannot tell for certain; as always, I am groundless.

Rosa seems to know. She is confident in her opinions and beliefs, a little too confident for the comfort of someone like me, who lives in uncertainty. We talk about Ramon quite a bit, since there is little else that binds us together, and on occasion I have probed the question of what he did to her. She insists that it was justified, and that it was her idea in the first place. Ramon, she explained to me, was bigger than her, bigger than his family. Not only would it have been wrong to stand in the way of his defection, she said, it would have been wrong not to give everything she had to achieve it for him.

"It doesn't make me a saint," she said. "Not at all. It is what I should have done, no more than that."

I may have, in some sense, agreed with her—in fact, I felt closer to her than I ever had before, since it occurred to me that I had done the same, that I had given him the only thing I could give in order to secure the success of his defection. Also like her, I don't feel especially noble for having made a sacrifice for him; it certainly does feel, as she said, that to do less would have been a great sin.

She reached out to me—we were sitting at a card table in the kitchen—and lightly grabbed onto my shirtsleeve, a move that was tender but avoided the awkwardness of a more physical touch. We looked at each other, commiserating.

Then she said, "It's the same with you, you know. It's that way for both of us. We serve and love Ramon, even if he doesn't serve us back." She did not say *even if he doesn't love us back*, but the words were in the air, given weight by their conspicuous absence, and she looked away from me and leaned back in her chair. "Ramon has a great destiny I think, but that doesn't mean there is any goodness in him. Sometimes I think there's not. What he did, agreeing to let me go to Charlie Dance, that was probably not something a good man would do. And that's why you're still here."

I shook my head to indicate that I didn't understand.

"You served him first by helping him get out. But now you're still serving him, by doing this, by being good to me. He couldn't have done it, but you can. You're good to me."

That was the last time we ever discussed our strange arrangement. I may be reading too much into what was really a brief and simple conversation. Maybe I'm mistranslating, maybe I heard just want I wanted her to say. In any case, she soothed me in this way, and for a while I didn't even think much about what I was still doing in Cuba. When I think about it now, I am able to dismiss it with a clear and satisfactory thought: I am not capable of doing great things—the grandeur and grace that are summoned when someone like Ramon steps onto a baseball field are inaccessible to me. But it may be that I am capable of doing a few good things, and maybe my life with Rosa in Cuba is some evidence of that.

Once I'd saved a few dollars, and no longer had to wear Charlie Dance's gargantuan Sansabelts, I began going to baseball games. The park is near our house, and it is August, and there are at least five games a week—not always the Toronados, sometimes another local team, sometimes one from the high school. I see Charlie Dance at the games, slouching and watching through binoculars even though he sits twenty yards from home plate. I don't think he'd do anything if he saw me, but I take care to sit far away from him. He writes things down in a leatherbound notebook. He drinks beer and eats. Sometimes he brings a radar gun. No one sits near him (I think he buys out the whole row), and he never takes his eyes off the field, even when he's buying food from the vendors.

The first day I went to the ballpark, I watched him almost as much as I watched the game. Somewhere around the fifth inning I began to wonder about Charlie's life. I wondered what he would do after the game that night, how he was going about getting hookers these days. I wondered if he watched the players with any kind of hope, or if he just tried to spot someone who was good enough to write reports about, so that he could pick up a few favors. I thought about his apartment and the posters of the great players on the wall. I thought about the magazines on the stained coffee table. I remembered how I thought at the time that he must get them mailed directly from a connection in the States, because they'd be unavailable down here. How those magazines were current, only one or two weeks behind the American news-stand date. How they brimmed with statistics and scores that are meaningful only to the most lunatic of baseball fanatics. How they were disposable to him, how he used them as coasters.

That night at two in the morning, I went to look for the magazines in Charlie's trash. I jumped the fence of an alley adjacent to his apartment building to get to the roofless wooden enclosure where the tenants threw their garbage. I stood among the reeking mound of trash bags for over three hours, untying and retying the sacks so that no one would notice I'd been there. I threw up twice early on, and dry heaved about once every half hour after that—everyone in Charlie's building seemed to subsist entirely on cheap seafood, and the trash was wet from morning rains. By the time dawn came, I still hadn't found Charlie's trash, and I was certain I'd have to dip myself in boiling alcohol if I ever wanted to smell normal again, but there were still quite a few bags I hadn't been through, and so I came back the next night.

I found Ramon at 4:30 in the morning in six-point type. I was dizzy and nauseated from the stench, and my pant cuffs were stained with trash juice. When I saw his name, I stuffed the magazine in the front of my pants, tied up the trash bags, and skulked out of the garbage enclosure, heading towards a cut-off that lead to the beach; I did not want to be surrounded by trash when I took in this information. I jogged a few blocks towards the ocean, then stopped at a street-light to savor my discovery.

Ramon was on page 87 of *Total Baseball Insider*, in a box score of the August 4 game between the Natchez Crayfish and the Montgomery Planters. R. Sagasta, left-handed pitcher, threw seven and a third innings, allowed one run on four hits, struck out eleven, walked two, and hit one batter with a pitch. The hit batter came in the eighth, and I took this to mean that Ramon's coaches had not pulled him out of the game because he was in trouble, but that he'd been ejected after hitting the batter on purpose. It surprised me how unquestioningly I believed this.

The Crayfish are Double-A; I'd played against them in the Southern League when I was with Chattanooga. I had hit in their stadium, scampered down their base paths, crouched on the chalky dirt behind the batters box in that park where Ramon had thrown this game. I remembered that a few men I'd played with in Chattanooga had gone on to the majors—while excellent talent was not common in the Southern League, it was far from the true hinterlands of minor league baseball.

Because I had played against them on this field, and because I had the box score in front of me, and because I was weary and almost immune to the stink of the trash, I was able to visit his game in my head, and insert myself in it. I could feel the hot wind from the Mississippi, I could taste the dust that exploded into my face when a sinker kicked in front of me. I could hear the scream of Ramon's fastball rising, leaping octaves and decibels as it bolted home, ending in a sonic boom on the leather of the catcher's mitt. I could see his grinning, toothy face beneath the scarlet Crayfish cap, the lean tall body awkwardly tucked into the gaudy home uniform. I could see the chief scouting director watching from the second row, tinkering with the radar gun, making the occasional note in a legal pad, enthralled with the performance but reminding himself not to get too excited. I could hear the collision of ball on bone in the top of the eighth as Ramon pegged the insolent batter, who had probably been crowding the plate. It was like I was there, it really was.

With a final image of Ramon's face—open-mouthed as he protested his innocence to the umpire, unspeakably indignant at having been ejected—my mind closed itself to this dream and I saw myself again as I was, on a beach in Cuba, imbued with the stink of Charlie Dance's garbage. I walked to the water to clean myself off.

As I swam, I told it to myself in logical terms, without the fantasizing and daydreaming. He had made it across, and he had made it to the organization—Natchez was indeed one of their farm teams. It had only been five weeks since I'd met him at the outskirts of the Rios meadow, and he was already starting in Double-A. A win like the one he'd recorded on August 4 doesn't necessarily mean much in the mid-level minor leagues, but after two or three such victories, especially if he kept striking batters out, they would move him up to groom him for next year. It was late in the season, and so they would hammer out contracts soon, make sure he signed with an agent they liked, coach him in their own facilities in the off season. They would work on his media skills, make sure the story of his defection was one they wanted to hear. But even the organization can't really know or control what Ramon will do; soon he will be beyond their reach.

I didn't tell Rosa any of this; I never will. Soon I may go back to Charlie's trash and try to scavenge more box scores, but I'll sneak out of the shanty even more carefully this time—she can't know that I have this. Her expectations are too large, they have not been tempered by repeated contact with various strains of greatness, as mine have been. Even if it happens, even if Ramon is at this moment sitting in a small apartment in Natchez scheming about how to channel his impending millions into her rescue . . . It may simply be an impossible thing.

I must keep reminding her of the contingencies, I must become more insistent that she resign herself to a certain fate. Perhaps I can even drop some hints that I've heard things from the fishermen on the shore, that Ramon might have been lost at sea, or thrown into the Prison Nacional. I would rather have her mourn than suspect she had been abandoned. If the sanctions are ever lifted, of course, she might see Ramon for herself in *Sports Illustrated*, but I can't look that far ahead. In any case, I don't think that her hope will last the off-season, and when it is finally lost, she will tell herself that he's dead. It will be the only Ramon Sagasta story she can accept.

I will be here when that happens. Maybe we will find a better house, maybe we will become lovers when she decides that Ramon is dead to her. There will never be love between us, just a kind of comfort and protection, but that doesn't seem so bad. It would make a kind of sense, after all. Just a few days earlier, I had pondered the injustice of our positions, how Ramon should have been in America all along, while I, with my groundlessness, my meager and forgettable talent, was more suited toward Cuba and the life Ramon had been shackled with. It seemed to me that we had gradually, inexorably swapped places, and that this was the real nature of my sacrifice—trying to correct the accident of our births. And Rosa was a part of this life, my life.

In truth, I didn't think about this much, nor do I worry

much about the police or the informers or the soldiers, though I still take precautions. All of my previous worries were exiled from my thoughts by the words and numbers in that six-point type, the three-inch clipping of the box score, which I keep in a pocket of my wallet. Those numbers are clear, indisputable, grounded—and they are what matters. I am tired of wondering, tired of planning and worrying, tired of acknowledging that I am groundless. I'd rather think about what I know.

I still go to all the games. In fact, I have begun taking notes. I keep my own box scores, and I am beginning to recognize the names and styles of the players. There is a kid on the neighborhood team—they play maybe once a week—with some raw batting talent, though he always pulls the ball and can't seem to keep his head down.

One afternoon, I saw him hit a home run and three doubles against a decent pitcher from a Havana club team. He plays third base well, and he is gangly and fast, perhaps seventeen years old. After the game I bought a typewriter in the market square, went home and wrote a scouting report on the kid. I wrote nine pages and included copies of all his game scores. The next day I found a Canadian tourist and paid him to mail the report to the organization when he got home—I literally cannot even imagine what they'll think or do when they get it.

What was this for? The kid probably isn't that much of a prospect. In the States they might give him a tryout, but he isn't even worth the risk of thinking about down here. Even if they thought they could trust my word, even if they connected me with the blazing talent they have down in Natchez. Even if they have prepared a place for me back in American baseball because of the gift I've given the organization, a place that I could claim any time I liked. What was I doing this for?

Simply this: it is what I do. I have fallen back into baseball. I stare at it languidly, stupidly, every afternoon and most evenings. I stare at it the way Rosa stared at the ceiling, the way she stares at the tiny print of the American baseball scores, waiting for Ramon to come and take her away. I have waited for this longer than she has, and in spite of her bravado and seemingly limitless certainty, I believe that I will keep my faith for longer than she can.

This may seem a strange thing, that I haven't lost my faith the way Rosa will soon, since I'm not really sure if I will ever be remembered, let alone acknowledged on a placard in the Hall of Fame. I recognize that I may very well rot anonymously down here, stupidly imagining that I am protecting something, looking for something, waiting for something. Rosa may be rescued or she may be forgotten, and I can honestly say that whatever happens will not surprise me, nor will it change the way I feel about Ramon, or about what I did for him. There are many things that I am unsure of, but that is not one of them.

My faith is this: I know there is greatness out there somewhere. I have seen it before, I have sacrificed for it. It may be true that it isn't here anymore, and that I may never find it again. Greatness will visit me the way it always has, in strange and unexpected moments, the way it visits most of us. But as for the other kind of greatness, the kind that might elevate even me in its reckless swath, I will watch for it always, I will keep its promise beside me.